ISBN 978-1-4477-3621-9

Big thanks to Pete Shovlin for reading the first draft and being brave enough to give constructive feedback.

Monkman, Matt and Thomma for buying a Kindle copy despite having read it already.

Everyone who has taken the time to give positive reviews and encouragement. Special mention to JanieP for this.

Marj for allowing me to write instead of working in the period when I got the writing bug.

Massive thank you to anyone who I met when growing up, you never know, you may have provided inspiration.

Craig Turnbull for finally giving me a professional cover.

To Joseph, Lorna and Florence Rose.

Don't grow up like your Uncle Alan.

"Be Good!" ET (The Extra Terrestrial) 1982

Even at the age of ten I took great delight in kicking Emlyn Hughes in the face. One look at his features, mutated after my Father had taken a hot knife to his eye socket was all it took. The chirpy, footballer turned personality, however, still grinned insanely through his deformity.

The field behind my home had become Wembley to the boy's from our neighbourhood and the plastic Emlyn Hughes Superstars football had been the ball of choice for the past two years now. The field, roughly the length and width of a small cottage, sloped off sharply in the right hand corner of what was known as the Back Lane End where the corner flag was replaced by a permanently muddy puddle. At the far side of the field we had the Bush End which had a privet hedge along its length. To the left of the field was a road that separated us from Tate's, a large wasteland surrounded by a seven-foot brick wall and to the right was the gable end of the Pritchard's house.

"I'm calling the police if you don't stop belting that ball off our wall. Our lass is trying to watch Coronation Street," Mr Pritchard was out again with one of his nightly rants. It was hard to take him seriously. He was five foot four and sported a bushy, black moustache that gave him the appearance of a schoolboy dressed up for a school play. "This is our field, I could get you done for trespass." Saliva sprayed from his lips as he bawled at us.

"It's not your grass, my M m m mam checked with the council. They said it belongs to them and we can p p p play on it as much as we like, " Elvis shouted and then took a step behind Bumper. Paul 'Elvis' Morris lived three doors up from me. He was tall and thin for his age and wore a pair of thick-rimmed spectacles that he tied on with old shoelaces when we played football. His stutter came and went depending on how excited he got. I'm not sure if his Mam had checked with the council but it sounded good to me.

"Don't talk wet son," said Mr Pritchard.

"You're the one talking wet. I'm bloody drowning here," Bumper pretended to wipe spit from his face. Pritchard climbed over the wall that connected his garden to the field and went for him. He stopped dead in his tracks when he caught sight of the imposing figure on the corner of the back lane. Uncle Tim was a giant of a man, six foot four in his tartan slippers, he was quite an intimidating sight. He wasn't my real uncle but he was a friend of my Dad's and always seemed to look out for us. He removed his pipe from his mouth, studying it briefly before ambling over to Mr Pritchard.

"Is there a problem?"

"Err no, no problem, " Pritchard was shaking. "I was just trying to explain that our lass can't hear the telly because of the noise they're making."

"Well tell her to turn the bugger up then." The thought of Tim slippering Pritchard to death did appeal to me. I glanced at Bumper and you could tell that he was silently willing Tim on to chin him as well.

"Yeah, good idea, I didn't think of that." Pritchard climbed back over the wall, taking his moustache with him and headed back inside.

"Don't worry lads, he won't bother you again."

"Cheers Tim," I said.

"No problem, you know where I am if you get any hassle." Tim replaced his pipe, glanced at the specks of mud that had gathered on his slippers then wandered off round the corner.

****

"Morning Mr Morris," Kevin Davison stood menacingly in the doorway of the shop, temporarily blocking out the light.

"Ah fuck."

"That's not a pleasant way to greet an old school friend now is it?"

"What do you want Kev? I've got work to do," Elvis put down his screwdriver.

"Glad to hear that you're busy. That means that you shouldn't have any problems paying the small rent increase that I'm going to have to impose."

"Again? It only went up t t t two months ago."

"That's inflation for you," Kev patted Elvis on the head. "It's only fifty pounds a week more."

"F f f fifty pounds? How am I going to afford that?"

Davison shrugged as he took Elvis' glasses from his face and tried them on. "Fuck me, how blind are you?" His two friends, who had just come into the shop, laughed. "You remember Mr Thompson and Mr Couzens don't you? I think you'll find that it's insurance day."

"Shit," Elvis shook his head.

"I trust you won't have any problems paying them," Davison went to hand the glasses back to Elvis but instead dropped them onto the floor before standing on them. "Clumsy me. Never mind, accidents will happen."

****

We'd kicked off again and it wasn't long before the ball was racing down the back lane alongside Tate's. Gilbert chased after it as we sat with our backs against Pritchard's wall, grateful for the rest.

"Fancy a swig?" Bumper handed me a bottle of Dandelion and Burdock that his mother had bought us. I took a swig of the bitter, sweet liquid and handed it onto Elvis.

"What's down the bottom of the bank then?" Bumper hadn't been in the area long but we had taken him under our wing.

"There's a garage at the very bottom and another road," I said, "that's why you have to be quick; if the ball goes on the road it's bound to be burst by a car."

"Do you think Gilbert was the best man to send after it then?" Bumper looked down the back lane to see how far Gilbert had got. "He's not exactly the quickest lad I've ever met."

"He was in goal, " I said. "It's the rules. Gilbert's ok, at least he makes the rest of us look like good footballers."

"Seems like a good lad, doesn't say much though. Has he been here long?"

"Yeah, he lives on the Marley Potts estate at the top of our street. He lives with his Mam and his two brothers."

"What about his Dad?"

"Don't know. I don't think anybody knows who or where his dad is but we've never bothered to ask. It's not something he talks about." Gilbert was just getting to the top of the bank. His face was bright red and he was out of breath. He was nearly as tall as Elvis but a lot chubbier and he sloped forward when he walked quickly, resembling a ski jumper speeding down the slope.

"What's on the other side of Tate's then?" Once Bumper started, he was full of questions.

"There's a big car park that used to belong to the Plessey's factory, " Explained Elvis. "At the far end of that is Inkerman Print."

"What's that?"

"It's where they print the football programmes"

"Can we go down there sometime? I'd love to see it." Elvis and me exchanged nervous glances.

"No, it's far too dangerous."

****

Elvis pedalled up to the front of the tower block and freewheeled to the foot of the stairs. He never took the lift. The smell of urine was even more overpowering than it was in the stairwell and along with cycling to work, taking the stairs was his only sacrifice to fitness.

He placed the bike over his shoulder. The old Raleigh racer wasn't as good as the mountain bikes people favoured these days but it did the job it was intended for. It was also cheap, £20 from the classifieds in the local paper. The bike had probably been stolen like most of the items featured in the classified ads but he didn't care. *If you can't beat them join them,* he thought. As he reached the stairwell of the fourth floor he had to push past the local gang of teenagers stood smoking on the stairs in their brightly coloured Kappa tracksuits and ill-fitting baseball caps.

"Nice bike. What is it, a penny farthing?" Elvis chose not to answer the junior comedian having long since learnt the lesson from entering into a debate with his sort. *Fucking little prick.* he thought and carried on along the corridor to his flat.

"Hiya love, good day?" Marie wasn't really looking for an answer and was already heading back to the kitchen where she was preparing the tea.

"Yeah, great now that you ask," Elvis removed his glasses that were now held together with sticky tape and rubbed his eyes. "First I found the rent for the shop had gone up, and then a couple of our friendly local insurance men came for their monthly payment, reminding me just how important it is to pay them on time. More important than putting food on the table it seems."

"What was that, love? I couldn't hear you, the kettle was boiling."

"Nothing, just saying how busy I've been. Nothing for you to worry about," Elvis picked up the paper and slumped into the armchair, realising that Declan had been sat alone on the couch.

"Alright son? Good day at school?"

"The usual."

"Got any homework?"

"Finished it," said Declan.

"Already? You'd better go and check that it's right seeing as you've finished it so quickly," Elvis flicked the remote control and after a few seconds, the television came to life. Declan trudged into the bedroom and slammed the door behind him.

"Mind that door, you'll have the bloody hinges off soon." Elvis scanned the channels on the television without anything registering.

Declan took his sopping wet exercise book from his bag and threw it against the wall where it left a damp stain. He lay face down on the bed and began to cry.

You haven't got a clue what it's like dad. Not a clue.

****

"Give us a swig of that will you?" Gilbert asked for the bottle of pop. "I'm absolutely knackered. Can we have a rest?"

"We just have," Bumper jumped up and took a swing at the ball. "Come on, you can stay in goal if you're still tired."

"No chance. I'm not running down there again."

"You can have the bush end this time." This offered a little protection as the ball would normally lodge in the hedge rather than roll down the bank.

Each goalmouth, as was the fashion in the late seventies and early eighties, was either a mud bath or baked hard by the sun. This accounted for numerous cuts and grazes and even more telling offs from our parents for coming in caked in muck.

Elvis, Gilbert and myself were ever presents the 1980/81 season, playing football every day during the holidays and most nights after school. Bumper made up the quartet when he moved into the neighbourhood that Christmas. He was of similar build to Gilbert and Elvis and was a bit of a joker but harmless with it. The lads liked him and so did I.

Whilst the four of us were involved in nearly every match there was a group of about ten other lads who joined in the games from time to time. During the holidays each match lasted a full day from when you got up until we were called in for tea. Half time was when we went for lunch. Occasionally we would have extra time that lasted until it got dark. Boots and shin-pads were optional although they were generally for the rich kids so it pretty much ruled out any of us from Southwick. It was also essential that you assumed the persona of your favourite footballer. We quite often had Johan Cruyff, Kevin Keegan and Gary Rowell all on the pitch at the same time. I always chose to be Mario Kempes, Argentine star of the 1978 world cup.

It wasn't long after we had kicked off again when the ball shot past Gilbert and into the bush.

"It's bust," he said as he retrieved the ball.

"Not again." My dad had already repaired the ball twice by heating a knife on the electric ring of the cooker and melting the plastic over the puncture. I wasn't sure if it would hold up to another restoration.

"Why don't we call it a draw and start again tomorrow? I got a ball for Christmas and I haven't had a chance to use it yet." Everyone agreed with Bumper as we left. All of us as deflated as Emlyn Hughes' now sunken cheeks.

****

"Fucking stupid cow."

"Will you stop that?" Marie was annoyed and Elvis knew she was right. He had sworn at the television an average of three times an hour tonight. It wasn't his worst performance but he could tell that things were getting on top of him.

"Well she is a stupid cow, the twisty faced old bat." Admittedly, Deirdre Barlow wasn't the normal target for a vitriolic attack but she was winding him up.

"It's make believe, Elvis. It's only a TV show," Marie laughed as she stood up. "Do you want another can, love?"

"Yeah, go on," he said, slightly embarrassed at his outburst. "We need a holiday Marie but I can't see when I can get the time off work, or the money to pay for one."

16

"Don't worry love. We'll manage." Marie headed into the kitchen.

"Boring old Twat," said Elvis as Ken Barlow walked onto the screen.

****

"Ah shit."

"What's up?" I headed onto the field.

"Dog shit, loads of it." Bumper was right. The field that had been spotless when we had left it the night before was now covered in dog turds. This severely hampered our football plans.

"I'm sure that the owners wouldn't be too happy if we shat in their gardens would they?"

"Good point Bumper but it's not going to help us is it? We're going to have to clear them away."

"How?" Asked Elvis but Bumper already had a plan and ran to the bush end of the field and snapped off four twigs.

"Come on, let's see who can get them the furthest up Tate's wall." He handed us each a twig and, excited at the new challenge, I opted to go first. I chose the stool nearest the road, which was quite solid. I placed my stick in it and flicked it over the road towards the wall. It splattered about half way up then dropped back down.

"Good shot." Elvis went next. He took the lead with a shot that was just two bricks short of the top of the wall. It was unlikely to be beaten and Gilbert didn't put up much of a challenge when his shot didn't even clear the road and landed slap, bang in the middle of the white lines.

"You spenk."

"Watch your heads," shouted Bumper as he launched his turd with some force. It cleared the wall with ease and ended up some way inside Tate's yard.

"The champion." I raised Bumper's arm above his head and he bowed to the imaginary crowd. The field was clear and we kicked off but the game didn't last long.

"What the fuck do you think you're playing at?" We were all rooted to the spot as Mr Tate came round the corner, a brown stain down the front of his overalls.

"Leg it!"

****

Claire felt the eyes watching her again. She had noticed it before but it seemed like it was becoming more regular these days. Maybe she was just imaging it. She glanced over her shoulder, half of her wanting to see a familiar face, the other half dreading who or what she may see. Nobody was there, nobody unusual anyway. The gang of kids were standing outside of Booze Buster but then again, they always were. Wearing their mismatched tracksuits and their baseball caps perched precariously on top of their heads. *Who ever told them that green and purple go well together?* Then she remembered something her dad used to say... "If his brains were dynamite, he wouldn't have enough to blow his cap off on a windy day." She laughed to herself. *I wish he could see this bunch.* She hadn't seen her father for a number of years now, not since she got married. She quickened the pace. Not that they had even registered her presence. *Too much dope.* The eyes were still there, watching. She flicked her hair back and smiled. Boredom was beginning to play tricks with her mind. She walked back towards Booze Buster. The Brady Bunch begrudgingly moved out of the way, dragging their feet as if they were wearing diving boots. Claire picked a couple bottles of white. *It's a nice day. I could fancy a glass by the pool.*

****

Elvis and myself had just got to school, St Christopher's RC Primary. We walked past the army of mothers dropping their precious kids of at the gates and took up position in the yard. Elvis had just got a new pack of Top Trumps and we called Bumper over for a game. We sat, cross legged on the concrete as Elvis dealt the cards. Just then there was a commotion at the gate. Fighting his way through the crowd was an unkempt, bearded man pushing a wheelbarrow.

"Now fucking behave yourselves," he said as he tipped his children out of the barrow. Seemingly unfazed by the experience, the brother and sister waved cheerfully and chomped into the pease pudding stotties that their father had made for lunch.

"Who's that?" Bumper asked.

"The scruffy bloke is Albert Davison," replied Elvis, "the local rag and bone man."

"The chubby lad," I added," is his son Kevin Davison. To be avoided at all costs. My mam says he's evil."

"He looks a bit strange but he hardly seems dangerous." It didn't take long for Bumper to regret these words.

****

It took me a while to find Elvis. Looking through the phone book for Paul Morris brought up nothing. It was only when I was flicking through the paper and stumbled upon an advert for Costello's Computer Repairs. It was worth a go.

I found the shop on the outskirts of town. All the units either side were boarded up and this appeared to be the only one with any signs of life. When I walked in Elvis didn't even look up.

"With you in a minute." Bits of computers lay about all over the place in some sort of organised chaos. Posters on the wall advertised Frogger and the VIC 20.

"Isn't it about time you modernised?" I asked.

"You what?" the thick rimmed spectacles peered up over the VDU screen. Elvis had filled out a bit since school but was pretty much identical to how I remembered him. His shoulders were slightly hunched which made him look a little smaller than his six feet two inches. He had been this height since he was fifteen making him stand out from the crowd.

"Bloody Hell, Pete I haven't seen you in years." A big grin spread across Elvis' face.

"Still wearing the Elvis specs I see." The thick lenses and black frames were exactly as I remembered.

"No, these are just safety glasses." He took them off and I realised it was possibly the first time I had seen him without glasses. His eyes looked uncannily small and squinted. He then proceeded to replace his glasses with something equally thick and cumbersome held together with an elastoplast. The old Elvis was back.

"Where have you been," Elvis moved from behind the computer, still carrying a slight limp from the accident, "and more importantly, what brings you back?"

"Thought I'd look up a few of the lads, maybe organise a bit of a school reunion." I reached over to shake his hand.

"Count me out, I fucking hated school and so did you as far as I can remember. What makes you want to meet up with all those twats?" Elvis concentrated back on the shell of a PC he was working on.

"It's been fifteen years now, Elvis. Water under the bridge and all that. Let bygones be bygones."

"Yeah, well they can stay gone as far as I am concerned. I just want to keep my head down and get on with my work."

"You seem to be doing all right for yourself, your own shop and all that." I looked round at the banks of computers and monitors lined up against the walls.

"If it was my own shop. Everybody seems to want a piece of it. I'm struggling to keep my head above water."

"Sorry to hear it. If there's anything I can do?"

"Yeah, p p p piss off with your stupid ideas about school reunions for a start. While you walked away from all that shit I've been up to my eyes in it for years."

"It was just an idea..." I didn't really know what to do next. Elvis had been pleased to see me but I seemed to have touched on a raw nerve. He came out from behind the computer and drew up a swivel chair for me to sit on.

"I'm sorry, mate. Been under a lot of pressure recently, you know how it is." He flicked the switch on the kettle and sat down beside me. "How do you fancy coming over for a bite to eat tonight? Marie will be made up to see you again."

"Marie?"

"Marie Johnson."

"Things can't be all that bad. Is she still as fit as she used to be?"

"Careful, that's my wife you're talking about." Elvis pretended to be hurt.

"It's just a bit of a shock. How long have been seeing her?"

"Since the thirty first of January nineteen eighty seven."

"That's a bit precise."

"Yeah, our first date was Elvis Costello's gig with the Confederates at the City Hall." Elvis pointed at the tour poster on the wall.

"You certainly know how to treat a woman." I said as Elvis passed me a mug of coffee.

"Luckily she's into the same music. We've seen every gig he's done in the north east. Our honeymoon was in Dublin in eighty eight. He did a gig with Christie Moore it was fantastic."

"What, the gig or the honeymoon?" We both laughed and Elvis was a lot more relaxed now.

"We've got a little lad now as well, although he's not so little anymore, he's nearly twelve."

"Let's guess, you've called him Elvis?"

"Not quite, he's called Declan. Anyway is 7.30 alright for you tonight?"

"Yeah great. Where are you living now?"

"Forest Court. Number 125. Your trip might be worthwhile," Elvis grinned, "I think I might have something you may be interested in."

"I'm intrigued. See you then."

"Sorry to have bitten your head off earlier. It's really good to see you again, mate. I've missed you." Elvis gave me a strong bear hug that took me a little by surprise.

"It's good to be back. See you tonight, I wouldn't miss it for the world." It was good to see Elvis again and I was looking forward to seeing Marie and little Declan. The thought of a miniature version of Elvis made me chuckle. "And I don't care how many gigs you've seen, none of them will beat eighty one with the Attractions."

"Can't argue with that, " agreed Elvis. "See you tonight, mate."

The four of us waited in the queue to go in for lunch. Bumper's mother had made him sandwiches, Elvis and me were going to buy our lunch and Gilbert was on free lunch, Nashy dinners as they were known.

As lunchtime approached, Kevin Davison realised that he'd eaten all of his sandwiches and he didn't have any dinner money. He was still hungry so he did what he knew best. He casually walked up to Gilbert, punched him squarely in the face and took his dinner ticket. He then went into Bumper's lunch box unchallenged and took his Tunnock's teacake.

"Don't mind do you?" he asked, then walked off without waiting for a reply.

"That's not fair," said Gilbert, "it's curry today."

It was the first time I had been on the Forest Court Estate. I had seen countless other's all over the world and they rarely differed. I felt sorry for Elvis. He was a good lad with his own business yet he was living on one of the most run down estates in the city. A burnt out Ford Sierra blocked the entrance to the car park so I left the car on the road opposite. The orange street lighting illuminated it to provide a little security. A young lad, about ten years old, rode by slowly on his mountain bike looking me up and down working out what he could scam from me. He doubled back.

"Look after your car, mister?" I remembered this from when I was a kid. We used to offer to look after people's cars when they went to the match. Patrolling the streets on the look out for potential wrong doers. This offer was more sinister.

"I'll give you a fiver if it's still here when I get back."

"Tenner."

"Five quid and I'll let you keep your kneecaps." He thought about it for a while then he must have realised that the only people driving a BMW Z3 on the Forest Court estate were likely to be drug dealers or connected in some way. He accepted my offer. I knew he wouldn't bother hanging about long waiting for a fiver but at least my car would still be in one piece when I got back. I walked past the burnt out Sierra and headed for the stairwell. Broken glass was strewn all over the car park and the usual graffiti covered the walls.

In the entrance of the stairwell sat a man in his forties with his head in his hands. Balding with an ear ring in one ear, he had a tattoo on the skin between the base of his thumb and forefinger on his left hand. The initials FC showed that he was an original Forest Courter. Like a borstal spot, it showed where you had come from and marked you for life. He had lived here all his life and was unlikely ever to move. He looked over at me but not in the threatening way you expect when confronted by a stranger in a dark stairwell. He looked a broken man, not caring who or what I was. Usually the appearance of a man in a suit would set the alarm bells ringing. Inevitably it would be the police or a funeral director. He looked as though he would be happy to see either as long as they took him away from here. I tried a half smile as way of a greeting.

"Alright Mate. Haven't seen you for a long time." His voice sounded familiar. I looked a little closer and realised I recognised this man. I couldn't put a name to the face but I knew that I had went to school with him. He hadn't aged well.

"And you can take your frigging clothes with you an' all." A woman's voice screamed from the balcony above us. A pair of jeans hit the ground at our feet.

"Meet the missus," he said as he picked up the jeans. The crotch had been crudely cut out with scissors. "Caught me playing away from home with the barmaid down the club. She'll get over it, it's not the first time." He shrugged his shoulders in a gesture of apathy.

"Here's the fucking rest of them." I looked up just in time to see a wardrobe being edged over the balcony. I dived into the stairwell as it came crashing to the ground, splintering all over the car park. He shrugged again.

"See you later, mate," he said, possibly expecting the marital bed to come flying down and join the wardrobe.

"Hope it all works out for you." I said as I headed up the stairwell to the fourth floor where I would find Elvis' flat. The light was out on the stairs but you could feel the ever-present dampness. It was slippery under foot due to the slimy residue that had built up on the concrete stairs over the years. The ammonia like stench of urine burnt the hairs on the inside of my nose. This place was depressing. Surely Elvis could do better than this.

****

In between holidays Elvis, Bumper, Gilbert and myself went to St Christopher's primary school. I enjoyed school, not that I would admit it but apart from football and watching Claire Pearson, it was my favourite pastime. Claire was in my class and she was beautiful. We were the two top performers in our year and always got chosen for the special tasks like doing readings in assembly. This was great as I always got to sit next to her. I knew I was going to marry her when I was older, I loved her.

"Pete, could you go down and see Sister Mary? She wants you to take a message down to the St Patrick's for her." It was always a bonus when I was sent to the big school as the school secretary. Mrs Patterson had a jar of swizzle lollipops and she always gave me one when I went down there.

I walked the couple of hundred yards from our school gate to that of St Patrick's, clutching the brown envelope in my hand. A stone bounced just in front of me and ricocheted across the pavement. I looked towards the far side of the road where a group of about a dozen lads sat on the wall next to the all weather pitch. They weren't from St Patrick's as they were wearing different ties; they all carried sticks or bats of some description. Mrs Patterson ran from the main entrance and ushered me inside.

"Are you alright, Pete love?" she asked with concern as she took me into her office. The stone throwing hadn't bothered me but she seemed to think it was serious. "Phone the police, Linda. They're back again." The three women in the office stared out of the window as Linda picked up the phone. "It's ok Linda, Mr Swinbank's going to have a word with them."

I watched as a great hulk of a man, bigger than Uncle Tim, walked across the road towards the group of lads. He had two other teachers with him; they each carried a hockey stick and a brief discussion followed. The young lads walked off grudgingly, scuffing their shoes on the ground as they left. Mr Swinbank came into the office to make sure that everyone was alright.

"I'll walk you back up to school, son. You never know what that lot will get up to next." I agreed with Mr Swinbank, disappointed that Mrs Patterson, who was now busily munching on a cream cake, had forgotten to give me a lollipop.

****

A good wine may have been a bit pretentious so I settled on a bottle of plonk and eight cans of Boddingtons. I was quite taken aback when Declan answered the door. He was the double of his dad even down to the specs. I got even more of a shock when I saw Marie. Short cropped hair and another pair of thick glasses. I was beginning to feel under dressed. They were all clones.

"Hi Pete, good to see you again," Marie gave me a hug and a peck on the cheek. "What have you been doing with yourself?"

"This and that, you know how it is."

"I don't actually. You disappeared fifteen years ago and nobody has heard anything since"

"Yeah I've been busy. How are you anyway?" I handed over the wine and cans. Marie seemed pleased with my choice.

"Good, good. Elvis's doing well at the shop and Declan is doing well at school, right little bright spark he is. Chicken all right for you?" She shepherded me into the sitting room. "It was all a bit short notice. You could be a vegetarian or anything."

"I haven't changed that much, chicken's great. Do you see many of them from school then?"

"Yeah, now and again. Down at the shops and that. Elvis says you were wanting to get a school reunion going."

"Well it was an idea."

"I thought you hated school and most people in it. Why do you want to go over old ground?" Marie took my jacket.

"Just interested I suppose. See how people are doing now. Gilbert for example I wonder how he's getting on."

"Bank Manager."

"Fucking Hell, Gilbert Douglas is a Bank Manager?" I was shocked.

"Mind your language in front of the kid," Marie slapped me on the arm.

"Sorry, it's just I can't believe that Gilbert's a Bank Manager."

"She's pulling your leg, he's a gardener," Elvis walked back into the sitting room carrying a bottle of Bordeaux that put my plonk to shame.

"Thank God for that. You had me worried for a moment," I thought the world had been turned on its head.

"We were keeping this bottle for a special occasion. I guess a visit after fifteen years warrants a special occasion." I suddenly felt quite embarrassed by the bottle in my hand and tried to hide it. Elvis noticed so I attempted an excuse.

"It was the only wine they had. If I had a bit more time I would have got something better."

"No problem. Marie loves Liebfraumilch," she looked at him quizzically.

"Yeah. I'll just pop it in the fridge," they obviously thought I had fallen on hard times and didn't want to embarrass me.

"Let's eat. I'm starving and I can't wait to show you your surprise," Elvis looked excited "Another face from school you might recognise but possibly not quite as you may remember it."

****

The four of us were lucky enough to all be in the same class. Elvis and myself always sat together although Bumper and Gilbert generally stayed apart. They were friends outside of school but Gilbert was what was known as a 'Special Child' who needed extra attention. They sat in the corner of the classroom in their own group however as I was always top of the class, I sometimes got to help him with his Maths.

I'd never been to Gilbert's house but it was rumoured that they didn't have a television. He didn't have a dad either; I wasn't sure which was worse. The lack of a television, however, might explain why he wasn't very bright.

Mrs Matthews was a pleasant woman who always had time for us. She had a jar of sweets in her desk and she used to give them out for good work. Bumper was always good at painting. Elvis and myself were good at Maths and I also excelled at English. Gilbert was good at remembering to turn up but very little else.

We were in the middle of an art lesson when Karen Walker, who was Claire's best friend, raised her hand.

"Please Miss, Kevin Davison's escaped," and he had. As we looked out of the first floor window we saw the tubby shape of Kevin disappearing over the school fence. He removed his elasticated red tie and threw it to the floor.

"Let the Bugger go," said Mrs Matthews.

****

"Come on then. What is it that you're so desperate to show me?" The meal had been lovely. Chicken with Basil and cherry tomatoes in a cream sauce. The wine had relaxed me and I was feeling at ease.

"Do you remember Mr Burns?" Elvis moved over to a PC in the corner.

"I could hardly forget him, the old bastard," I replied. "I was hoping he was dead."

"He'll probably wish he was soon. You know I fix computers?"

"Yeah?"

"Well, the other day I was sitting in the shop doing a bit of work and who should walk in but old Burnsy. He's got this top of the range PC. Bit of a surprise really considering what an old fart he is," Elvis tapped away on his keyboard.

"Anyway, his hard drive was buggered and he wanted to know if I could fix it. Cheeky Bastard wanted a discount because he used to teach us. I should charge the twat double for what he put us through."

"Too bloody right," I agreed as Marie started clearing the table. I headed over to the PC.

"I went round to his house but it was a bigger job than I had expected and I had to take it back to the shop," Elvis inserted a disk into the drive. "I got it up and running but being the nosy bugger I am, I decided to have a bit of a poke about in his files. See if there was anything in there about any of his old pupils. I came across a couple of files that were password protected. It made me think because there's only him and his old bird in the house and I'm sure she doesn't know how to work the computer. Well passwords are a doddle to override when you know what you're doing."

"Enough of the computer master class, Elvis. Are you going to get to the point?"

"Yeah, I was just about to. Have a butchers at what came up when I got into the files."

"Fucking Hell!" My jaw dropped when I saw the screen. I had to grab the back of the sofa to regain my balance. The wine must have been stronger than I thought.

"Makes interesting viewing doesn't it?"

"Interesting viewing? I can't believe it."

"And that's not the best of it," Elvis clicked on another file.

"Jesus, that's fucking sick."

"Yeah I don't think it would go down to well with the PTA would it?"

****

"Jesus," we watched as Kev ran across the road and flicked the Vs to the bus driver who honked his horn at him.

We found out the next day that Mr Rowcroft had invited Kev to the front of the class to get his backside warmed by his trainer. This was due to the fact that Kev had attempted to set fire to Kelly Atkinson's hair. He deemed this an unfair punishment and decided to go home. Whilst Gilbert was a 'Special Child' there was something a little more special about Kevin Davison as we were all eventually to find out.

****

Claire put on her swimsuit and took a glass of wine out to the pool. She knew she still had a good figure, although she had let herself go a little bit recently. Gilbert was working in the garden and she noticed him looking. It always embarrassed him when she wore her swimsuit. Without letting on she had seen him she adjusted the top of her swimsuit showing off her cleavage to full effect. *If he's going to look, he might as well see something worthwhile.*

Gilbert could feel his cheeks glowing as he dug a hole with his trowel. He could virtually dig it with the bulge he had in his pants.

****

"Have you s s s s seen this?" Elvis waved a copy of the Echo at me frantically.

"No, what's up?"

"Elvis C c c c costello is p p p p playing at the City Hall. We have to go and s s s see him." His eyes seemed to double in size beneath his glasses.

"How are we going to manage that?" I asked. "I get ten pence a week pocket money and the tickets will cost at least a fiver."

"I've got a p p p plan." Elvis said eagerly. "We can take all the empty p p p pop bottles back to the shop and make money that way. Then we can do odd jobs for people, gardening and stuff. We'll make a f f f fortune." He wasn't going to be distracted from his task.

"Who's Elvis Costello?" Gilbert looked confused.

"Who's Elvis Costello?" Exclaimed Elvis. "Are you joking? He's the greatest p p p p pop star ever. Oliver's army, Accidents will happen, you must know who he is."

"No, never heard of him."

"Tall bloke, skinny, with thick glasses, ring any bells," Bumper joined in nodding in Elvis' direction.

"I never knew you were a pop star, Elvis." Gilbert was more confused than ever.

"He's not the pop star, idiot," Bumper shook his head "he's just named after him."

"I wish I had a pop star named after me, it must be great." We looked at each other in disbelief; this was going to be harder than I thought.

"Come on, we'll explain it on the way," Bumper put his arm around Gilbert as we headed down the street. We were off to work.

****

I had been sat in the car for over an hour now and was beginning to drift off. The knock on the window took me by surprise.

"Pete?"

"Gilbert, I didn't see you there, mate. How are you?" I straightened myself up and tried to look awake.

"Good, I haven't seen you in ages. It must be at least two or three..."

"Fifteen, Gilbert. It's been fifteen years since I've seen you."

"Is it? I never was that good at maths. What are you doing back here?"

"Thought I'd look up a few mates. Maybe have a bit of a reunion."

"Good idea. Were you going to see Kev?" asked Gilbert. "I've just finished his garden. He's doing all right for himself now, making a mint. Not that I'm sure what he does mind but he has got a big house."

"Kev lives round here does he? I didn't realise. He is doing well isn't he? Anyway I'm glad I've bumped into you. I've got an invite to the school reunion for you," I took an invite from the glove box and handed it to Gilbert.

"Fancy dress? Great, I love fancy dress. I might go as Batman."

"Fancy dress? What makes you say that?" I was confused.

"Mr Burns being dressed as a frogman. I just thought it was fancy dress."

"It's not a frogman's outfit it's...oh never mind. You will be coming won't you?"

"Yeah try keeping me away," with that Gilbert turned away to walk down the road. I noticed that he had his name imprinted on the back of his black leather biker's jacket in metal studs. GIBLET it proudly proclaimed. He stopped for a moment, turned round and headed back towards to the car pushing his wheelbarrow in front of him. "Wrong way," he said, pointing in the direction he was going. "I've got shit for brains."

****

"Sorry son we don't have a garden," the old woman shut the door on us.

"Who's stupid idea was this," Bumper looked at us all, "deciding to become gardeners in a street of terraced houses? We'll be lucky if we get a window box to work on." We'd been trying all day and hadn't earned a penny.

"I knew it was a waste of time," said Elvis.

"No you didn't," I said, " it was your idea."

"B b b bugger off." Elvis stormed off down the street in the huff. I looked at my watch; it was nearly tea time.

"I'm off home, see you tomorrow."

Gilbert and Bumper were left leaning against the wall. "I still don't get it," said Gilbert, "if Elvis is a pop star, why can't he get us free tickets?"

****

The rain had been falling steadily for nearly two hours now. The windows of the BMW were a torrent of water. I didn't want to use the wipers too much in case I drew attention to myself. I was parked just down the street from the large detached house I was watching. I was convinced it was Claire I had seen. I possibly should have asked Gilbert; if he was working round here surely he would know which house Claire lived in.

At first I had thought my eyes were playing tricks on me. After what Elvis had shown me last night I didn't believe anything I saw anymore. Fifteen years hadn't dulled my memories though. Admittedly she was a little plumper than I remembered, then again who wasn't? Her hair was different, bobbed but still modern. I'd always worried that when I returned she would be somehow different, maybe fatter, or tattooed or anything. I wasn't sure what I'd thought. She was still as beautiful as I remembered and was obviously doing okay for herself. A big house on the seafront, she always said she was going to become successful and I was happy for her.

It had been a chance sighting. I had headed down towards the beach as I had wanted to check out the lighthouse and see the changes that had been made to the seafront. It had been one of the first things on my 'To Do' list when I returned. There was a new pub that was made out of a railway carriage. The Pullman Lodge sat alongside the Seaburn Centre, a small but tidy sports centre. The supermarket was also new, everything had changed and I was amazed at the transformation. I had started at the bridge and walked down past the university and the Glass Centre, stopping to try out the glass roof I had heard so much about. It was a magnificent structure but a sign of the times that the first thing the national press picked up on was the fact that you could see up a woman's skirt if she walked on the transparent roof. I checked out the sculptures as I headed down to the harbour to look around the new marina. The yachts and penthouse flats suggested that there was more money in Sunderland than I thought. The dog shit that covered the marina suggested that some people didn't deserve it.

****

I slammed the door behind me as I walked into the house. "Don't slam that bloody door," my mother shouted. I slumped on the settee and noticed Tim sat there.

"Alright, Tim?"

"I'm ok, what's the matter with your face?"

"We've been trying to earn money all day to go and see Elvis Costello and we haven't made a button."

"Just as well," my mother had just come into the sitting room, "if you had made the money you still wouldn't have been able to go."

"How?"

"You're eleven years old, Pete. I wouldn't let you go to Newcastle on your own."

"I wouldn't be on my own. I would be with, Elvis, Bumper and Gilbert."

"That doesn't exactly fill me with confidence. You're not going and that's final," my mother headed back towards the kitchen to finish the tea.

"That's a shame," said Tim, "seeing as I've got these." He produced four tickets from his pocket.

"Are they what I think they are?" I asked excitedly.

"They are but your Mam said you can't go on your own and I've got to agree with her."

"It's not fair."

"It's lucky I got one for myself then, isn't it?" Tim smiled as he took a fifth ticket from his pocket. I somersaulted off the settee and gave him a hug.

"I'm going to tell Elvis," I shouted as I ran for the door. "Oliver's army are on their way."

****

I had returned to the car and continued along the coast past the now derelict fountain and the refurbished Seaburn Hotel. The spouts of the fountain sticking up like a metal thistle. I was on my way back past the park when I saw her going into the off licence. I wasn't sure at first but as she got closer I knew it was Claire. The walk, everything was the same. Except for the smile. The smile seemed to have gone. If it had been anyone else I would have gone straight up to them to introduce myself, invite them to the reunion and do a bit of catching up. Basically what any normal person would do after they hadn't seen an old school friend for fifteen years. Not Claire though, I couldn't do it. *Bugger.* The shyness took over and I couldn't understand why. We had been friends years ago after all. It just wasn't that easy. Instead I followed her home and parked in the bus stop opposite her house. The advert on the bus shelter was encouraging people to use their mobiles more to contact old friends. I watched her cross the road and go into the large building on the corner. It was a bit tacky for my liking, lions on the gateposts and a mermaid fountain in the garden but it was Claire's and I had to admit that I was pleased to see her. Maybe she had just moved in and was planning to change it. I switched off the engine and tried to pluck up the courage to cross the road.

****

Bumper picked at the hot tar with a lolly stick as we sat in the lane against my back wall. It was a hot day so we had decided to take a break from the football.

"I'm not sure I understand this, why do we want to fight?" Asked Elvis.

"We have to find out who is the hardest," I replied.

"But why? We're all friends. We don't need to fight. I don't want to fight," Elvis removed his glasses, using the lenses to magnify the sun's rays and melt the tar.

"Are you bottling it?"

"No. I'm not b b b bottling it. I just don't see the p p p point. Who's involved?" As with all young lads, some in our group were harder than others. The trouble was we didn't know which ones. As we had never fought each other we could only assume. With this in mind we decided we would have a boxing competition to decide.

"Everyone's involved. We want to see who is the hardest lad in Southwick," I knew this wasn't strictly the case.

"But we don't know everyone in Southwick and if you think I'm f f f fighting Kevin D d d davison you can get lost." Elvis was losing his temper, which I have to admit wasn't good for whoever was going to fight him.

"Ok. Fair enough," I had to agree with him. "It will just be the lads we play football with. The winner will still be the hardest lad in Southwick we just won't tell anybody else in case he gets beaten up."

****

I had spent nearly four hours trying to pluck up the courage to go and speak to Claire. Only the intervention of Gilbert had interrupted my silent vigil. Well it was now or never. I grabbed an invitation from the glove box and got out of the car. The rain was lashing down now and the seafront was deserted. I pulled the collar of my suit jacket up around my neck and jogged across the road, dodging the puddles. I headed up the drive and to the front door and could feel my face burning up as I got closer to the house.

Stay calm. I said to myself. When I rang the doorbell I looked down at the invitation in my hand and suddenly had a panic attack. *Jesus, what if she doesn't recognise me? She'll think I'm some kind of pervert.* Quickly I stuffed the invitation in my pocket.

"Yeah?" The size of the man answering the door took me completely by surprise. He was about six two and quite obviously worked out. In fact he was huge.

"Err, erm.... I was just."

"Look, we don't need new windows, kitchen, conservatory or fucking cuddly toy so if you're selling something you can fuck off. If you're the Police I want to see your warrant card and then you can fuck off." This bloke was a one hundred per cent dickhead but he had really thrown me off guard. Everything I had planned to say turned into mumbles and stutters.

"No I'm not selling... I was looking for...maybe I've got the wrong house, sorry." I turned to leave. I was half way down the path when he shouted after me.

"Hold on. Pete? It's Peter Wood isn't it?"

"Yeah but how..." I turned back, surprised, then the truth dawned on me.

****

Elvis reluctantly agreed to the fight and wrote everybody's name on a piece of paper. As it had been my idea, I got to draw first.

"Who've you got?" Asked Bumper, who was shadow boxing against the wall. I unfolded the small square of paper and read the name to myself. A look of relief spread across my face.

"Gilbert." Gilbert had a reputation for being soft so I was quite confident that I could take him.

We took our shirts off and stood in the middle of the field. Gilbert was far bigger and heavier than me but I was quicker and brighter. I would defeat him with cunning. Everybody crowded round.

"How do we start?" Asked Gilbert.

"I'm not sure." It was at this point that I realised that I had never been in a fight before.

"Most of the older lads just shout come on then," said Elvis.

"You could just hit him," suggested Bumper.

"What do you mean hit him?"

"It's a fight. That's what you are meant to do. Punch him," I looked at Elvis. "Go on. You can't have a fight without hitting each other."

I threw a wild punch at Gilbert and he hit the ground like a ton of bricks.

"He's out cold," Bumper stood back and looked on in amazement.

"What are we g g g going to do? His Mam'll kill us." Elvis started to panic.

"Get some water."

"What?"

"Throw water over him. That's what they do with boxers." Just as Bumper said this, Gilbert came round to relieved cheers from everyone.

"I'm not sure I want to fight, " said Bumper.

"Me neither, " said Elvis. Nobody had considered the fact that you could actually get hurt fighting. "Fancy a game of football?"

"Bags eye I'm Gary Rowell!" shouted Bumper.

When Elvis had gone chasing down the bank after the ball I took Gilbert to one side.

"You took a dive didn't you? I never touched you."

"You won't tell anyone will you?"

"Course not, but why did you do it?"

"Who wants to be known as the 'Hardest Lad in Southwick' when Kevin Davison finds out?"

****

"Kev?" I was gob-smacked.

"Fucking hell mate, how are you doing? It must be four, five…."

"Fifteen, Kev. It's been fifteen years since I've seen you."

"Well you might as well come in then." Despite his earlier greeting and previous form he was being quite sociable. I wondered if he remembered what had happened at St Patrick's. Then I realised, what had been a huge deal for me, engulfing my life for the last fifteen years, probably meant nothing to him. Judging by the size of the house he was obviously doing very well and had bigger things to worry about.

"What are you drinking? I've got just about everything." He opened the lid on his globe drinks cabinet. It looked antique but most probably wasn't. "Straight from Nelson's drawing room," he said pointing at the cabinet.

"Whisky please." I hoped it was a strong one. I needed it.

"What was it you said you were selling?"

"I'm not. I was just back here for a couple of weeks. Thought I would look up a few of the lads. I was planning a bit of a reunion. You know, a party?"

"Alright, I see and you were wanting me to organise the security?"

"Security?"

"Yeah, I know a couple of lads who'll watch the door for you, good lads. I'll do you a canny deal, being old mates and that." Kev poured a generous measure into the tumbler.

"Bloody Hell, Kev. It's a school reunion not the Hells Angels' summer bash."

"You're probably right, maybe one lad will be enough."

"No Kev, I think we're at cross purposes here."

"Cross what?"

"I was just wondering if you fancied coming along," the words nearly stuck in my throat. This had been quite an unwelcome surprise. I fumbled in my pocket for the invite.

"Yeah I see, I suppose if I was there nobody would dare cause any trouble. There will be drinks on won't there? I couldn't stand it if there wasn't any booze." Kev stared at the invitation. "Fucking Hell, is that who I think it is?"

"Yes, the legendary Mr Burns. I couldn't believe my eyes when I saw it. Fucking class isn't it?" I was annoyed at myself for swearing; I was already sinking to his level.

"You're telling me? There's a lot of money in blackmail these days. I bet Mrs Burns hasn't seen it." Kev examined the invitation carefully.

"I hadn't thought of that. Anyway, most of the invites are out now so half the town will know soon. What do you reckon then?"

"Blackmail is always an earner." I could see the cogs moving round in his head.

"Not about that. Do you think you'll come along? It will be good to see how all the old lads are getting on." I hated this man but started warming to the idea of the overgrown orang-utan showing himself up and proving what a Neanderthal he had become. Just as me and everybody else had thought he would.

"Most of the lads work for me now anyway in one way or another but yeah, I'll be there," Kev scratched his arse. "Our lass would love a night out as well, she doesn't get out much. She's in the kitchen, I'll give her a shout." Kev left the room and headed for the kitchen. I took a big swig out of the whisky he had given me. I was confused maybe I had got the wrong house.

"Pete?" The voice was just as I remembered. I went red again.

"Claire?" I could feel my face burning up. The whisky started to have an effect. What had earlier been a dream was suddenly turning into a nightmare.

****

We were about four hours into the second half when Elvis had his accident. My side including Gilbert and Bumper was in quite a commanding position with us leading thirty-five goals to twenty-four. This was mainly due to Elvis's team including Gilbert's older brothers Gerald and Bernard Douglas. You would think that experience would have given them an advantage over us however they seemed to have just learnt more mistakes and clumsy challenges. Whilst most of us attempted to wear some sort of football kit, Bernard took us all by surprise with his outfit. He wore a patterned, woollen sweater, paisley boxer shorts, the like of which we had never seen, we were used to Spiderman y-fronts, and a pair of navy socks and brown brogues.

"What's he come dressed as?" asked Elvis.

"His todger's going to come out of those shorts if he's not careful," observed Bumper. We just shrugged and got on with the game. I had run down the right wing and chipped the ball to Gilbert who attempted what could only be described as a tricycle kick with arms and legs flailing everywhere. The ball, which should have been nestling in the imaginary net at the back of the bush end, had flown in quite the opposite direction and had gone out of play on the Tate side. Elvis chased after it.

 He wasn't looking where he was going when he slipped.

That's when the car hit him.

****

"Are you all right Pete?" My head was thumping and my eyes were just about focusing. I felt the back of my head and there was an egg-sized lump but luckily there didn't appear to be any blood. I could make out two fuzzy heads, they started to become clearer, and I was starting to remember. Claire and Kev. Yes, that was it Claire and Kev. The slow realisation didn't do much for my bad head. I was beginning to feel nauseous; the salty saliva was now forming in my mouth. I was going to be sick.

"Can't take his drink, that's his problem. One sip of whisky and he's on his arse."

"Shut up, Kev. He's not well."

"I'm Ok. It's just a bit hot in here," I was starting to come round." Can I use your bathroom?"

The cold white porcelain in the spacious bathroom had been a relief. I threw up once, seeing Marie's lovingly cooked meal in front of me again. I got up washed my face and drank a glass of water, noticing the photo of Kev and Alvin Stardust on the wall.

I realised that last night had taken it's toll. I'd stayed up all night with Elvis making the invitations and we managed to polish off best part of a bottle of Bells along with the Boddingtons and wine. We even drank the Liebfraumilch. Marie had gone to bed and left us to it. I'd felt a bit sheepish when she woke me up on the couch in the morning.

"We don't see you for fifteen years and then you come here, get drunk and fall asleep on the couch. What impression is that to give Declan, or Elvis for that matter?" Marie gave me a telling off.

"I'm sorry, I think we got a bit carried away."

"Don't worry about it. Elvis seems happy to see you and that's good enough for me. He's been a bit down lately."

Why hadn't Elvis and Marie warned me about Claire and Kev? It wasn't that I hadn't asked. I'd mentioned Claire a couple of times to both of them. They just avoided the question, saying that they saw her about occasionally but didn't speak much. They were even less forthcoming about Kev I'd put it down to the fact that there wouldn't be anything interesting to tell about the ape-man. Even if he had been inside it wouldn't have been newsworthy. It was the least that was expected of him.

"So what's this Kev was saying about a school reunion?" Claire sat me down on the sofa. "Sounds like a good idea. I get to see quite a lot of people from school but they never really have the time to speak. You know how it is, everyone lives their life at one hundred miles an hour now."

"I'm off to do some business. Don't give him anymore to drink; we don't want him to be sick on the carpet. Cost me a fucking packet, well it would have done if I'd actually paid for it."

"See you Kev, be careful," Claire waved him out of the door, eager for him to go to work.

"So what business is he in then?" I asked.

"Oh just this and that, you know. Do you want a coffee or something? We've got a lot of catching up to do."

"No thanks, not at the moment. I've got quite a lot to do, people to see. Maybe catch up later?" I wanted to get out and clear my head. I needed some time to take everything in. "Maybe another time."

"Yeah, everybody lives their lives at one hundred miles an hour." I noticed a sadness in her voice that hadn't been there before. "Do you need a taxi?"

"No, I've got the car thanks."

"And you're sure you are all right to drive?" Claire looked worried. Her concern was justified seeing as I collapsed as soon as I walked through the door then threw up in her bathroom.

"Yeah. Sorry about earlier. I think it's the jet lag and late nights catching up with me."

"Well make sure you get some rest before the reunion because I'll be expecting a dance from you. Great invitations by the way."

"What? Oh yeah Burnsy, excellent aren't they? I'll see you later then."

"Take care," Claire gave me a peck on the cheek and opened the door. The smile that I remembered returned to her face.

"See you later." I noticed the garden as I left. Despite the lions and the fountain it was really impressive. *Maybe Gilbert does have his uses.* I thought to myself.

****

To say that Mrs Morris was less than pleased was an understatement.

"What have you done to our Paul?"

"I haven't done anything. He ran out into the road," I protested.

"You're his friend. You should have been looking after him." The police were now redirecting the traffic down the back lane as Elvis was loaded into the ambulance. The sirens and blue flashing lights had brought out the crowds. Elvis was a celebrity. "Why don't you have ball boys like they do at real matches?" I think she was being a little bit unreasonable now.

"I've got to go now. Your mother will be hearing about this, Peter Wood." Mrs Morris followed Elvis into the ambulance.

"What's that smell?" She climbed back out of the ambulance pinching her nose. I could smell it from where I was. It really was a pungent stink. I desperately hoped that Elvis hadn't disgraced himself and had two accidents for the price of one.

"It's his trousers Mrs Morris, " said the ambulance man. I feared the worst.

"Looks like he slipped in some dog muck." I glanced at Gilbert. It was his poor shot in the chod chucking competition two days earlier that had caused the accident.

"Isn't that meant to be lucky?" asked Bumper. "Next goal the winner?" he shouted as we kicked off again.

****

"This is a strange place to hide." I was surprised to hear Claire's voice but didn't react. "I followed you. I could see you were upset."

"I wasn't upset."

"You didn't know about me and Kev did you?"

"No, it did come as a bit of a surprise. You seem happy enough though," I said. Claire shrugged.

"Things change, Pete. You left fifteen years ago, things move on, people move on."

"I'm happy for you," I lied.

"I wish I knew what you were really thinking. You never have shown any emotion have you? Nobody can be as cold and heartless as you pretend to be. There must be something bursting to come out. Come on why don't you say what you really feel, just for once?" Claire placed her hand on my face. "What is it? Are you scared of getting hurt? You're safe with me, I won't hurt you." I turned and stared out towards the sea.

"I used to come here when I was a kid. Any shit at home or school and I would just walk away, come down here and stare at the sea for hours. Nobody ever missed me. I sometimes sneaked out at night and came here. It's so peaceful. I would watch the light searching across the sea. Funny thing about the lighthouse is, while it appears to be looking for something it's actually trying to warn people off, keep them away. Save them from getting hurt."

"Is that what you're trying to do. Save me from getting hurt? Or are you actually searching for something? I'm a big girl now I can take the knocks. I've learnt to roll with the punches."

"There's things you don't know about me, things that you wouldn't like."

"You're not that complicated, Pete. You have to forget about the past, leave it all behind. Then you might actually find what it is you're looking for."

"I've tried that, remember? I left fifteen years ago and I'm still no further forward. I came back hoping to find some answers but I'm just finding more questions."

****

"Why can't we go?" Asked Bumper.

"We've told you. It's too dangerous," Elvis had returned after his accident. His mother had been reluctant to let him play with us but I think she relented when she got sick of him being under her feet all day. He had a chalk on his leg that we had all signed and also a pair of crutches.

"I don't get it. How can going to a printers be dangerous?" We had to have regular breaks from the football now that Elvis was back. Whilst he was on crutches, he still insisted on playing in goal. He couldn't stand for too long so we got to enjoy the rest. I sucked the moisture from a piece of grass.

"I bet a dog's peed on that," said Elvis. "The way they shit all over the place I wouldn't be surprised." I tried to act like I wasn't bothered when I threw it away.

"Come on, why is it dangerous?"

"What do they print there, Bumper?" I asked.

"Football programmes, you've already told me that part."

"And what is on the back of the programme?"

"I don't understand."

"On every football programme you've ever seen, what is written on the back page?"

"The teams?"

"Exactly," said Elvis and me in unison.

"You've lost me," Bumper was confused.

"What day is today?"

"Wednesday."

"And what day is the next match?"

"Saturday," Bumper replied.

"That's our point!"

"Your point is that it's Wednesday?"

"How do they know what the team is going to be on a Wednesday when the match isn't until Saturday?" I asked. The penny finally dropped with Bumper.

"You mean that Ken Knighton works in the printers?"

"Not exactly but he must tell them the team early in the week. That's why the security is so tight."

"Imagine knowing the team before Saturday. We would be celebrities. We have to go," I stared at Bumper. He obviously hadn't listened to a word I had said.

"He's right though isn't he?" Said Elvis. I couldn't believe what was coming from his lips. "It's got to be worth a look."

"It will be suicide."

"Not if we have a plan," said Bumper.

****

Two burly men passed me as I entered Elvis's shop, each one carrying a P.C. "Business picking up?" I asked.

"Not quite. Didn't you recognise them? That was Tomma and Couzens from school."

"What were they doing here?"

"Come to collect their insurance payment. I didn't have the cash so they took stock instead."

"How much are you paying them? Those computers must be worth a fortune."

"Too much," Elvis rubbed his eyes. "What can I do? They work for Kevin Davison."

"Why didn't you tell me about Claire and Kev?"

"You're obsessed, Pete. You always have been. Why can't you just move on and forget about her?"

"It's not that easy, Elvis. Do you fancy a pint tonight?"

"Can't really afford it mate."

"No problem, I'll get them in, seven thirty in the Ivy? I've got a little business proposition for you."

****

"What do you mean we just go and ask for a look around?" I asked with amazement.

"They'll not be expecting it. Who has ever heard of spies knocking on the front door and asking to have a bit of a nose about? It's foolproof, we'll tell them it's for a school project." Bumper had a point but I still wasn't sure.

"What if they do realise what we are up to? We'll be dead men."

"It's a chance we've got to take. It's our only way in." I considered this for a while.

"Ok. I agree. Is everybody else in? Let's see a show of hands." Three hands rose slowly. One didn't.

"How about you, Gilbert?"

"I'm not sure," Gilbert had sat silently through the whole conversation.

"Come on, what are you scared of?"

"I'm not scared. It's just…."

"It just what?" I was raring to go now and couldn't understand why Gilbert was holding us back.

"The skip. What about the skip?"

"What's the skip?" Asked Bumper. I shuffled up closer to him as I explained, trying not show any fear.

"I've seen it, when we drove past one day with my parents but I knew about it long before I saw it." We had all heard about it.

"It's a large, red, m m m m metal container about eight foot high by ten feet long and about three feet across the m m m m middle," stuttered Elvis. "There's a door on one side with a bolt and large p p p padlock on it."

"That's where they put the Missing Boys," added Gilbert.

"The what?" asked Bumper.

"The Missing Boys. Boys who have attempted to break into the printers in the past to get their hands on the programmes. They were locked in there and never came out."

"You're joking. They can't get away with that. What about the police?"

"They are in on it as well. You can never escape the skip," Gilbert was obviously scared.

"What's inside the skip?" asked Bumper.

"N n n nobody's sure as n n n nobody has ever got out of it alive b b b but I've heard that there are two over grown Alsatian d d d dogs that they leave hungry until they feed them children, " replied Elvis. Bumper was shocked but persistent.

"I still want to go. We'll be heroes." We all nodded.

Gilbert took a felt pen from Elvis and started to draw a map on his chalk.

"If we are going to do it, we might as well do it right."

****

"Well, what do you think?" Elvis and me were tucked in a quiet corner of the Ivy House. The pub had been refurbished a number of times over the years but the feel of the place was still the same despite two rooms having been knocked into one. At the bar end stood a pool table and alongside that was the entrance to the Gent's toilets. Whilst the Ivy House was by no means a drugs den, it did have that element within it's clientele and they chose to congregate at this end of the bar. The regular procession of sniffing, edgy twenty-something's emerging from the cubicles would seem obvious to anybody who bothered to take the time to notice. Elvis and myself chose the far end. There was a coal fire and comfy armchairs along with a big screen showing Sky Sports Centre. "Fuck off you twat." Rodney Marsh was on the screen yet again, annoying the viewers.

Elvis had said that you could feel the pub get warmer the further up the bar you went and I knew what he meant. It wasn't physically warmer; there were radiators at the pool end. It was the warmth of atmosphere and the lack of the distrusting paranoia that emanated from the drug takers further back. We needed to talk so the fire end suited us fine.

"You can count me out, no Fucking way. Absolutely not." Elvis had gone pale.

"I thought you were on my side. I thought you felt the same."

"I do. No I don't, well to a certain extent yes but not this. No, definitely not. You're on your own with this one."

"What have you got to lose?"

"What have I got to lose? You self-centred, fucking prick. I'll tell you what I've got to lose." Elvis was glowing red, like the blazing coal fire behind him. He leaned over the table and started to raise his voice. The angrier he became, the higher pitched his voice was.

"All right, all right, keep it down. People are beginning to look."

"Let them f f f fucking look. What will they see? One m m m man who has a wife and a child to feed. A home albeit a modest one, b b b but a home all the same. Don't forget the b b b business, I've built that up since I left school. They'll also see you. Someone who disappeared f f f fifteen years ago and has now returned under the pretence of meeting old friends but really you had a hidden agenda all along. You wanted to use these so-called friends to do your d d d dirty work." Elvis threw a beer mat across the table. "Well f f f fuck you and your stupid fucking ideas. I'd appreciate it if you kept away from my family and me from now on. You might as well have this back." He handed me the invitation for the reunion. "I was right all along."

We sat staring at each other for a few minutes whilst I composed myself.

"Well if that's how you feel I'll respect your wishes. Just remember the next time some hired thug comes round to the shop asking for money that should be really going to your wife and child. Money that should be putting you in a home that isn't modest. Money that should be invested in a business that after fifteen years should be huge with your talent but instead is a little boarded up shop on the outskirts of town. Remember, when that business goes bust and you lose your home and your wife and child. Remember that you had a chance to change all of that and you turned your back on it."

I was now also shouting, angry that Elvis couldn't see the chance he was about to throw away.

"Yeah, well I'll take my chances along with everybody else thank you very much." With that, Elvis downed his pint of Guinness and headed for the door.

I slumped back in my seat and contemplated my pint. I looked up at the screen where Rodney Marsh's mug was grinning down at me.

"Will someone turn that cunt off?"

****

We waited until it got dark and headed down to the car park. We wanted to show Bumper the area before we went to the printers the next day. There was only one car in the car park. It had a light on inside so we decided to take a look. Elvis had stayed at home due to the effort of walking on his crutches. Bumper, Gilbert and myself edged towards the car. We weren't entirely sure what the couple were doing in there but we were fairly sure they should have had some clothes on.

Whatever they were doing they didn't take kindly to three, eleven-year old boys having their faces pushed up to the glass. The man went for the door handle. We didn't need to hang about to see that he was unhappy so we legged it. When we got to the bank we looked back. He was standing there completely naked with his thingy hanging down. He was screaming and shouting and jumping up and down making it swing even more. It was hilarious.

****

The black Shogun swept into the car park and clipped the edge of the fruit and veg stall, sending the oranges and grapefruit tumbling to the floor.

"For fuck's sake," shouted Bumper as he scrambled around, picking up the fruit that was now rolling across the ground.

"Morning Bumper, lovely day for it," the shaven headed figure of Kevin Davison emerged from the 4 wheel drive. "I take it you have something for me?"

Bumper went into his money belt and counted out five twenty pound notes. He handed them over reluctantly.

"I think you'll find you're fifty short, Bumper."

"There's a hundred pounds there. It's the right money."

"Silly me. Did I not tell you that the rent had gone up? It's now one fifty a week. Come on, chop chop, I haven't got all day." Bumper took another fifty from his pouch and handed it over.

"Don't mind if I take these do you?" asked Kev as he took a bag of bananas. "Don't worry about the oranges, I'm sure you can claim on your insurance."

****

"I wish I'd seen it," said Elvis as we relived the tale of the previous night.

"What? You wanted to see the man's willy?" asked Bumper.

"No, do you think I'm a woofter or something?" Elvis looked hurt.

"I don't think that it was us that made him angry," said Gilbert after we stopped laughing.

"How do you mean?"

"I once walked in on my Mam and the bloke from next door. They were doing the same thing on the settee. They didn't see me but my Mam was screaming her head off." We were all confused about this but Gilbert agreed to ask his Mam what she was upset about when we got back from the printers.

We were glad that Gilbert had been persuaded to come with us and we headed down the bank alongside Tate's. With Elvis on crutches, we all had to take turns in offering a shoulder to support him. He slowed us down but he had to be there. Sapling trees grew on the steep grassy bank leading down to the car park. At the far side, another bank led down to the main road.

"Right, has anybody got any questions before we get there?" I asked.

"I've got one," said Bumper.

"What's that?"

"Why do they call orange jam, marmalade?" We all pushed him down the bank and he took out a couple of trees as he rolled down the hill.

Discussing the man and woman in the car had luckily kept our minds from what we were about to do and we shortly arrived at Inkerman Print. We crossed the short strip of grass and out of the sun and into the cold of the shadow behind the large red skip.

Nobody spoke. I noticed that although there was a large bolt on the skip there was no padlock. This could mean anything. Had they just put somebody in there? I couldn't hear any screams but this didn't comfort me. I decided to keep my thoughts to myself.

****

Tomma wasn't surprised when he got his visit. It was long overdue. He'd been careless and somebody was bound to notice. He was just glad it was Nick.

It was a couple of days ago when he found out, Friday afternoon it was. Tomma normally went to the bank on a Thursday to top up the Oz account but he'd been busy running errands for Kev. Friday was always a nightmare in the banks, all the factory girls cashing their paycheques then pissing it all away on the Friday night. He got caught in a queue and was therefore late getting to the Whistle. Usually he wouldn't take the Oz book anywhere near the lads but he was late. When he arrived most of the lads were already there. Tomma took off his jacket to play pool and the book fell out. Nick had picked it up and gave it back to him but Tomma hadn't been sure whether he had seen inside it. He was now.

"I've been watching you Tomma and I've got to admit I'm impressed. Making all this money for the lads and they love you for it but there's something that's been bothering me," Nick took a swig from his can. "I've seen how much cash we make and everybody takes a cut and goes home happy. You've got Kev wrapped around your little finger and that means you've got every little wannabe crawling up your arse. But I know you're stitching us, I know your cut's just that little bit bigger than everybody else."

****

Just as we reached the roller shutters of the printers and were about to knock, they clattered open. A large tattooed man with a moustache was stood behind it. Suddenly this didn't seem like such a good idea.

"Alright lads. What are you after?"

"Sounds quite friendly for a mass murderer," whispered Elvis.

"Perhaps after you've killed a few young lads it becomes second nature to you," replied Bumper. Everybody stared at the moustached man without speaking.

64

"Cat got your tongue?" He asked.

"We would like to have a look around if you don't mind?" Elvis spoke calmly and clearly.

"Look around? At what?" The man looked puzzled. I hoped we hadn't upset him.

"At how you make err...p p p programmes?" Elvis' stutter had returned.

"At p p p programmes eh?" This man was pure-bred evil.

"It's for a school p p p p p p project."

"Why not? I'm going for lunch now but one of the other lads will show you round." "Stan," he shouted. "There's some young lads here want to have a look around. Can you show them what they want to see? It's for a school project or something. I'm going to get the sarnies."

"Stan will show you around. See you soon lads." We all just grinned back stupidly.

****

"I've got you sussed and I want a part of it," Nick leaned back in his chair. "I'm not a greedy man, fifty, fifty will do. But if I ever think you're trying to stitch me then a little birdie is going to have a word in Kev's ear."

This was going to delay Tomma's plans. He had just over twenty thousand pounds in there, not quite enough to get him away for good. Not now that he had to hand over half of that to Nick. It wasn't fair he thought. After all he had done for these lads he deserved a bit extra. He just wasn't sure that Kev would see it that way. He slumped back in the chair. He wasn't going to try and lie his way out of it. Any of the other lads would have gone straight to Kev but Nick was different. He was only in it for himself.

"Ok, it will take a few days though."

"That's ok, I can wait." Nick drained his can and threw it in the bin.

Tomma watched Nick from the door and thought about disappearing straight away. He could easily do it he had the money after all. But he wanted to do it right. He knew how much he needed for his house and he wasn't going to leave before he got it. He would just have to work that little bit harder. Corners were going to have to be cut.

****

Stan took us through the whole process and appeared to be quite friendly. The whole printing thing, I have to admit should have been quite interesting but I didn't take any of it in. The machines clanked loudly as we walked past them. Stan's lips were moving but I couldn't make out what he was saying and my hands had started to get clammy with sweat. The anticipation was too much. When would he get to the end of the tour so we could see the finished product?

"I suppose you'll want to see a completed programme then?" He said as we had finished looking at the guillotine. We nodded enthusiastically. Stan ambled over to a box in the corner and fished a programme from the hundreds that were lying there.

"Here you go son," he said as he passed it to me. I wiped my hands on my pants before I took it from him. The other three crowded round me as I anxiously turned to the back page. And there they were, Saturday's teams in black and white, in my hands. I started to shake with excitement.

"Come on, that'll have to go back in the box with the others," said Stan as he snatched it cruelly from my hand. "They're all counted. I'd love to give you one lads but I'll be for the high jump." I tried to hide my disappointment but Elvis noticed.

"We've seen the teams. That's what we came for," he said.

"Did you have any questions?" Stan asked after he showed us round.

"Do you know what I don't understand?" said Bumper.

"What's that son?"

"Chinese writing," he laughed. I slapped him on the back of the head.

"Very funny, son. Has anybody got any serious questions?" We exchanged glances seeing if anybody would ask the question that had been bothering us all day.

Nobody spoke.

Except for Bumper.

Oh Shit!

"What's in the skip?"

"Idiot," Elvis kicked him, which was quite an achievement as he was wearing a cast on his left leg.

"Off cuts," Stan answered dismissively as he examined a random piece of printing. We looked at each other and shrugged our shoulders.

"What, like at the butchers, feet and things?" Stan seemed to find Bumper's question amusing. My heart was racing in time with the printing machine now. I began to realise how warm it was in there as the sweat started to gush out of every pore.

"Not quite," he said with a smirk. "Any programmes that aren't printed straight or when the colours aren't right. They all go in there."

"You must make plenty of mistakes, the bloody thing's huge," Bumper muttered. Luckily Stan chose to ignore, or did not hear his glib comment. Elvis kicked him again.

"What about dogs?" Gilbert spoke for the first time. I glared at him.

"No, we don't print dogs son," he laughed. "Or chop them up. The only dog here is the guard dog."

We breathed a collective sigh of relief. I had been holding my breath for what seemed like hours. There were no dead kids in the skip. No giant Alsatians, just a few old bits of paper and old programmes. We waved at Stan as we left. The moustache man had just returned with a box full of sandwiches.

"See what you wanted, lads?"

"Yes thanks," we replied cheerfully. The shutter clattered down behind us as we left and we all burst into laughter. It couldn't have gone any better.

"I can't wait to tell everyone about the skip," laughed Elvis.

"Me too. I can't believe I was so scared, " said Gilbert.

"Anyone remember the team?" I asked.

"Are you kidding?" We started to reel them off in unison. "Turner, Hinnigan, Munro, Buckley…."

"There is one little problem though," interrupted Bumper. "We don't have proof. We've seen the teams and we can recite them without thinking but who is going believe us? Everyone's going to think we have guessed," he was right, "we need a programme."

"Where will we get one?" Asked Gilbert. Bumper raised his eyebrows. We all knew the answer but didn't want to say.

"We could always go back and ask for one," I suggested.

"They'll never let us have one. We're lucky they even let us see one. Stan told us they were all counted." Bumper was right. I was just delaying the inevitable. There was only one place we were going to get a programme from.

"The Skip."

****

It wasn't difficult to find Bumper; after all there weren't that many six-foot bananas in the health club's car park.

"Alright, Bumper?"

"Pete? Jesus it must be at least ten years…."

"Fifteen, Bumper. It's been fifteen years since you've seen me."

"Yeah, fifteen eh? Bloody long time. You seem to be doing all right for yourself, very smart I must say."

"Thanks, you haven't changed a bit I see."

"The outfit you mean? It's my trademark now. Bit of a pain in the arse to tell you the truth but it keeps the punters happy," he held out his hand and shook mine firmly.

"How did you get the idea to dress as a banana?"

"I've worked on the market stalls since I left school. There hasn't been much money in it up until now. Then I had the idea to open a stall here. You know what they're like, all these fitness freaks, more interested in looking like they are being healthy rather than becoming fit. That's where I come in." Bumper offered me an orange, I shook my head. "They've got to be seen to eat a lot of fruit so I hit the jackpot. The outfit was just meant to be for the first day, get myself noticed. It had such an impact I decided to keep it for a while. I couldn't get rid of it now even if I wanted to. All the young lasses come out of the club and they can't wait to come and see Bumper the Banana boy. Sad really. I know they're taking the piss but as long as they are spending, who cares?"

"So you are making a bit of money then? It's good to see someone from school doing well for themselves."

"Not as much as I would like unfortunately. One of our school's other success stories is making a mint out of me." The bitterness in Bumper's voice was all too evident.

"Davison?"

"How did you guess? He owns this place you see. Charges me rent for using his car park and also gives me the benefit of one of his insurance schemes. Basically I give him money and he doesn't beat me up. Pretty much the same as school, nothing ever changes that much."

"I bumped into him the other day. It's surprising how far brute force and ignorance will get you these days."

"I take it you know about Claire then? It's a shame, she used to be such a nice lass." At least Bumper didn't try and hide it from me.

"Yeah, it was a bit of a surprise. Anyway, the real reason I'm here. How do you fancy coming to a school reunion? See how everybody else is getting on."

"I thought you hated school, why do you want to go back? It's all a bit depressing if you ask me."

"So you'll come along then?"

"Yeah, wouldn't miss it for the world," a big grin now spread across Bumper's yellow face.

"Best have an invite then," I passed him one of the invitations.

"Jesus, is that who I think it is?" he asked.

"The very same."

"Classic. Does he know you've got a copy of this?"

"Not yet but he will when he gets his own invite. It would be rude not to invite the teachers along wouldn't it? I think it's only fair that his wife receives an invite as well," I said.

"Definitely. You've turned into a bit of a bastard since you've been away." I think this was meant as a compliment.

"I try my best. It's quite fulfilling this revenge business. I'm starting to get a taste for it."

"Wouldn't mind a bit of it myself. I've got a few on my list who I'd quite like to pay a visit to in the middle of the night."

"It's funny you say that. I might just have something you maybe interested in."

****

"What could be simpler? There's no padlock on the door of the skip. I checked on the way in," I put the plan to everyone.

"We know that the skip doesn't contain any Alsatians or dead children," chipped in Bumper, "all it contains is programmes and hundreds of them as far as we know."

"What if they were lying? What if there are Alsatians?" Gilbert wasn't convinced.

"If they planned on killing us we wouldn't have got this far. Come on we're going back," I led us back along the pavement and across the strip of grass towards the skip. "Now's the best time to do it, they've just started dinner. We'll have about half an hour." We lined up at the back of the skip and checked that nobody had decided to have their lunch in the sun.

"The shutter's down. We should be safe," I could tell that Gilbert still wasn't happy. "Look, you can stand outside and keep watch if you don't want to come inside. Just shout if anybody comes and we'll leg it."

I edged round to the front of the skip pulled back the large red bolt. The door was huge and it needed both Bumper and me to edge it open. It creaked but not loudly enough to alert those inside the factory.

"Who's going to be first?" Suddenly I wasn't so brave.

The heat inside contrasted sharply with the shadows outside. It was stifling. The sun had been belting down on it all morning and with no air, it had built up like a pressure cooker.

"I'll go," said Elvis. "If there are dogs in there I'll kick them with my cast." We all laughed nervously.

I pulled the door open a little further and Elvis cautiously stepped inside.

"Jesus Christ."

"What is it?" Images of gnawed bones and big dogs raced through my head.

"P p p p programmes, m m m millions of them." I didn't need a second invitation. I opened the door fully and pushed Elvis inside. He fell into the mounds of paper that lined the floor of the skip. The light from the door wasn't great but there was enough to show that the skip was about three foot deep in programmes.

"Whey Hay!" Shouted Elvis whilst he lay on his back throwing programmes in the air. "They're perfect." What Stan had described as off cuts turned out to be near perfect programmes with only slightly tatty edges or smudged colours to differentiate them from the real thing.

"Jesus. We could make a fortune," said Elvis.

"What do you mean?"

"If we take these and them sell them at the match we'll make a mint. Who's going to notice that they've gone?" He was right. I called for Bumper and he climbed into the skip.

"The plan has changed. Grab as many programmes as you can carry. There's millions of them and they're near perfect."

"What did I tell you?" He said triumphantly slapping me on the back.

Using the half-light from the door we started selecting the best programmes and discarding the ones that didn't meet our meticulous standards. Gilbert stayed outside and stood guard. We stuffed them everywhere we could, down our pants, up our jumpers.

"Look at you," laughed Bumper. "You look like the Michelin man."

Then it went dark.

"What's happened?"

"Why's the door closed?" I heard someone start to whimper at the back of the skip. I didn't know whether it was Bumper or Elvis.

"Where's Gilbert? Why didn't he shout?"

"I'm here," Gilbert spoke up timidly from the front of the skip.

"What are you doing in here? You're supposed to be keeping guard."

"There's something outside." His voice was wavering, I could tell he was fighting back tears.

"What's outside?" I was frantic.

"A dog."

"A dog? What do you mean a dog? What type of dog?"

Gilbert sniffed loudly before answering.

"An Alsatian."

****

Before we discussed business Bumper had an invite for me.

"Look mate, I know it's short notice but I'm getting married next Friday. One of my Aunts has dropped out, varicose veins playing up or something. Anyway there's a meal going to waste. I'd be chuffed if you could make it. Elvis and Marie will be there."

"I'd love to. Congratulations. Who's the lucky girl?"

"Bernadette McLaughlin. She was a couple years below us at school."

"Bumper and Bernie's bananas. I can see why you're marrying her?" We both laughed. "Are you having a stag night?"

"Just a couple of pints with Gilbert and Elvis on Saturday, you're welcome to come if you're up for it." Bumper replied.

"Definitely, I'll be there."

"You said you had something that might interest me," said Bumper, "what was it?"

"It can keep." I didn't want to upset him before his big day. I was also a little concerned about seeing Elvis again. He had been quite upset the last time I had seen him and I hoped he hadn't told Marie of my plans.

****

Nobody spoke. Only the breathing and whimpering could be heard. "This is serious," I broke the silence. "We're trapped. We're going to die."

"Have you not got a p p p plan?" Said Elvis with a little too much stuttering sarcasm for my liking.

"I'm scared Elvis. More than I ever have been before." Not only was there an angry dog baying for our blood outside but it was also pitch black and like a furnace inside the skip.

"You said there weren't any dogs," Gilbert shrieked. "You promised! It's all your fault." I was choked by the accusation but the stories about dead kids became more feasible now. I started to think of the children's bones I might now be standing on.

"I'm sorry. I'm sorry," I felt the air being drained from the skip. My throat was getting drier. Every breath we took was one breath closer to our deaths. "I'll think of something."

"Well make it quick, I can't breathe," Bumper shouted.

"Ok give me a chance. I'm thinking." I slumped down against the wall of the skip and tried to collect my thoughts. I racked my brains for ideas but could only come up with one.

"We're going to have to make a run for it," I croaked.

Silence.

"It's the only way. What else are we going to do? If we don't do something we are all going to die. Can't you feel the air disappearing?" Somebody coughed. My chest tightened.

"Everybody get as many programmes as you can and stick them down the front of your pants. That way we will be protected if the dog goes for us." I was desperate for a response but didn't get one. "If one person gets attacked the rest of us might able to fight it off."

"And if we can't?" Gilbert asked.

"I don't want to think about that," I was struggling to get the words out now.

"Jesus Christ, Pete," Bumper shouted.

"It's our only option. If we don't go now we'll all suffocate within the next ten minutes. It's your choice. Are you with me or not?" I knew I was going regardless of the reply. As it happened nobody spoke. I took this as a sign of agreement. "Is everyone ready to run?" I shouted as I edged towards the door. "This is it."

One voice spoke up. It was Elvis.

"I can't."

"What do you mean you can't?"

"My leg. It's b b b b broken. I can't run."

"Shit," I never thought. "But you have to come, Elvis, you're my best mate."

"We can't go without you. It's everyone or no one. You're coming with us," agreed Bumper.

"You g g g go. I'll distract the d d d dog while the rest of you get away."

"You're not serious. You'll be killed."

"Like you said, we're all going to d d d d die anyway. It's the only way." I fought back the tears as I shook his hand.

"I'll never forget you, Elvis."

"We can't leave him here. We have to go together," Bumper was now screaming hysterically.

"No, Bumper. I'll go out first to d d d drag his fire. You just run as fast as you can. D d d don't look back. You m m m might not like what you see." We were all sobbing now. Elvis shuffled towards the door.

"Let's d d d d do it!" Elvis slung open the door and jumped outside. A mass of fur and fangs leapt towards him and he screamed. I ran past him as fast as I could with the others following me. My legs were turning to jelly but I had to keep on running. I had my eyes shut but the tears still streamed down my face. I couldn't imagine what was happening to Elvis.

"What am I doing?" I shouted. "Elvis is my best mate." I stopped running but couldn't look back. Gilbert and Bumper passed me without a second glance. I shouted after them. "What's the dog going to do after it's finished with Elvis? It's going to come after us. We can't leave him."

****

"Haven't you noticed how much money he's spending? How do you think he could afford that jacket? Four hundred quid, he has to be taking the piss," Tomma lent across Kev's desk. "Look at the

78

amount of Charlie he's getting through as well. Something has got to be done and quickly."

"You're right Tomma but he's been one of my best mates since we were at school, how could he do this?" Kev sat back in his leather chair and sighed. Tomma sat uneasily in his seat and looked around the office. There were numerous pictures on the wall of Kevin with various B- List celebrities. These were only outnumbered by the amount of photos of Claire. Kev sat behind an oversized mahogany desk in a luxurious leather swivel chair. In the corner of the room sat a life size porcelain tiger. No doubt as expensive as it was tasteless.

"People get greedy, they're not satisfied with what you're offering so they choose to help themselves. It could happen to any one of us but he's your mate you're going to have to sort it out. It's him or the business Kev, you decide."

"Who'd have thought one of your mates would do that to you? I suppose it's the game we're in and I'm going to have to deal with it," Kev was devastated at being ripped off however he was not going to let it get the better of him.

"Ok, I'll sort it. I'll make sure the thieving bastard never gets caught with his fingers in the till again. Promise me this doesn't go any further, I don't want it to look like any little Johnny Fuckwit can come and have a go."

Kev went to the drinks cabinet and took out a bottle of Jack Daniels. "Fancy a quick one before you go?"

"No thanks. I have to be off." Spending this long with Kev was beginning to make Tomma feel uncomfortable. He knew he wasn't too good with a drink inside him and didn't fancy slipping up.

****

I looked back reluctantly and saw the Alsatian stood on it's hind legs with it's front paws pinning Elvis to the Skip. The dog was licking his face, he wasn't dead.

"Elvis is alive," I shouted. "The dog's harmless." Neither Bumper nor Gilbert stopped running but they slowed and glanced back. I walked back towards Elvis laughing. He saw me coming and managed to push the dog away. It ran off into the car park and started to chase it's tail.

"Some guard dog eh?" he was laughing as well. He used his sleeve to wipe away the snot and tears that the dog hadn't already licked off.

"I'm sorry we left you like that."

"So you should be, I was nearly licked to death."

We walked back along the bank of the car park towards where the other two had stopped running and were lying on the grass waiting for us.

"We all have to agree," I said, "what happened today stays between us, nobody has to know about the tears." Everyone nodded in agreement.

"Jesus that was some day wasn't it?" Said Bumper. We were all now lying on the grass slope leading onto the car park. We stared up into the cloudless sky.

"All for some bloody football programmes," laughed Elvis.

"The programmes." Bumper and me shouted. "Come on let's see if it was worthwhile. Get your programmes out." I started pulling the programmes from up my jumper and down my pants. I laid them out on the grass. Bumper and Elvis did the same.

"We've got hundred's of them." It had been some trip but it had been worth it.

"Come on Gilbert how many have you got?" He pulled them from under his jumper; I think he was going to have the most. Then he pulled them from his pants.

"Jesus Gilbert, they're soaking. How did you get them so wet?" He didn't need to answer. The poor lad had peed himself.

****

"Quick, phone for the Fire Brigade." I threw my mobile at the old woman walking her Yorkshire terrier. She was oblivious to the smoke coming from beneath the front door of the large house that we were passing. Two faces peered out helplessly from the upstairs window. They were young girls; I had to act quickly. I ran round the side of the house where a pair of ladders were standing against the half-built extension. Awkwardly I carried them back round to the front of the house and placed them against the main wall.

"Open the window!" The girls were either unable to hear me or too scared to take anything in. Flames were now licking at the front door and had spread to the curtains at the downstairs window. I banged furiously on the window but still got no response from the girls who just stared back blankly. I was going to have to break the window but had nothing to smash the glass. I heard the window below me crack as the flames took hold. I was heading down the ladder to get a rock from the garden when the upstairs window opened. A woman in her late twenties whom I assumed to be the girls' mother was standing there.

"Take the kids. Quickly, the fire's spreading." The older of the girls who appeared to be about four, climbed onto my back whilst I took the younger one in my right arm. Steadying myself with my left hand, I carried them both down to safety, returning for the mother just as the fire engines arrived.

"Step back please. We'll take over from here."

The two children cuddled into their mother as I gave her my jacket.

"How did it start?" I asked.

"I don't know. I was on the phone. The first I knew of it was when I heard the girls screaming. I ran through from my bedroom to find you at the window. Thank God you were passing."

A silver Range Rover pulled into the drive behind the fire engines.

"What the Fuck is happening here?" A shaven headed hulk climbed down from the car. "Who are you?"

"I was just passing when I saw the smoke," I replied.

82

"He saved us, Joe. He got the bairns out. They would have been dead."

He shook my hand. "Joe Ingham. Looks like I owe you a big thank you. I don't know what I'd do without Elizabeth or the kids," he picked up the youngest, kissed her and put her back down. "Can I have a quick word, mate? What did you say your name was?"

"Pete Wood."

"Hi, Pete," he led me away from his family and the crowd that had started to gather. "If there's anything I can ever do for you, just let me know. I've got a lot of contacts in this city." He handed me his card.

"There's no need. I just did what anybody would have done."

"Just the same, let me know. Did you notice any cars or anybody acting suspiciously when you were passing?" I thought back to before the fire.

"I don't think so….no."

"Bastards!" He kicked a plant pot over and it smashed against the ground. A few people looked over. "I'll fucking kill whoever did this." I backed off a few paces as he seemed ready to kill right now.

"Do me a favour. If you remember anything, let me know before the police. I need to take care of this myself."

"No problem." His family had just been attacked and I wasn't about to interfere.

"Someone's going to pay for this."

We had been playing football on the field for most of the day when Bumper was called in for his tea. It had been a great game and everyone had turned out in full kit. Bumper in his Ipswich Town replica strip, Elvis in his Liverpool one and me in what my parents had told me was the Sunderland goalkeeper's strip. It was in fact just a green T-shirt and a pair of black football shorts but I was convinced. Whilst I sported the goalkeeper's strip, Elvis still played in goal due to his broken leg.

He asked if I wanted to go round to his for tea and I gratefully accepted. I quite enjoyed my little conversations with Mrs Morris and looked forward to one day meeting her husband. Mrs Morris occasionally invited me round for tea. I think she was glad that Elvis had a friend and she had long since forgiven me for Elvis' broken leg. She didn't know about the Skip. We could chat about most things, school, television, well we could chat about those two anyway. The one thing Mrs Morris and I could not agree on was currants. She loved them I hated them. She made fruit cakes, currant buns. I think she would have made currant sandwiches if she could get away with it. This was a difference of opinion that no amount of arbitration was going to solve so in order not to upset my mate's mother I did what any polite young boy would do. I accepted the cakes gratefully and when Mrs Morris wasn't looking, I picked out the currants and put them in my pocket.

Elvis' mother had owned the budgie for about five years now. It was called Chirpy and lived in a cage in Mrs Morris' sitting room. I was never one for pets so couldn't really see the point in having a noisy, brightly coloured bunch of feathers stuck in the corner of your room. At night, to ensure that the budgie went to sleep, Mrs Morris placed a blanket over the cage. For me, they could leave it on all day to stop it from annoying us when we were round Elvis' house.

As usual, after some polite conversation and a couple of beef paste sandwiches, Mrs Morris produced the fruitcake. I accepted politely and when she headed back to the kitchen I started to pick out the currants. I went to put them in my pockets then I realised. I didn't have any! I was wearing my new football shorts instead of my school ones that normally masqueraded as football kit. I started to panic. Where could I put them? Mrs Morris would think I was a madman if I announced that I didn't like currants after I had been accepting her fruitcake for the past two years. Then I remembered Chirpy. I had seen a few nature programmes on the television. If I was honest, they had bored me senseless but if I had learnt one thing from David Attenborough it was that little birds like berries.

Mrs Morris was still pottering about in the kitchen and Elvis was lying on the floor watching Blue Peter. I sidled up to the budgies cage and stuck a couple of currants through the bars. Chirpy seemed to like them and whilst I wasn't a pet lover I was happy to be giving a treat to my little feathered friend.

I settled down to watch Blue Peter with Elvis as his mother went over to the corner shop. When the programme finished Elvis asked if I wanted a glass of orange.

"Yes please."

I used the opportunity to see if Chirpy had eaten all of the dried fruit. The sight I encountered when I got to the cage, I have to admit, came as a bit of a shock. Chirpy had indeed eaten all of his currants, however instead of perching on his perch as budgies do he was lying flat on his back with his feet sticking straight up in the air.

****

"They've attacked my family, Kev. What's going on?" Ingham was furious.

"They tried to kill Elizabeth?"

"Fucking bastards. What's happening, Kev? You better not have anything to do with this."

"I can't believe you're accusing me. We have history but I would never attack a man's family."

Tomma shot Kev an anxious glance. The bad blood between Kev and Ingham ran deep. He hoped Kev wasn't involved.

"Okay, okay. I'm just a bit wound up. If you hear anything let me know."

"Of course, I'll put the feelers out," Kev put his arm round Ingham and led him to the door. "Don't worry, Joe. We'll get the bastards."

"I need to get everyone together," Ingham looked Kev in the eye. "I want everyone to know how serious I am."

Tomma looked worried. He could do without this. When Ingham pulled away from the drive Tomma turned to Kev.

"You're not involved are you?"

"Of course I'm not you stupid twat," Kev looked worried. "Don't you get it? If they are willing to attack Joe's family in their own home, they won't think twice about coming after us."

****

I knew this couldn't be my fault. I had seen Wildlife on One. What was I going to tell Mrs Morris?

Elvis hobbled back from the kitchen carrying two glasses of orange and holding his crutch under his left armpit. He handed one of the glasses to me.

"Thanks, four eyes."

"What?"

"I said thanks, Binocular face."

"Who do you think you're calling?" He was going red in the face.

"You, you four eyed peg leg." After I said this I knew what was coming. Elvis lifted his crutch and swung it at me. I ducked and the crutch crashed into the budgie's cage.

"You've killed Chirpy," I said without looking round.

"What?"

"Look. Chirpy's dead." As it slowly dawned on Elvis he hobbled frantically over to the cage. We both looked in and Chirpy was indeed dead.

"What am I going to tell my Mam?"

"We'll just say he died in his sleep. Put the blanket over his cage and say he wanted an early night. She'll find him tomorrow and she won't suspect anything." I had it all worked out.

"Promise me you won't say anything to my Mam?" Elvis was horrified.

"It's our secret." I knew that this made us even. Elvis had saved my life at the Skip. I had now saved his. It was never mentioned again.

****

"Shit," the barman cautiously eyed the crowd that had just come through the door. Tomma was at the front, closely followed by Nick Couzens and about twenty other unpleasant looking men.

"Is your boss in?" asked Tomma.

"No, he's out for the night."

"That's a shame. I'll have a bottle of Becks." The barman went to the fridge a little apprehensively and retrieved the bottle.

"That will be one eighty please."

"Yeah, whatever," Tomma took the bottle without paying and went to sit down.

"I'll have the same," Nick was now at the bar.

"I'm sorry but I'm not serving you until your friend has paid for his beer."

"Look son, you have two choices. Either you get me my beer now or you get seriously hurt. What's it going to be?"

"I don't want any trouble but I can't give beer away, I'll lose my job." A bottle flew past the barman's ear and smashed into the optics behind him. Tomma grabbed him by the shirt and dragged him over the bar.

"Your boss owes us money so be a good boy and do what you're fucking told."

Nick jumped over the bar and emptied the till as Tomma landed a kick in the barman's stomach. This was the cue for the rest of the lads to start smashing the bar to bits. The Guinness mirror behind the bar shattered as a stool hit it. Customers ran for the door as the glasses started flying. Two lads had thrown the fruit machine to the floor and were attempting to smash it open. Two more attempted the same with the cigarette machine. The barman lay, cowering on the floor. The sound of breaking glass nearly drowned out the sirens of the police cars that were approaching.

"Police, let's do one." Everyone started pushing for the door, smashing everything in their path.

"Nick, quick let's go this way," Tomma was holding open the fire exit.

Nick looked at the crush at the main door and ran towards Tomma. As Nick went through the door, Tomma slammed it shut behind him and joined the crowd at the main door.

"Tomma?" Nick looked back at the closed door then he felt the presence of someone beside him.

"Kev, what are you doing here?"

****

There were two playgrounds at St Christopher's. Originally they were to separate the Infants and Juniors however since the school had grown, the Infants had moved further down the road. There was the main playground that we tended to use and the smaller playground was generally unused. This was apart from the presence of Kevin Davison and his associates.

The larger playground was surrounded on three sides by grass and on the fourth was the school. The main playing field was at one end whilst the other two pieces of grass were little more than verges leading to the fence of St Patrick's Senior school. Every playtime and lunchtime we used to play football along the full length of the yard.

On more than one occasion the ball would go flying over the fence into St Patrick's and would have to be retrieved by whoever had put it there, unless it was a goal. Then it was the goalkeeper's fault and he had to get it. There were two ways of getting the ball back. The first was to go to the staff room and ask for the key to the gate leading to St Patrick's. This was a risky business depending on which teacher answered the staff room door sometimes resulting in the ball being confiscated for the rest of the day. It was to be avoided if at all possible. The second was even more dangerous although it was ultimately quicker and more likely to gain respect amongst your peers.

There was a small ditch that ran along the length of the fence. I have never been sure of its purpose however it was the ideal size for a little boy to duck under the fence, reminiscent of somebody out of the Great Escape, and retrieve the ball. If caught, not only would the ball be confiscated but you would also be in serious trouble. And if Mr Rowcroft caught you, well it didn't bear thinking about!

****

"Evening, Nick."

"Kev, I thought you weren't coming tonight."

"I had some urgent business to attend to. Have you got the money?"

"Yeah, here," Nick handed over the bundle of notes. " Shouldn't we be getting out of here? The pigs are round the corner."

"Is that all of the money?"

"Yeah, of course it is. What's up, Kev? Come on lets get a move on."

"Sorry, Nick. You're not going anywhere." Kev produced a blade, his eyes glazed over as he stabbed Nick repeatedly in the chest.

"You fucking little bastard. Did you think you could get away with it? Nobody, but nobody messes with Kevin Davison." The stabbing became more frantic then with one final lunge, Kevin stabbed him in the eye.

"Do you hear me? Don't ever fuck with me again."

Nick wasn't listening, he was already dead.

****

This particular game had been going on for nearly the whole lunch hour. It was a special one for me as I was wearing my new anorak. It was split into two diagonal halves, one red and one blue. It had a racing car on the left-hand side and was finished off with a red hood. As I had never owned a real replica football strip, I had convinced myself that this was a match for the Barcelona strip. I was now Johan Cruyff.

Inspired by my new persona, I had already scored ten goals and set up another four. Using a fair bit of wing wizardry on the right I played in the perfect low cross for Bumper to finish. I had never been confident of Bumper's skills as a goal poacher and my fears were realised when he spooned the ball high over the imaginary crossbar and into the neighbouring field.

"I'll go and get the key, " said Bumper dejectedly.

"We haven't got time," I said desperately.

I knew that if we didn't get the key in time, or worse still if the ball was confiscated, the game would be abandoned as a draw. We had a commanding lead and I didn't want to give it up.

"You'll have to go under the fence."

"You're joking. How do you think I am going to get under there?"

He was right. Someone of Bumper's size was never going to get under.

"Ok then, I'll go. Create cover for me and I'll go under."

They formed a crowd that blocked the view from the staff room window. To offer encouragement they all whistled the theme tune to The Great Escape and shuffled about as if emptying soil from their shorts' pockets. I was no longer Johan Cruyff. I was Steve McQueen. I rolled down the bank and straight into the ditch and went to get out at the other side.

Then nothing.

I couldn't move.

I was paralysed.

****

"Don't forget you've got church in the morning," said Bernie, "I don't want you getting drunk tonight and not turning up. I'm stopping at Colleen's tonight so I won't be here to wake you up."

"Don't worry love," Bumper reassured his bride to be, "it will only be a couple of quiet pints with the lads."

"Ok then, have a good night." A car horn beeped outside.

"That'll be the taxi, " said Bumper as he kissed Bernie goodbye. He walked down the stairs from the flat to the waiting car.

"Fuck me," he exclaimed. Elvis, Gilbert and myself were standing with our heads sticking out of the sunroof of a white, stretch limousine.

"Evening, Bumper. Ready for a night on the town?" I asked

"Too bloody right," he said as he stepped into the car and took a glass of champagne from me. "But you have to promise to get me up for church tomorrow morning, Bernie will kill me if I don't turn up."

"You big puff," laughed Elvis, "this is your stag night, you can't be worrying about church."

"I'm not worried about church," Bumper explained, "I'm worried about Bernie chopping my knackers off if I don't turn up."

"Let's have a toast," I shouted, "to Bumper's last week of freedom."

"Bumper's freedom," shouted Elvis and Gilbert.

"Can you take us to Southwick please, mate?" I asked the driver.

"But make sure you don't stop when you get there," added Bumper, "they'll have your wheels off in no time."

The driver took us for a ride round all of our old haunts. The field was now two small houses, Tate's was a car showroom and Inkerman Print was no more. Perhaps it was a mistake to come here, they always say that you should never go back.

****

"Little shit alert," Mr Rowcroft said to nobody in particular as he sipped his tar like coffee.

"What's that?" Mrs Matthews asked him as they both looked out into the yard.

"Barry's spooned the ball over the fence again. He's got to be the worst footballer I've ever seen. He'll be coming in here for that bloody key again."

"We should get him his own one cut, " said Mrs Matthews. "He's in here more than I am."

"What **is** he doing?" Bumper was now shuffling around with his hands in his pockets. "He looks like he's wet himself!"

"Well if he has, all of his friends have as well. Look at them." All of the teachers were crowded round the window now.

"Go on, Bob. Your turn to go out." Bob Rowcroft absent-mindedly picked up the hammer he had been using to repair the bookshelf as he headed for the door.

"I'm going to kill the little bugger."

****

After our drive around Southwick, the driver took us into Sunderland City centre. It had only been a town centre when I left. I tipped the driver and said I would give him a ring when we needed picking up.

"Eeeh, are youse famous?" a young girl asked as we stepped out of the limo.

"Aye pet," replied Bumper, "this lad here is Elvis."

"Frig off you cheeky bastard," was her less than cheerful reply.

We climbed the flight of stairs that took us into Gillespies and I was taken aback when we got to the top. The place was packed and I suddenly felt old, everyone was about fifteen years younger than us. We fought our way to the bar and I got the beers in. Kylie Minogue blasted out of the speakers and the atmosphere was electric, a smile spread across my face. This was a side of Sunderland I had never experienced and I knew I was going to enjoy tonight.

The next pub was Sinatra's and Gilbert was bursting for the toilet. "Here get them in while I go to the bog." He handed me a twenty pound note. I got the beers in and slipped a couple of extra twentys into his change. He wouldn't notice and even if he did I could claim that the barmaid must have made a mistake and thought he had given me a fifty. On his return, Gilbert slipped the change in his pocket without checking.

We went on a pub crawl. Marlowe's, The Borough, Chaplin's, Fitzgerald's (definitely more to my taste and our age group), Baroque, Master's, The Londonderry then I don't know, it all became a bit hazy. Perhaps the shooters in Fitzgerald's were a mistake, the tequila in Baroque definitely was.

We sat slumped in the kebab shop. I'd ordered a pizza, the other three had ordered kebabs with extra chilli sauce. Bumper asked for a side order of cheesy chips while we were waiting for my pizza. I phoned for the limo and we could tell the driver wasn't overly pleased with our choice of takeaway food but I tipped him well so he let it go.

We cracked open the cans when we got back to Bumper's flat but I knew I was done in. It wasn't long before I drifted asleep on the couch only to be woken by the ringing of the phone.

****

As much as I tried to move, I couldn't. I was lying face down in the ditch unable to move the top half of my body. Had I been shot?

The whistling stopped. Although I couldn't see properly, I could feel the crowd move away.

Then it went cold and dark.

"What are you doing down there, Wood?" Said a loud, booming voice. I recognised it instantly. I was in the shadow of Mr Rowcroft. With hindsight I realise that a group of lads who had, no more than two minutes ago, been happily playing football, shuffling around and whistling as if they had invented some new low-key dance was likely to arouse suspicion. Mr Rowcroft had a fearsome reputation. He was known to beat kids to within an inch of their lives with whatever he could lay his hands on. Trainers, large wooden rulers, football boots. It was even rumoured that he had hit Kevin Davison with his running spikes although this had never been confirmed. Did he now have a gun? Was it Mr Rowcroft that had shot me? I had held the record as being one of the only boys in the school never to have been attacked by him but I knew my time had come to an end.

Then I was free, Mr Rowcroft un-snagged my hood from the bottom of the fence. I wasn't paralysed.

As I was marched across the playground back towards the school, all of the lads bowed their heads not wanting to make eye contact with Rowcroft. Bumper did begin to whistle the Great Escape theme again but a sharp clip to the back of his head soon put an end to it. He was joining me on the trek back to school.

Now I have no idea why a Primary school teacher would have a hammer in his hand but it certainly added to the tension in Mr Rowcroft's classroom.

"What do you think I am going to do to you both?" He asked menacingly. I went for the obvious answer.

"Hit us with the hammer?" He just grinned. Bumper didn't.

"No, not this time. You and Barry are now banned from the large playground for one week. You, for being stupid enough to think that you could get under the fence without me knowing and your friend here," he said pointing the hammer at Bumper, "for being such a bad player that he should never be allowed near a football again."

As we left Mr Rowcroft's classroom we were both relieved.

"A week in the small playground?" Said Bumper. "Can't be that bad? I thought we were definitely going to get the hammer."

"Me too," we both laughed.

Then Bumper went white. "The Small playground."

"Kevin Davison."

****

I awoke on the settee, pizza still in hand. The phone was still ringing but there was no way I was going to answer it. Gilbert roused from his slumber at the other end of the sofa. Chilli sauce stained his previously white shirt. Elvis was asleep on the floor beneath Bumper's IKEA rug.

"Bumper, phone," I shouted.

98

"I know, I know," he muttered as he stumbled from his bedroom in his boxer shorts. Red cabbage and kebab meat stuck to his hair. He tripped over Elvis and woke him as he went for the phone. "Fuck."

"Hello," he croaked down the phone. "Bernie?" I wasn't sure what Bernie was shouting but it didn't sound pleasant. "I wasn't drunk, honest," he pleaded. Bumper held the phone away from his ear as Bernie screamed at him. "I'm sorry, love. I thought you wouldn't mind, I've decided to go to a later mass as the lads wanted to come along."

"We what?" The three of us said, shocked. He waved his hand to shut us up.

"The priest won't mind," said Bumper, "he said he would like to see us in church more often, he didn't say we had to be together." Bernie had another outburst on the other end of the phone. "Ok love, see you later." Bumper shook his head as he came off the phone, sending kebab flying everywhere. "Best get you arses into gear lads, we're going to church."

****

For afternoon break Mr Rowcroft had found some chores for Bumper and me. This was great as it delayed our meeting with Kevin Davison. At least it would give us time to say goodbye to our parents.

"I'm not well," I said pleadingly.

"I don't care. You're going to school." My mother had no heart. I was genuinely sick. Sick with worry. A few doors away Bumper was playing out the same scene with his mother, with similar results. We met at the top of the street and headed to school. Nobody said much. Elvis and Gilbert knew what we were thinking. I'm not sure what was said in Assembly that morning or in Mrs Matthews' lesson. When the bell rang for first break we knew it was time.

"Good Luck, " said Elvis. Shaking my hand knowing that he might not see me again.

"You've been a good friend. One of the best," I said.

"I wish I could take your place." It was a nice sentiment but I knew he didn't mean it. Bumper and me met at the classroom door and headed downstairs together.

"Take one of these. It might make it easier," I said as I handed Bumper a prayer card that I had stolen from Mrs Matthews' desk. It was of St Christopher, they all had been. He was the patron Saint of travellers but it would have to do. He offered me one of his last two Cola Cubes.

The sun blazed down on us as we walked out of the side door and into the yard. It was a lot more compact than the other one and had no grass surrounding it. The school was on two sides. There was a hedge at one end that cut off the view to the road. The hedge then went round the corner, only broken by the path to the caretaker's house. At the far end of the privet was a path leading to the main yard and playing field. We checked out our escape routes.

The yard was empty at this stage. Davison was probably committing a murder or something on his way to the playground. We headed for the far corner where we thought we would be safest. We waited for about five minutes without speaking and then the unmistakable figure of Kevin Davison emerged from the school. He had three henchmen with him and headed straight for us. I fingered the prayer card in my pocket.

"What are you doing in my yard?" He threatened.

"We're banned from the Main Playground, " said Bumper nervously. I had chosen not to say anything at the risk of upsetting someone.

"You two? What for?" Suddenly ducking under a fence didn't seem so dangerous. I didn't want to embarrass myself.

"It was either this or the hammer from Rowcroft." Bumper avoided the question brilliantly.

"The hammer?" They were impressed. "He's never got me with the hammer before. You must have really upset him." Kev was laughing. I think we were safe.

"Fancy a tab?" Kev offered us a cigarette from a box of ten.

"No thanks I said. They stunt your growth." I tried a joke as I was beginning to feel comfortable. I regretted it instantly when I realised that he was no taller than me.

"Whatever," he said, not appearing to be insulted. Before Kev could light his cigarette I noticed Mr Rowcroft approaching.

"Rowcroft," I said. Alerting him to the danger.

"Quick, grab these. I'll get them off you later." He handed me the cigarettes and the matches. I shoved them in my pockets quickly as Mr Rowcroft approached.

****

We didn't have time to get cleaned up before we got to church.

"I'm sorry lads," explained Bumper, "we're getting married here next week but the priest said he wouldn't marry us if we didn't start attending regularly."

We all nodded resignedly. I hadn't been to church since I was at school and I had certainly never been to church with a hangover. I wasn't looking forward to the experience.

We shuffled into one of the back rows and the elderly lady who had been sat there moved away as soon as she smelt us. Stale beer and old kebabs isn't a pleasant combination.

"What do we do?" asked Gilbert.

"I don't know, it's that long since I've been." I said. Elvis shrugged his shoulders. "Bumper?"

"Just follow everyone else," he explained, "stand up when they do, sit down when they do, it's a bit like the Hokey Cokey."

The first hymn started and the woman in front passed us a hymn book under the misapprehension that we were actually going to sing along.

Gilbert nudged me. "Have you seen who's at the front?" I craned my neck to see. I elbowed Elvis who in turn nudged Bumper.

"Mr Burns," we laughed.

****

"You're not smoking again are you, Davison?"

"No Sir," he said. Sounding quite offended at the accusation.

"Empty your pockets." Kev emptied his pockets to show nothing more than a few loose coins and a key.

"And your friends." I was in serious trouble now. I had gone from being star pupil one day to being destined to a life of crime. Not only was I banished to the small playground but I had also befriended a known criminal and I was now a smoker. My descent into criminality had been rapid.

"You two go and play elsewhere. This lot are nothing but trouble." Mr Rowcroft had let us off the hook. Bumper and me didn't need a second invitation and headed to the other end of the playground. We spent the rest of the break using Kev's matches to set light to sweet wrappers under the bush in front of the caretaker's house. A surprisingly rewarding experience we found. We headed back to the school when the bell rang relieved at how painless the whole experience had been. Kev was waiting just inside the door.

"Thanks lads. You saved my skin out there."

"No problem," I said as I discreetly handed over his cigarettes and remaining matches.

"See you later." We had gained a very powerful friend.

Mr Burns sat uncomfortably in the front row. *Perhaps I should have bought the extra large after all.* He thought. *You can never be sure when you are buying off the internet.*

Burns had been at a bit of a loose end since he had retired from the school but he had now found something to occupy his time. Giving out communion at church was right up his street. It was a high profile position and fuelled his holier than thou attitude. He was the priest's right hand man and he loved every minute of it. Perhaps the job should have rightly been Mrs Turner's. Perhaps Burns had embellished a little when he told Father McAllister that there had been complaints about her smelling of fish but the job was his now and he wasn't going to let it go without a fight.

It was time to hand out the communion and he shuffled awkwardly onto the stage, sorry altar, to do his duty. His new PVC underpants were beginning to chafe a little.

****

The blue flashing lights of a fire engine always caused excitement for schoolchildren, today was no different. We all rushed to the window as Mrs Matthews tried to contain us. It came as a great surprise to me to find flames leaping from the caretaker's bush. I looked at Bumper and felt a knot form in my stomach.

We eventually went back to class but I couldn't concentrate. I was waiting for the knock on the door to take me away.

It was a relief when the bell for dinnertime went and we headed down to the canteen. It also came as a great surprise when we arrived there to see Kevin Davison being loaded into the back of a police car in the car park. We were even more relieved when we were told that he had been searched again and was found to have matches on him.

We'd got away with it…. for now.

****

"Hair of the dog?" asked Bumper.

"What?"

"Hair of the dog, they're giving out free wine at the front. If you feel half as bad as me you'll try anything."

"Got to be worth a go," I agreed.

"Come on it'll be a laugh," said Gilbert, "imagine Burns' face when we get to the front of the queue." We shuffled out into the aisle and joined the queue for communion, barely suppressing our laughs.

Burns had bigger things to worry about; his pants were really beginning to cause him problems.

"Body of Christ?"

"Amen." The eager child took communion from him.

Christ on a bike thought Burns *I can't go on like this for much longer.* Sweat poured from his brow as his black mini briefs dug into his flesh. He raked beneath the elasticated leg and gave his testicles some breathing space. *That's better.*

"Body of Christ?" he said as he offered the communion host.

"Err I don't think so," replied the young mother, "that was disgusting." She ushered her son into the next queue as she explained to the elderly woman behind her. The whole of Burn's queue shuffled across into the next one leaving him embarrassed and ashamed. The colour drained from his face as he realised the only four people left were Elvis, Gilbert, Bumper and myself.

"Body of Christ?" he murmured.

"No thanks," I replied, "I'll go straight for the free wine if it's ok with you."

He dropped his communion wafers and ran for the side door humiliated. This church lark was turning out far better than I could have ever imagined.

****

After the caretaker's fire we didn't see Kevin Davison again for the rest of term. Bumper and me were restored to the main playground and everything went back to normal. We had a brief brush with the criminal underworld. It had been exciting but neither of us wanted to go back.

Elvis had his plaster removed however his leg hadn't healed properly and he still walked using a crutch. That summer, whilst he made the odd foray up field as a running goalie, he became a bit of a legend in between the sticks.

Our last few weeks at St Christopher's had been quite eventful but we were all looking forward to starting St Patrick's. I had come top of the school in the end of year exams and was quite proud of myself. It looked like Elvis, Bumper and me would all be in the top stream in St Patrick's. Gilbert unfortunately would not, although he had managed to avoid going to the Special School over the road. Kevin Davison, fortunately for us, had not been so lucky.

****

Cold, uncaring eyes stared out from the Polaroid pictures on the wall. Davison, Ingham and Tomma all had their mug shots up there. Joined by a number of arrows and black lines. The eyes were no colder in the Polaroid of Nick Couzens lying, blood covered on the pavement.

D.I. Carter was a confused and worried man. "I just don't see how it works. We've got two dead bodies and one burnt out house but nothing to link them to Davison other than the fact we know they have to be. Davison is in competition with Ingham and Nick Couzens worked for Davison. Ingham is in the protection business but couldn't protect his own home. Davison's never made a move onto Ingham's patch before so I don't see why he would start now. It doesn't make sense." He shook his head.

"Couzens died in a pub brawl. Unfortunate but hardly pre-meditated. I would have thought he would have moved on from that sort of stuff by now. Then there's this joker. He pinned another photo to the board. Why did he choose to kill himself now?" Carter picked up his paper cup and took a swig of coffee. "Urghh! It's fucking cold." He threw the cup in the waste paper basket and headed to the door, grabbing his coat on the way.

"I'm going out, see if I can get anything out of Davison's wife. If nothing else it might shake him up a bit."

****

I was quite content, lying on the floor of the front room watching Grange Hill. My parents were both sat in their reclining chairs, my mother reading the paper, my father reading a book. We'd had quite an exciting game that day that my side had lost narrowly by forty-five goals to forty-four. Whilst the television was on I wasn't really watching. I was reliving the game in my mind, particularly the Brazilian like, curving free kick I had scored with.

It was quite a hot summer that year and the field had become rock hard over the last few weeks due to the lack of rain. We played football nearly every day. Occasionally changing to cricket when the mood took us. There were a couple of times whilst Wimbledon was on that some of the lads brought out tennis racquets but it never really caught on.

"I see they are going to build houses out the back," my Mother said to no one in particular.

"Are they? How many?" Questioned my Father. They regularly had conversations like this. Neither of them looking up from whatever it was they were reading. Sometimes they might not even get a response.

"Two. It's amazing how small they build houses these days."

"Means you will have to find somewhere new to play football now, Pete."

"What?" I was confused.

"Aren't you listening? They are building houses on the grass out the back. Looks like you'll have to use one of the proper football pitches."

"It is a proper football pitch."

"It's not. Who ever heard of a footballer playing on a little bit of mud like that?"

"Pelé learnt to play on the beach and Kevin Keegan used to practice against the back wall of his house. They didn't even have grass. I know because I've read the books."

"That's beside the point. Football field or not, they are building houses on it." My Dad always had to be right.

"They can't! That's our field," I protested.

"They can do what they like and they would like to build houses. Therefore that is exactly what they are doing." I was disgusted that my father wasn't taking this as seriously as me.

"It's not a bad thing. It's getting far too dangerous out there. Look at the state poor Paul is in. Mrs Morris is beside herself." My mother had now decided that the field had some strange power of it's own that had willed Elvis to run out onto the road.

"They can't. We won't let them. I'm going to see Elvis."

"Not until you've finished your tea." I rammed the remainder of my ham sandwich in my mouth and ran out of the door with my cheeks bulging. I hated ham sandwiches.

****

I left the car at Bumper's and walked back to the lighthouse. There had been so much to take in over the last few days that I needed a walk to clear my head. The car was all right where it was; I would collect it in the morning. I looked at Joe Ingham's business card and put it back in my pocket.

When I got back to the lighthouse the decorators were still there. Most of the restoration had been completed before I had returned to Sunderland but they were adding the finishing touches, claiming overtime for working a Sunday. The builders had recommended Jim and Dave and, although they were only half joking when they commented that there wasn't a straight wall in the house, they had done quite a good job. They were the classic double act, the fat loud one and the skinny one who was the foil for the humour. The larger one had a mop of brown curly hair, which was speckled with white paint. I headed to the bathroom to freshen up and was hit by the overpowering smell of air freshener that was still only barely disguising the smell from the toilet.

"Sorry about that mate. Bit of a wild night last night," said the larger of the two painters proudly. The combination of these smells along with the paint fumes and cigarette smoke made me feel nauseous. That was the last thing I needed so I headed to the balcony at the top of the lighthouse to get some fresh air.

The main light was still in working order although I hadn't had it switched on yet; it was part of the agreement I had with the council when I was granted planning permission. Over the past few months I had visited the lighthouse on a number of occasions with the planning officers. My visits were always brief and I left Sunderland as soon as they were finished. Ideally I wouldn't have visited at all however they were being difficult so I needed to meet them personally to persuade them. The oval sitting room was positioned around the central light with a specially built, curved sofa at one side of the room. I had panoramic views across the city and out to the North Sea and on a clear day I could see all the way down the coast to Cleveland.

"We're away mate. We'll finish up tomorrow." I thanked the decorators and watched them leave, waiting until they were nothing more than specks at the end of the pier.

The air was sharp and refreshing on the balcony. I took a few deep breaths and composed myself. I had purchased a telescope, mainly to watch passing ships and to look down the coast. I had always wanted one as a kid and it was one of the first things I bought when I knew I was getting the lighthouse. I turned the telescope round and pointed it towards Seaburn. I could clearly see Claire's house, Kev's house, Kev and Claire's house. There was a feeling in the pit of my stomach, not the nausea but something different, emptiness perhaps.

The rain had stopped some time ago but the night was drawing in and it was becoming colder. I put on a woollen Paul Smith jumper and my fleece and sat with a cup of coffee, black as usual, watching, waiting, and hoping to find some clue as to why Claire had chosen to live with such a Neanderthal. Admittedly it was a lovely house and the MGF on the driveway suggested that Claire didn't do without but how could she be happy, with him? It made me all the more determined that I was going to have to carry through with my plan.

The purchase of the lighthouse now seemed more like a good idea for a number of reasons. I had bought it on a whim when I realised it was coming up for sale. Nostalgia, something I generally tried to avoid, had taken over and I got into a bidding war with someone who was obviously being just as nostalgic as I was. Now that I had it though, I could see the possibilities. First and foremost it brought back a number of memories from my childhood, not many of them good admittedly but the lighthouse portrayed a sense of calm in an otherwise turbulent period. It was also converted into a luxury seafront home with undisturbed views up and down the coast. Now, it would appear, most importantly of all it offered a view of the palatial, if somewhat tacky residence of Mr and Mrs Kevin Davison.

****

Elvis couldn't believe it either.

"They can't do it. We'll have to stop them."

"How?"

"We'll go on strike." I had to admit it was a great idea. Elvis may have walked with a crutch but his brain had obviously had a nudge in the right direction during the accident.

"Fantastic," I said. "How?"

"I don't really know. I've seen a few on the telly, they just seem to shout a lot and wave banners around."

"Well that's right up our street. We can all shout and wave banners, even Gilbert."

"My Mam was right when she said I should watch the news. It's an education in itself," Elvis was proud of himself.

"That's the thing about strikes, they're always on the news," I said confidently. "Nobody's going to take a field away from kids who have been on the news."

"Come on, I can't wait to tell the others." Elvis hobbled towards the door.

"I can't believe it. We're going on strike," I shouted. "and we're going to win." I leapt triumphantly in the air, accidentally rapping my knuckles off the doorframe.

"I'm going out Mam," shouted Elvis as we headed for the door.

"Where are you going?"

"On strike," we replied.

****

As Tomma opened the door he could hear the theme music from Eastenders coming from the television.

"All right mate," he shouted through to Jamie.

He didn't get any response so popped his head through the door. The television was on but nobody was there. He walked through to the kitchen and filled the kettle. It was still warm. Tomma took a walk upstairs, the toilet door was open but the bathroom was empty. He knocked on Jamie's door and walked straight in. He wasn't expecting the sight he was greeted with. Sat on the bed were Ingham and two henchmen, all three brandishing shotguns.

"Good evening Mr Thompson, I think me and you need a little chat." Ingham pulled back the barrel on his gun. "We helped ourselves to a cuppa, hope you don't mind."

"No...." Tomma was still trying to take it all in. "...what do you want, what have I done?"

"Oh, I think you know the answer to that one Tomma. The small matter of a failed delivery."

"But I delivered the parcel to Cullen yesterday, like you said."

"Yes, you delivered **a** parcel to Cullen just not the one we were expecting. It was a little light if you know what I mean."

"No, I fucking don't know what you mean you mad bastard."

"Now there's no need for foul language, just tell us where the money is and we'll think about letting you keep that filthy tongue of yours."

"Why have you come to me? Why haven't you gone to Cullen?"

"We have and after we conducted extensive enquiries we are satisfied he is not the culprit." Ingham raised his eyebrows.

"What do you mean, extensive fucking enquiries?" Tomma looked worried.

"Well we removed each of his nails, one by one, starting with his toes and then moving up to his fingers." Tomma started to feel

114

sick. "When that didn't produce any answers we started to get a little bit nasty, sticking knitting needles where you wouldn't want knitting needles to go. Do you understand now?" Tomma retched and threw up all over the bedroom carpet.

"Now you are really starting to annoy me. Where's the bleeding money?" Ingham was now standing with his gun pointing straight into Tomma's face.

"I swear it was all there. Nick counted it, every last penny it was there."

"What the fucking hell is Nick Couzens counting the money for?"

"He wanted to make sure that we weren't being stitched. You can never trust anyone these days."

"That's exactly my point. It appears that Mr Davison and friends are trying to have my pants down."

"I swear, I'm not involved."

"Glad to hear it but it's all a little convenient isn't it. Someone attacks my family and then a delivery turns up short and the one person you put in the frame is now dead. That is why I don't believe your little story about Nick Couzens." Ingham smacked the butt of the gun in Tomma's face, knocking out one of his front teeth. "If Couzens was involved, it was through direct orders from above. He's greedy but not stupid. He wouldn't try it on without back up."

"I swear I know nothing about it. You have to believe me."

"I don't have to do anything. You're lucky I haven't killed you already. I'm going to do some more investigating before I visit our mutual friend Mr Davison. If you breathe a word of this conversation to him I'll kill you. I trust you know not to take any holidays in the near future, I wouldn't like to have to come looking for you." Ingham headed for the door but first he launched a fierce kick into Tomma's groin that left him doubled up in his own vomit. "See you soon."

****

"We'll be famous when we go to St Patrick's. There's not going to be many kids who've been on the telly during the school holidays." Bumper seemed to like the idea.

"Apart from James Duffy, " said Elvis, " He was stuck on the cliffs at Seaburn when the tide came in. He started crying for his Mam and the helicopter had to be called out."

"I would love to go in a helicopter, " said Bumper.

"Me as well, that would be excellent," Gilbert agreed.

"Not if you're James Duffy," explained Elvis, "his Mam knacked him when he got home, he was grounded for the rest of the holidays. They even had a close up of him with tears streaming down his face, the big lass! You can keep your helicopters, I would rather go on strike."

****

Carter knocked on the door and waited. He avoided the doorbell as he knew it played the theme from the Godfather. He waited patiently and eventually Claire came to the door. Her hair was scraped back in a ponytail and she wasn't wearing any make up although she did have on a pair of dark glasses.

"Hello, Mrs Davison. DI Carter, Southwick. Mind if I come in for a few minutes? I've got a few questions I'd like to ask you." He moved to get past Claire but she blocked his path.

"Got a warrant?" She knew the drill.

"Look, I'm not after anything. Can I call you Claire?"

"Mrs Davison is fine."

"I'm just a little worried about your husband. He seems to have been under a lot of stress recently."

"Nice of you to be concerned. This community policing has come a long way." She didn't normally speak to the police, she usually left that to Kev and she couldn't be bothered today. "If you want to know anything about my husband I think you had better ask him."

"I would usually but as I said, he seems to be under a lot of pressure. Are things ok at home?"

"I don't think that's any of your business, do you?" She went to close the door but Carter placed his foot in the way.

"I wouldn't ask normally, it's just I couldn't help noticing the glasses. Had a little accident have we?" There was no point in denying it; the bruising had spread far enough for it to be obvious.

"Walked into a door."

"As I thought. The thing is, there have been a lot of people having accidents recently. I have two dead bodies on my hands; both of

117

them linked to your husband. Now I'm not suggesting for one moment that he is involved but he could well be in danger. Has anything changed recently, is there anybody new on the scene? Is there anything at all that you want to tell me?" There was only one new face but he wasn't involved with Kev.

"Not that I know of. I don't get involved in his business. Like I said, you should speak to Kev."

"I will, don't worry about that. I just hope I get to him before somebody else does. If you do think of anything at all please give me a ring." He handed her his card.

"Goodbye constable." Claire closed the door.

"Detective Inspector, " said Carter. Claire threw his card in the bin.

****

"Where did you get them from?" Elvis asked. I was carrying two bed sheets.

"From the airing cupboard. My Mam won't miss them. There are only two beds in the house, my parents' and mine. They've both got sheets on so the ones in the cupboard serve absolutely no purpose whatsoever. I've no idea why my Mam has them."

"Wasn't your Dad on strike a few years ago down the shipyards," Elvis suggested.

"You're right. He must have intended to use them as banners and never got round to it."

"You'll never believe what I found," Bumper produced two tins of paint from behind his back. "I couldn't believe my luck when I

118

found them in the cupboard under the stairs. The house is already painted so I've no idea why they were there."

"We couldn't be luckier if we tried."

The plan was starting to come together. All the other lads were getting involved. Some, I must say, were a little more reluctant than I would have liked especially Gilbert.

"My Mam'll knack us."

"Look Gilbert, she'll be proud of you. How many of your brothers have been on the news?" He still wasn't convinced but Bumper intervened.

"I know we said we would never mention this again but this is an emergency. Remember the programme incident, Gilbert? You wouldn't like that secret to get out now would you?"

"That's not fair."

"True but like I said, this is an emergency. Are you with us or not?" Gilbert reluctantly agreed.

"Right everybody go home and watch the news," I ordered, "we need ideas." We all ran home excitedly.

****

Claire read the newspaper; Mr Burns was on the front page. She hadn't really liked him at school but it was sad that he was dead. The paper said it was suicide; he had hung himself. She wondered if this was one of the bodies that Carter had referred to. Kev had his faults but he could hardly have been involved in a suicide. She remembered the invitation that Pete had given her. Maybe Burns had been involved in some sex game that had gone wrong. She looked in the mirror as she poured herself another glass of wine, hoping that the bruising would have gone down by the time she went to the reunion. She didn't want to field any awkward questions.

Claire picked up the flowers that were in a vase on the sideboard. Kev had sent them. He always did when he had hit her; he thought it made everything ok. She moved them into the dining room where she couldn't see them.

Noticing Pete's number on the post-it note by the phone, she thought of ringing him for a chat but she knew Kev would be in soon expecting to be fed. Anyway, she didn't know what she would say if she did ring.

Claire placed the pan on the hob for the pasta and started chopping the vegetables, the onions making her cry.

"Alright love?" asked Kev as he came into the kitchen. He glanced briefly at the paper and put it down again. "What's for tea?"

"Pasta." She couldn't be bothered to make anything else. He wouldn't care either way.

"Good. Been up to anything today?" He took the orange out of the fridge and took a swig from the bottle. She handed him a glass.

"Had a visitor earlier."

"That's nice, who was it?" He was looking in the fridge for something to eat while he was waiting for his pasta.

"Tea will be in a couple of minutes. Don't eat anything now; you'll ruin your appetite." He grunted and closed the fridge door. "It was DI Carter from Southwick."

"What was?" asked Kev dismissively.

"My visitor today."

"What the fuck did he want?" Kev slammed the glass down and moved towards Claire. She edged backwards towards the bench.

"You know not to let anyone in here unless they have a warrant."

"I didn't let him in. He just wanted to talk." Claire eyed the pan of boiling water and wondered if she could reach it.

"How many times do you have to be told woman? You never talk to coppers."

He was now standing right above Claire pinning her into the corner. She had nowhere else to go.

"He said he was worried about you. He wanted to know if there were any problems at home."

"And I suppose you told him that I did that to you?" He pointed at her face. His voice was getting louder, more aggressive. The water in the pan was beginning to bubble over.

"I didn't tell him anything but I could hardly hide this could I?" She pointed at her eye with her left hand, with her right she had found the knife.

"So what did he say exactly?"

"He said there were two bodies, said that you were connected to them." He punched the cupboard above her head as the water sizzled on the hob. Claire grabbed the knife tightly.

"He has no right coming round here saying things like that to my wife. I'll fucking kill him."

"He thought you were in danger. Said you had to be careful."

"Do you not think I can look after myself, think I'm turning soft?" He raised his hand.

"Take one more step and I'll kill you. I swear I will." Claire swiftly pulled the knife from behind her back and pointed it at Kev.

"What the fuck do you think you are doing?" He took a step back.

"I don't know what your involvement is with these deaths and I don't want to know but I'm warning you, if you ever raise your hands to me again, yours will be the next body he's looking at."

"Ok, ok," he edged back another step. "What bodies was he talking about?"

"He didn't say, just said you were connected. I'm scared Kev. I think Mr Burns might be one of them."

"Mr Burns?"

"From school, remember? He's dead; it's on the front of the Echo." She lowered the knife as he picked up the paper. He read the story slowly and then threw the paper across the kitchen.

"It was fucking suicide. How could I be involved in a fucking suicide? They know who the killer is already."

"I just thought you were connected to Mr Burns even if you weren't responsible for his death. Maybe that's what he meant."

"I don't know any more. Whatever it is he means I'm still going to kill him if he ever comes round here again without a warrant."

Kev suddenly made a lunge for Claire and grabbed her right arm. He squeezed it tightly until she dropped the knife.

"And I swear if you ever threaten me again I'll kill you, you stupid bitch. That's one murder he will be able to solve." He stormed off towards the door. "I'm not hungry any more, I'm going out."

Claire shook as she took the pan from the hob. It had boiled dry and the pasta had stuck to the bottom of the pan. She started sobbing as she knelt down to pick up the knife.

****

We met up the next day, dismayed that there hadn't been any strikes on the news the previous night. We had to make the slogans up ourselves.

"Builders go away," suggested Elvis.

"Stick your houses up your bum," offered Bumper. We all laughed at this one. Except Gilbert who was a bit concerned at the logistics of it all.

"Keep off the Grass." It was inspired, it was my idea and everybody loved it. Better still, I knew where I could get some signs that were already printed up. We were off to the park.

The park keeper wasn't pleased to see us stood on the grass.

"Get off there," he shouted. I thought it was a good idea to do as he said. Bumper had other ideas.

"Why?"

"Because you're not allowed on the grass. That's why." He was going red.

"Where does it say that?" Asked Bumper.

He had a point. There were no signs. We had them all in our bag. It was time to run.

****

The whole house shook as the door slammed, making the windows rattle as if in the beginnings of a Los Angeles earth tremor. Gilbert was trying to ignore the row that was coming from indoors. They had become more frequent recently and however hard it was for him to do so, he tried to switch off. He created a little hole with his trowel and lovingly took the flower from it's pot and placed it in the soil. The clouds were gathering and he wanted to get this finished before the rain started.

He surveyed the garden, his garden. Gilbert had been working here for nearly two years now and he was proud of his work. He knew he was never going to win Mastermind but when it came to gardening, he had few equals. Yes this was truly a great garden and it was all his creation, except for the fountain and the lions of course. They were Kev's idea, then again, he who pays the piper and all that. Gilbert took a step back and took a photo with the camera he always had around his neck. Maybe one day he would get it into one of the gardening magazines. He only bought them for the pictures although Claire would sometimes read a couple of the articles for him. She was good like that. She hadn't changed that much since school, despite what other people said.

He heard the crash and turned to see Kev storming through the door, slamming it behind him and nearly taking the glass out.

"What are you looking at, you fucking retard?"

Gilbert had grown used to the insults by now. After all, he'd been getting them since school. Best just to say nothing. Kev was coming towards him now, his face scarlet, the vein that ran across the top of Kev's head was now more prominent than ever. Gilbert hadn't seen him this angry in a long time.

"I said what are you looking at?" Gilbert realised he was staring and tried to avert his gaze. It only succeeded in making him off guard when the blow came. The punch knocked him clean off his feet.

"Think you're better than me, do you?" Kev aimed a kick at Gilbert's stomach. Gilbert's mind was racing now, trying to think what he had done.

"I don't know what possessed me to employ a fuckwit like you in the first place. Look at the fucking state of this garden. Flowers everywhere. Are you trying to say I'm queer or something? Do you fancy me? Is that it?" Kev ripped out a handful of roses, the thorns piercing the flesh of his hands, and threw them at Gilbert.

"I'm going to have the fucking place concreted over. I should put you beneath it. As from now consider yourself unemployed."

Kev ripped out a young tree and thrashed Gilbert with it; blood was now seeping between the fingers of Kev's right hand and down the bark of the tree.

Gilbert realised he hadn't done anything wrong at all. This was normal Kev behaviour. Something goes wrong and he blames anyone but himself.

Well fuck you, you fucking arsehole. Gilbert wished he could say what he was thinking. He now realised he was in pain as well. He wasn't sure whether his jaw was broken; he couldn't, or didn't want to move it. Kev was now systematically destroying the garden, Gilbert's garden. That hurt more than anything else.

"What's this for? You haven't got any family you haven't got any friends. What do you need a camera for?" He ripped the camera from Gilbert's neck and threw it against the fountain where it smashed into little pieces. Gilbert forced back the tears.

"Fucking retard." Kev jumped into the Shogun and reversed, full speed down the drive, hitting the gatepost and knocking one of the lions to the ground.

"Gilbert? Are you all right, Gilbert?" He didn't want turn round. He didn't want Claire to see him crying.

"Don't take it personally. It's me he's angry with not you." Gilbert picked up the remains of his camera and headed for the gate. The tears were now rolling down his cheeks.

126

Why did you have to marry a prick like that?

"Take care of yourself, Gilbert." He could tell Claire was also crying. As he passed the fallen lion, the rain started to come down again.

****

After a pretty fruitful trip to the park we painted the remaining banners. We decided against Bumper's idea on the grounds that our parents would definitely kill us and stuck with Builders go away and Football not Houses. We got to work painting the banners then hid them in the bunker. We needed an early night, as tomorrow was strike day.

****

Big, heavy raindrops lashed the windscreen as I drove along the seafront. Two minutes ago the sun had been shining and then the black clouds appeared and the heavens opened. *It seems to have done nothing but rain since I came home.* I thought to myself. Through the rain I could make out the blurred figure of a man walking down the middle of the road. "Who's this fucking idiot?" I was about to beep the horn when I recognised the walk, shoulders hunched against the rain, and the black, biker's jacket. I pressed the button, lowering the electric window.

"Gilbert?" I got no response. "Gilbert, it's me Pete."

"Fuck off." His jaw wasn't broken but it took a lot of effort to speak.

"Not the most stimulating conversation I've had recently."

"Don't take the piss, I've had enough of it." Gilbert winced at the pain.

"Sorry, I was joking."

"Yeah just like everybody else."

"I've said I'm sorry. Now are you going to get in the car? It's pissing down." I noticed the blood on Gilbert's face. He headed for the passenger side door.

"Nice car."

"Thanks. Are you going to get in?"

"I'm soaking now. I'll mess up your seats."

"Sod that. Get in." I leant over and opened the door. We didn't speak for about five minutes then I broke the silence.

"What happened to you?"

"Don't ask."

"You look like you've been run over by a train. Nothing to do with your illustrious employer was it?" I handed him a handkerchief.

"How did you guess?" Gilbert wiped the blood from his face.

"Some things never change. Are you all right? What was it about?"

"I've no idea. Like you say, some things never change. When Kev's in one he always takes it out on someone who can't fight back."

"What if you could fight back? What if he couldn't push you around anymore?"

"I wish," Gilbert stared out of the window.

"You never know," I replied, "I might just know someone who could help. What's that in your hand?"

"A camera. Well at least it used to be. I saved for ages to get this and now that pig's ruined it."

"What do you take pictures of then?"

"What do you care?"

"I'm your friend Gilbert, I'm showing an interest. That's what friends do."

"Nobody's taken an interest in the past, except Claire. But she's the only one."

"You don't have to tell me if you don't want to."

"Anything really," he explained, "people, places, anything that catches my eye."

"Sounds like it means a lot to you."

"Yeah, it used to." We pulled up outside Gilbert's house.

"Why don't you take this? Get yourself a new one." I took a handful of notes from my wallet.

"No, I don't want your charity. You can keep it; you've obviously worked for it. Smart suits and flash car. You must be doing really well," Gilbert went to open the door. "Thanks for the lift."

"All right. If you don't want to take charity, as you call it, how about selling me a couple of photos?"

"What?"

"Well, I'm assuming you're good."

"What would you want with my photos?" Gilbert was chuffed but didn't like to show it.

"I've just bought the old lighthouse. I've converted it but it's still lacking something. I was hoping you would have some pictures to make the walls a little less bare."

"Fair enough. Do you fancy a coffee then?" Gilbert seemed quite excited at the prospect of being a professional photographer.

****

I was up as soon as my father left for work. I had taken the precaution of going to bed with my clothes on so I didn't waste any time in the morning. The rest of the lads had obviously done the same as they were at the front door when I got downstairs. They had done well. Not only did they have the banners but they had also brought supplies, Penguins, cola cubes and a big bottle of pop. We were going to be there for the long haul so the provisions were welcome.

"Bye Mam," I shouted through to the kitchen as I ran out of the door. She won't have been happy that I didn't have breakfast but this was an emergency. It was 7.45 and we headed for the field and set ourselves up for the day. It was a good turn out. Every lad who ever played football with us had turned up. The signs from the park fitted nicely along the side of the grass beside the road that had now been named the Elvis Morris left leg memorial Stand. It was a mouthful but it meant a lot to us. A couple more signs were placed along the Back Lane end. Bumper and Gilbert held up the banner proclaiming Builders go away and Elvis and myself held up the one with Football not Houses.

"How long do you think we will be here?" asked one of the other lads. "My Mam's taking me to the Town this afternoon."

"All Day at least," I told him. "We need to give the news crews time to turn up. We'll be on the telly tonight."

It didn't take long for us to gain our first supporter. A silver Escort drove past and honked his horn in a sign of solidarity. Either that or he wanted Gilbert to get out of the way after he had gone to recover a five pence piece he had seen in the road. After a couple more cars honking we were satisfied that we had the locals on our side. I have to admit that having Elvis stood there on crutches did help us to get the sympathy vote.

A JCB approached and the driver also honked his support. We waved back cheerfully.

He wasn't smiling. He was coming straight for us.

"Christ it's the builders."

"Stand your ground lads," I shouted. He didn't seem to be slowing down. "He'll notice that it is a legitimate strike and go away."

The teeth of the digger were getting closer. The ground shook beneath us as it rumbled towards us. I don't mind admitting that Gilbert wasn't the only one on the verge of repeating his programme incident.

The giant yellow digger ground to a halt just in front of us with the shovel hovering menacingly above our heads.

"What are you doing?" shouted the driver.

"We're on strike," I explained.

"What?" I think driving a noisy digger must have turned him deaf.

"We're on strike. This is our field so I'm afraid you can't build any houses here. You will have to go elsewhere," I explained rationally and politely. Completely in contrast to the reaction it provoked.

The builder, who was roughly seven foot tall and twenty stone, jumped down from his cab brandishing a spade in his muscled, tattooed arm.

"Now FUCK OFF the lot off you!" It's not often that you hear a word like that when you are eleven years old however in my limited experience I had learnt that it usually preceded a good beating.

"Leg it!"

The strike was over. The summer was over. The field was gone.

We started St Patrick's next week and I knew that somehow, life was never going to be the same.

****

Kev drove round the streets not knowing where he was going. Tomma sat in the passenger seat beside him.

"What do you think he knows? He was talking about two bodies."

"I don't know, Kev. You never liked Burns but nobody did. They can't pin that on you."

"What about the other body though? How does he know it's us?"

He pulled into the parking space at the end of the pier and looked out to sea. He had to think quickly. He had killed Nick, it was the

132

only way but nobody could prove it was him. He deliberately did it where there were no close circuit television cameras to capture the act. Tomma was the only one who knew and he was part of it so he couldn't say anything.

"Carter's guessing; he has to be. What does he mean about you being in danger? We would know if someone was trying to move onto our patch," Tomma was as confused as Kev. Whilst he was happy that Nick was out of the way, the last thing he needed now was a turf war. He wanted to get away with as little fuss as possible. He was sure that Kev had nothing to do with the attack on Ingham's house. He wanted to tell him about Ingham's visit but knew he couldn't.

"I could lie low for a few weeks and let it all blow all over," Kev looked out to sea.

"If somebody is looking to make a move on you, the last thing you should be doing is lying low. They'll walk all over you."

"I could take the money and run. I've got enough tucked away to last a long time. I don't need the hassle any more."

He ran this over and over in his head trying to think of a reason why he shouldn't leave. He wanted to take Elizabeth with him but that would mean taking her kids and having to look over his shoulder all of the time waiting for a visit from Ingham. It was worth the risk. He would take care of Claire; she could keep the house. He knew that Claire would never leave with him; he had already lost her. Then he thought; if Claire didn't love him, why would

Elizabeth? Was there any reason for her to move away? She already had everything she wanted. He had no options.

"I'm staying put and going to act as if nothing had happened," Kev had made his mind up. "If someone is going to have a go then let them try. Bring it on. If there's going to be bloodshed then so be it."

"You know I'm with you all the way don't you?"

"Cheers, Tomma. I appreciate it." Kev started the engine and indicated to pull out.

"What's this?" Tomma picked up a card from the dashboard.

"Fucking school reunion. That's all I need."

"How come I didn't get invited?" Tomma looked hurt at his omission.

****

"Are you alright son? Do you need a cup of tea or a glass of pop or anything?" Kev shook his head.

"Can you tell me in your own words what happened? Take as much time as you like."

DI Carter looked at the young lad in front of him. Barely eleven years old and he had spent the previous night sitting with his dead father as he lay in a pool of blood. Carter fully understood why the boy was silent. Kev sat staring at the table, occasionally biting his nails. The social worker tried to put her hand on his shoulder but he shrugged it off.

"Where's my sister? Is she alright?"

"She's being looked after. You'll be able to see her as soon as you've given us a statement."

"What's going to happen to us?" asked Kev. "I'm not going in a home."

Carter looked at the social worker who shrugged resignedly.

"We've got plenty of time to discuss that Kevin. Do you want to tell me what happened?"

"My Dad had been out. Just for a couple of hours mind, he wasn't drunk."

"It's ok, son. We know he'd been down the pub, we've spoken to the bar man. What happened after he returned?"

"He'd brought me a bag of nuts back from the pub, dry roasted they were. He told me I could eat them and then I had to go to bed. Elaine was already asleep. He poured himself a whisky, just to help him sleep."

Carter already knew how drunk Albert had been when he left the pub. The interview with the bar man had revealed that he had been asked to leave the pub after a fight over a card game.

"I went to bed after I'd eaten my nuts but I wasn't tired. I decided to read my comics for a bit. My Dad wouldn't have been happy if he'd caught me, so I used my torch under the blankets. I'd been in bed for about half an hour when I heard my Dad arguing with someone. "Who are you looking at?" He shouted but nobody answered. "I said who the fuck are you looking at?" but still nobody answered. I knew that my Dad would only get angrier when this man didn't answer. I heard him get up from his chair. I got out of bed and went to the top of the stairs. My Dad was in the hall. He was pulling his shoulders back, the veins bulging in his temples. I tried to stop him. "Dad. Who are you shouting at?" I tried to tell him that that there was nobody there." Kev was now crying and the social worker handed him a tissue. He refused it and wiped his nose on his sleeve.

"He kept on shouting "This Bastard here! Who do people think they are, staring at me? Not good enough for them eh?" He was staring at the door. I tried to tell him. I tried to tell him that the face he thought he saw staring at him was just the light of the moon reflecting through the door. He took no notice. It was as if I wasn't there. He went to head-but the face that was looking at him. His head went thought the glass in the door and it sliced his neck open. There was nothing I could do."

"Why didn't you phone for an ambulance?" asked Carter.

"My Dad would have killed me. He told us that you never call the police. No matter what the reason was. I knew that if I called an ambulance then you lot would turn up. You would put us in a home, saying he couldn't cope. I tried to stop the bleeding but nothing worked. I sat with him all night, I don't know when he died." Kev took the tissue from the Social Worker and dried his eyes. He sniffed loudly.

"Thanks son. I know how difficult that must have been for you."

****

"Hello Geordie, long time no see," Mike Teale welcomed an old friend. Mike was in his late forties, overweight but immaculately dressed. His black hair was slicked back; he wore grey slacks and a navy blazer over a pale blue shirt and yellow tie. His brand new Mercedes SLK was parked outside.

There was a small crowd gathering now. It had been a long time since all of the faces had been seen in the same place. Junior Carling, Ingham's right hand man, came in blocking out the sunlight from the door momentarily. At six foot six, he was easily the largest man in the pub and also the only black man. His muscles filled out his tight, white polo neck jumper. His hair was receding but tidy and he had a large black moustache. He was one of the few people who could carry it off. Both the jumper and moustache did little to cover the large white scar he received when he was at school.

Ingham was in amongst the group sitting alongside Teale. He had offered to introduce me but I had politely declined explaining that I just wanted a quiet pint and to watch the match. Ingham had gone back to the crowd, seemingly not offended and carried on with his conversation, occasionally nodding in my direction.

The group of 'Businessmen' took up most of one corner of the pub. The greetings were all loud and exaggerated. Mobile phones rang incessantly, constantly interfering with the picture on the televisions. The regulars were clearly annoyed but said nothing.

After about ten minutes the younger crowd arrived, Davison's gang.

Aged between early twenties to early thirties they looked altogether more aggressive. Most had short, cropped haircuts and sported tattoos. The younger ones wore Stone Island jumpers and jackets, the uniform of the football hooligan. They stood on the outskirts of the crowd, not sure how close to get. Handshakes were exchanged and drinks were purchased, the mood became a lot less jovial and more business like. I couldn't hear what was said but did observe that the one noticeable absentee was Kevin Davison.

As quickly as the crowd had arrived, it dispersed. Mike Teale was the first to leave. None of them knew me but must have heard about me from Ingham. A fleet of Mercedes, Porsches and BMW's screeched away from the seafront pub. The only group remaining now, along with the regulars, was Davison's gang. They tried to look moody and aggressive but failed to impress the fishermen and lifeboat men that frequented the pub. I laughed to myself and wondered if they still called themselves the 'St Pat's casuals.' I drained my pint glass, and still thirsty, headed back to the bar.

****

"At least we don't have to wear short trousers anymore."

Elvis and me were making our way to St Patrick's for the first time. My mother had wanted to walk me to school but luckily she had to go to work so I avoided the embarrassment. On arrival we were ushered into the hall where Mr Burns, head of first year, greeted us. I sat cross-legged on the floor as he introduced himself and told us how proud we should all be to be there. Elvis had been given a chair to sit on, as his leg hadn't properly healed yet. I searched along the row looking for familiar faces and smiled at Bumper and Gilbert.

Mr Burns told us all to stand for the first hymn. As he was booming out the first few lines, the door to the hall opened. I glanced round to see who it was and was horrified to see the familiar face. Whilst he was slightly taller now, there was no mistaking Kevin Davison. I tried to attract Elvis' attention but it was no good. Sitting with the teachers, he had no choice but to sing along. I was convinced that Kev was going to be sent to Maplewood special school after the fire but was obviously wrong. I looked to Bumper. He looked straight ahead but I knew, through the lack of colour in his face, that he had also seen him. My mind raced with excuses for the fire. I'm sure he would understand that it was all a big accident. My heart was racing and I began to feel sick.

Karen Walker nudged me.

"That's you."

"What is?"

"Mr Burns. He's just said your name."

"Well then, Peter. Do you not want to be in the top class?"

"Sorry sir?"

"Wake up Wood. I'm reading out of the name of people who are going into 'Class A' and you are first on the list. Come up to the front, son."

I stood but my legs were like jelly and I nearly fell straight back down again. I headed shakily to the front of the hall where Mr Burns ruffled my hair.

"We're not afraid of the big school are we, Peter?" The hall echoed with the sound of laughter. I didn't like this man.

****

Elvis had been drinking heavily since his meeting in the Ivy. He wasn't a big drinker usually. A couple of cans on a weekend, maybe a trip to the local every once in a while with Marie. He couldn't really afford it. Marie hadn't seen him this drunk in a long while and she was worried. She knew he was having a couple of pints with Pete, after all he had been working hard and he deserved it but she wasn't expecting this. He'd been drinking all weekend. Music was blasting out of the Hi-Fi and Mrs Corby was already banging on the ceiling. Elvis was oblivious to the thumping from upstairs.

"I can't stand up for falling down..." he sung along with the music then realised the irony of the words. "Did you hear that pet, I can't stand up for falling down?" He then stumbled onto the floor in a fit of hysterics, taking the contents of the table with him. "Do you get it? I can't stand..."

"Yes, I get it. Now are you going to be quiet? The neighbours are complaining."

"Let them complain. The only reason the piss stained old bag is moaning now is because it's us. Don't you see if it was any of the other hundred and one families on this estate she wouldn't dare? Too scared of the consequences." He tried to stand but just ended up breaking the chair.

"What are you talking about? Mrs Corby's never complained before. The music is too loud."

"Yeah take her side. Just like everybody else. It's only because you know I'll not fight back. I'm a coward. Didn't you know? Scared of my own shadow, that's me."

"What's Dad doing, Mum? He's not still practising for 'Stars In Their Eyes' is he?" Declan had wandered into the sitting room.

"Go back to bed, Declan."

"I heard him singing. I thought he was practising. He is good enough Mam."

"I know pet. Now go back to bed."

"Yes that's right, son. I'm practising, practising being a doormat, letting everybody walk over me."

"What does he mean, Mam?"

"Nothing. Now get to bed, this is your last warning."

"Goodnight son, sleep tight," Elvis waved at his son.

"Night Dad," Declan went back to his room but stood listening at the door.

"I hope you're proud of yourself, scaring the bairn like that."

"Well he'd better get used to it because it gets a lot scarier the older you get."

"I don't know what's got into you lately. You're moody, you never listen to your music anymore...." Marie shook her head in disgust.

"You've just told me to turn the fucker off."

"You know what I mean. You haven't been the same recently. What happened to the old Elvis?"

"He's gone. He got trampled on and died. This is the new Elvis and you're going to have to get to like him."

Elvis opened the door of the cupboard and started raking through the mess that lay inside.

"Maybe I don't have to get to like him," Marie shouted at him, "maybe I want the old Elvis back."

"Well you can't have him. It's new Elvis or nothing."

A pile of boxes now lay behind Elvis as his backside stuck out of the cupboard.

"Well it might have to be nothing. If you don't buck your ideas up you're going to lose Declan and me. You think about that when you're trying to get over your hangover tomorrow. I'm going to bed now. You can have the couch."

"Got it."

Elvis backed out of the cupboard and slumped against the wall. In his hand he held a plaster cast that appeared to have come from a child's broken leg. He laughed as he read the names of everybody who had signed it. He also studied the map that had been drawn in red felt-tip pen. Everything was there, the field, Pritchard's house, Tate's and most importantly, Inkerman Print. It had been over twenty years since he had broken his leg. A tear formed in his eye as he remembered when they were kids. 'Man out of time' was now playing on the hi-fi. As always, Elvis Costello's timing was perfect.

****

The first punch took me by surprise, the second I saw coming but I could do nothing about. By the time I hit the floor the kicks had started, each one aimed with precision on my temples. *Curl into a ball, curl into a ball.* I kept telling myself but it was too late, my senses were going. I knew I was bleeding but I didn't know where from. The last thing I remember before I passed out was the fire; the bastards had set me alight. *For fucks sake. My Mam is going to kill me.*

I heard the bells as I was coming round, the Police? The Fire Brigade? No, I remembered, the dinner bell, dinnertime's over.

"GOD, I HATE SCHOOL!"

Foolishly I had thought that Kev would have forgiven me. For a brief moment at St Christopher's we had been friends. Then I threw it all away by setting fire to the bushes. It was all an accident but there was no reasoning with Kevin Davison. From day one at St Patrick's I had been public enemy number one. We had all mistakenly thought that Kevin Davison was going to Maplewood, the special school over the road. We were wrong. Kev's Dad had died during the summer and I think the authorities must have taken pity on him. The rumours had been flying around but Elvis had heard his Mam telling the woman next door the story. The whole thing did his reputation no harm whatsoever.

****

I thought about the meeting in the Whistle. Why had all the main faces in the shady, Sunderland underworld got together now? All except Davison that is. It bothered me that they could be planning something that could ruin my plans. I needed to speak to Ingham to find out what they were planning. I took his business card out of my wallet and rang the number. A young female answered.

"Outlaw Entertainments, how can I help?" I smiled when I noticed the name of his company.

"Could I speak to Mr Ingham please?"

"Who should I say is calling?"

"Pete Wood."

"I'm not sure if he's in, he's a very busy man," she obviously didn't recognise the name and was trained to treat anyone she didn't know with suspicion.

"I appreciate that he's busy. Would you mind checking anyway please?"

The phone went silent for a moment then a voice appeared on the other end.

"Pete, how are you doing mate?" He then proceeded to have a side conversation with his secretary. "This is the man who saved the bairn's life. Don't ever put him on hold again." I heard her apologise in the background.

"Sorry about that Pete, that's what happens when you give barmaids a bit of responsibility. What can I do for you?"

"Look it doesn't matter if you're busy."

"I'm never too busy for you. What are you after?"

"I was planning on going out for a spot of lunch. I'm a bit out of touch with the restaurant scene in Sunderland and I was wondering if you could recommend anywhere."

"Why don't you come over to the club at lunchtime? I'll show you around then take you out for dinner."

"Sounds good."

"Don't expect much of the club mind. It's a bit of a dump during the daytime. About one suit you?"

"See you then."

****

"What do you reckon," I asked Elvis, "hearts and flowers or something funny?"

"You're wasting your time. She'll never look at you."

"She smiled at me the other day," I argued.

"She didn't smile at you, she was laughing at you. Exactly the same as everybody else."

Elvis didn't understand. Claire Pearson felt exactly the same about me as I felt about her. This Valentine's card was going to cement our relationship.

"Love or laughs, what do you think a girl goes for?"

Elvis shook his head.

"If you must get one, get something funny. Girls like a laugh."

I ignored him and bought the soppiest card I could find.

I'd been at St Patrick's for nearly four months now. I was still trying to find my feet and Kevin Davison wasn't making it easy for me but most other people seemed to be leaving me alone. Everyone was giving out Valentine's cards, it seemed like the thing to do at the time. If I started going out with Claire I would be accepted by everyone in the class.

"Can you give this to Claire please?"

I handed the card over to Karen Walker. She was Claire's best friend and sat next to her. The message read 'All my love P'. I wanted to be a bit mysterious but not too much. After all I was the only lad in my class whose name began with a P except for Paul 'Elvis' Morris and he was far too immature to have an interest in girls. Claire would definitely know who it was from.

"Are you sure you want to give this to Claire?" asked Karen.

"Of course," I replied.

"Okay then, if you're sure."

I'd fancied Claire since St Christopher's but hadn't quite built up the courage to tell her. She was beautiful, a perfect specimen. I knew that I was taking a big risk but Claire was always nice to me. I thought I could be in with a chance.

How wrong could I be? She waited till the class was full before standing up and tearing the card up right in front of my eyes.

"Why on earth did you think I would want a card from you?" Everyone was pissing themselves by now, laughing at me. It was the first and last valentine's card I ever sent.

****

Ingham had been right about the club. I rang the buzzer on the main entrance and a young girl in shorts and T-shirt opened the door. There was a strong smell of bleach where the cleaner had sluiced the steps down to get rid of the smell of vomit and piss. She took me up stairs and we walked across the dance floor to the back of the club. The lights were all on and Radio 2 was playing out of the PA system. The carpet was almost black with a combination of spilt beer, chewing gum and cigarette ends.

"Depressing isn't it?" Ingham came out of his office and shook my hand.

"I've got to admit, it isn't what I was expecting."

A cleaner was vacuuming in the far corner trying to see if she could find a pattern on the carpet.

"We've tried to have them steam cleaned but it doesn't work. They're just too filthy. We wait about eighteen months then replace them; it's all tax deductible. Or at least that's what my accountant tells me. Come on, I'll show you around."

It was all as he predicted, pretty dull although I couldn't help but be impressed by the DJ stand. He had to be an engineer to operate it. There were two P.C's, a huge mixing desk and also the controls for the lighting.

"The lighting is automatic but the DJ can override it if he likes."

He flicked a couple of switches and the strobe lights streaked across the floor. The rest of the place was as expected. I could tell Ingham was just humouring me by showing me round. I made enough agreeable noises to look like I was interested but I wanted to get the conversation around to Sunday's meeting and Kevin Davison in particular.

"Do you fancy lunch then? I have a friend with a restaurant. He doesn't normally open at lunchtime but he makes an exception for a few close friends and me. You'll love it."

****

"I might as well talk to the bloody wall. A class of thirty kids and not a sign of life from any of them."

A copy of the Guardian rustled at the other end of the room. Someone marked off one of the last days on the 1985 calendar.

"It can't always have been like this, I'm sure that when I was at school we at least pretended to listen. Now they're either hung over, drugged up or just plain, bloody stupid," Mr Burns had started on one of his speeches. "Take that Kevin Davison for instance," he said to no-one in particular," personality of a house brick and all the girls love him, can you believe it? I know he's had a hard life,

148

his dad dying the way he did, but he just sits there, with about as much get up and go as a koala bear on dope."

Burns tipped his cigarette in the general direction of the ashtray, missing and dropping ash on the already worn and stained carpet.

"At least his dad was interesting, an insane alcoholic admittedly but interesting all the same." He slurped at his coffee and shook his head.

"Then there's Peter Wood, strange little bugger. He's got all the brains in the world, has two lovely parents and what does he do? Sod all. Walks about like he has the whole world's worries on his shoulders. What's a young lad like him got to worry about? School days are the best days of your life so start bloody well enjoying them."

Burns had gone red in the face and had started spilling his cigarette ends and coffee all over. He brushed the ash from his lapels.

"Do you know that he refused to play in my chess team? He should be honoured that I even asked him. I'll not let him get away with it. Nobody ever crosses Jackie Burns and gets away with it."

He shrugged his shoulders and scanned the yard. He turned for recognition of his latest put the world to rights speech but found the room empty and his tweed jacket with a large coffee stain down the front.

"Bollocks to you all. Set of Bastards. You'll see I'm right."

He placed his now empty cup in the sink at headed back to class.

Ingham was spot on with his review of the restaurant. The food was first class and, for someone who doesn't open at lunchtime, he appeared to do quite a good trade. I recognised a few faces from Sunday. Most people appeared to know each other and nearly all of them came over to acknowledge Ingham.

"Was it somebody's birthday on Sunday?"

"How do you mean?" Ingham was struggling with a particularly awkward oyster.

"It's just there was a big crowd of you out on Sunday. The pub was packed."

"Oh that. It was just business. I'm not going to kid you Pete, I'm sure you have worked out what type of businessman I am. I hope you don't mind but I took the precaution of checking you out. It was little bit difficult at first; you were the man with no past, disappearing for fifteen years. I have a lot of friends around the country and I spoke to a few friends down south, I'm sure you know who I mean. I know enough about you to know that you're ok. As long as you pose no threat, you will be fine with me. Try any of that funny business and I'll kill you. Do we understand each other?"

I knew my past couldn't be hidden forever but I was glad that, despite his threat, Ingham appeared to trust me.

"I'd appreciate it if you kept my past to yourself for now. I'd rather people didn't know the full story."

"No problem, I'm just protecting my interests. You know how it is. Don't know why you need to keep it a secret though. Sunday was mainly just a social gathering with a little bit of business thrown in. We have a lot of business going on at the moment and I need everyone to be one hundred per cent on the ball. It was a bit of a team building exercise. I was a little disappointed that a friend of yours didn't turn up."

"I wouldn't really call him a friend as such. We just go back a long way"

"Whatever. I wanted to know who was making a move on me. You already know about the fire and then some money went astray. I think Davison's non appearance tells it's own story don't you?"

"You don't know for sure."

I found myself in the strange position of defending Kev.

"I know enough to know that he's taking the piss. That man is walking on very thin ice." Ingham gave me a stare that told me not to argue with him.

I hoped that Kev hadn't upset Ingham too much. I had plans for him. I had to be the one to finish it, not Ingham. I needed closure.

****

"Why are boys so immature? They're always farting, fighting or wanking. Then if they're not doing one of those three things, you can bet your bottom dollar they'll be talking about one of them."

Claire Pearson was leaning against the radiator in the girl's toilet. Surrounded by mini skirted, bubble gum munching friends who were almost indistinguishable give or take a few pounds. They were now the oldest in the school and hogged the radiator from the younger girls.

"I've got my eye on someone, not that I could tell you who it is, you would only laugh."

"You're joking, who is it, Claire?" Sara demanded. "Come on, we're your closest friends. You have to tell us."

"No, like I said, you would only laugh," Claire knew how to play to her audience.

Sara shrugged and edged her way onto the radiator as she took a drag from her cigarette. She blew the smoke skywards, an action that would eventually colour the pink walls with a tinge of yellow.

The door crashed open.

"What the frig are you doing, Wood?" shouted Sara.

"Sorry, I was pushed," I replied sheepishly.

"I don't care. Get out you little pervert," Sara aimed a kick at me.

Karen Walker gave me a hand up. I brushed myself down as I edged, blushing out of the girl's toilets. Davison and his friends walked away laughing.

"Come on then, what are they like?" Elvis was stood beside me.

"What do you mean?"

"The girl's toilets, what are they like? You've been in that many times you should be an expert by now."

"Very funny."

"I'm serious, what are they like?"

I have to admit that the girl's lavatories had always been a mystery to the boys at school.

"Claire was there," I replied.

It had been nearly four years since I had sent her that card. She had just about stopped laughing about it. I think she was beginning to warm to me.

"God, is that all you think about," said Elvis, "Claire, sodding, Pearson?" he stared at me through his milk bottle lens glasses.

"The girl's toilets are just the same as the boy's really, just pink," I said as I feared he was going to walk off if I didn't answer his question seriously.

"What so they piss in urinals?"

"No, obviously."

"So they're not the same then?" Elvis was beginning to annoy me.

"You know what I mean. All the girls stand round the radiators smoking and chatting, exactly the same as the boys."

"And that's it?"

"Yeah, apart from the cigarette machine."

"Cigarette machine?"

"Yeah there's a machine on the wall, it must be selling tabs."

Elvis stared at me in disbelief until a grin started appearing across my face.

"I was worried about you for a minute there, Pete." We both laughed and headed for the yard.

****

It was the usual Catholic wedding, went on a bit too long and there was a lot of hymn singing, or miming in my case. At one point the sun had come down through the stained glass windows, bathing Bernie's white dress in a rainbow of colours, she looked gorgeous. A number of 'oohs' ands 'aahhs' rang out around the church, the more religious among the congregation assuming that God himself had decided to shine down upon us and bless the wedding. Bumper thankfully went for a morning suit rather than his usual banana one.

I approached Elvis as the photos were being taken outside. We avoided discussing our meeting in the Ivy and we were, after the stag night, back on good terms. The weather had been kind it was a gloriously sunny day.

"Who's that?"

Bumper's granddad was pointing at the bride. He was in his late seventies now and the years had begun to take their toll. He was wearing an old brown suit jacket, the sleeves worn away at the elbows, a pair of black trousers, shirt and tie and a maroon v-neck jumper that was on inside out. He topped the outfit off with a flat cap.

"That's Bernadette, the girl I've just married," Bumper tried to explain.

"And who are you?"

"I'm Barry, your grandson." Bumper raised his eyebrows and headed towards us.

"Right, I see, " said his granddad, nodding as he walked away as if it was all beginning to make sense.

"He's going senile. Not a great deal we can do about it. Thanks for coming Pete, I really appreciate it."

"Thanks for inviting me." The sentiment was genuine. I was really pleased to be here.

"You know where the hotel is don't you?"

"Yeah. I'll see you there." Elvis and Marie had already arranged transport.

We had been lucky enough to be sat on the table next to Bumper's Gran and Grandad. She was a sprightly woman in her seventies with bright pink hair. She appeared to have all of her faculties intact so she must have had the patience of a saint to put up with all of his eccentricities. I suppose that's what comes with fifty years of marriage.

"I'm not having bloody turnip in my fruit salad," Bumper's Grandad shouted loud enough for everyone's heads to turn. The waitress tried to explain that it was in fact paw paw not turnip but it was all to no avail.

"I don't care what fancy name you give it pet, I'm not having turnip in my starter. I wouldn't expect Yorkshire puddings in a fruit cocktail so I wouldn't expect to see turnip either."

"Don't worry love, I'll take care of him."

Bumper's Gran reassured the waitress as she removed the paw paw from the glass. Elvis and me were trying to stifle our laughs when Marie kicked him under the table.

"You'll be like that one day so don't think I'll be looking after you when you lose your marbles."

Bumper was also having problems with his fruit cocktail.

"I'm not eating that."

"What's wrong with it?" asked Bernie.

"It's got bloody pineapple in it."

"Of course it's got pineapple in it. It's a fruit cocktail."

"I hate the stuff. I won't even have it on the stall."

"You mean you have a fruit stall and you don't sell pineapples?" Bumper's new bride was amazed.

"It's the Devil's invention. On the same day that God was inventing Jaffa Cakes Lucifer invented pineapples."

"Ok, I'll take them out for you. Stop making a scene."

"I'm not eating anything that's come·in contact with it. They'll be contaminated."

"Don't push your luck."

Even Marie had to laugh when the main meal arrived. It was a standard roast beef dinner, with turnip, and Bumper's granddad chose not to argue about the choice of vegetable this time. Having lived through the war and rationing, old habits died hard. He took a generous slice of roast beef and placed it in a serviette. While he thought nobody was looking he took the meat and placed it under his cap for later.

"It'll do for sandwiches," he told his wife in a conspiring whisper.

She nodded her head in full agreement; maybe her faculties weren't as intact as we thought. We howled with laughter at the spectacle, him blissfully unaware at why we were laughing.

****

"I plan to do something with my life," continued Claire, "get a decent job away from here. I might even become famous, who knows? I don't mean become a model or an actress or anything like that. I want to use my brains, really make something of myself," Claire waved away the smoke from Sara's cigarette.

"I don't want to sound big headed but I know I'm good looking, the amount of lads following me about tells me that but I've also got the brains to get me where I want and I don't care what I use to get there."

"Shut up will you," Sara broke Claire from her daydream. "Let's get back before somebody misses us."

****

Bumper had wanted Elvis to be his best man but family politics dictated that it was to be his brother Damien who had the honour. Damien was five years younger than Bumper and was commonly acknowledged as the black sheep of the family. His mother had hoped that the responsibility of the speech would make him behave for the duration of the wedding. She was wrong. Nervous at the prospect of standing up in front of scores of people he either didn't know or didn't like held no appeal for him at all.

"That Bumper's brother?" I asked Elvis as we returned from the toilet. I'd noticed him earlier when he was stood round the side of the church attempting to avoid the photographer. He was taking big swigs from the hip flask he had stored in his morning suit.

"He's going to be a mess before he does his speech, " replied Elvis. "He was drinking like that before the wedding. Fancy running a sweep on how many people he insults?" We headed back to the table.

"First of all I'd like to say what an honour it is to be best man today for my older brother Barry," everybody let out a sigh of relief. Whilst Damien was swaying he was at least coherent. "At least that's what my Mam says. I was quite happy to sit in the corner and get pissed. Anyway the sooner I get started the sooner I finish so here goes. I'll get the formalities out of the way so could you all raise your glasses and toast the barmaids for the wonderful job they are doing today?"

"The bridesmaids you idiot," Bumper hissed.

"Yeah, them as well. Thanks to the bridesmaids even if some of the larger ones did take up more space on the photos than they should have done. The photographer needed his wide angled lens at one point."

"Oh Christ," Bumper put his head in his hands.

"I've always known our Barry had an eye for the ladies," Damien rested his hand on the shoulder of the bride's father, more to steady himself than anything else. Bumper wondered where this was going, "ever since I caught him wanking over a copy of Razzle when he was fourteen."

There were a few sniggers from the back, some of the older aunts gasped in horror and Bumper just glared. I was quite enjoying myself.

"I'm glad to see that he has moved on from magazines and has actually got the real thing, not that I'm saying she's been a model in Razzle or anything." Bumper was wondering how he could stop the speech while he still had a little bit of respect left. "In fact I've always quite fancied Bernie myself."

Bernie's sister, Colleen, started laughing and pointing at Damien. The other bridesmaids started giggling as well. Damien continued until the whole of the front row was laughing. He thought it was his speech at first until he looked down. There was a black patch slowly spreading across the crotch of his morning suit. The speech finished abruptly and he plonked himself down in his seat hurriedly.

"Looks like you've sprung a leak there Damien," shouted Colleen.

He blushed as he tried to dry his pants with the tablecloth, leaving a pale yellow stain.

It had been a great day and I was really enjoying myself. It was a shame I was going to have to ruin Bumper's honeymoon by telling him the plan.

****

Mr Burns addressed the class, "I want you to write a short story. A story about what you think will make you happy."

Claire sat at her desk busily scribbling away. *If you love someone, you have to marry them. It's the law. I'm in love with someone but he doesn't know yet. I'm going to marry him when I grow up.* Claire looked over to where Kev and me were sitting. Kev was trying to pull my book away from me. I hated Burns for putting us next to each other. I put my arm around my work, not letting Kev see what I was writing. Claire smiled. *It's the law,* she wrote, *I'm going to tell him at the Christmas disco.*

Karen looked over Claire's shoulder and laughed when she read what she had written.

"You're mad if you fancy him."

****

Bumper and Bernie sat watching everyone on the dance floor. Despite Damien's speech, the day had gone really well.

"You never did tell me the reason why you wear a Banana outfit."

"Oh it helps pull the birds. Phallic symbol and all that," Bumper answered.

"And you find that it works do you?" She nudged him gently, laughing.

"Beating them off with a shitty stick love."

"Ooh, you have such a way with words you little charmer."

"Tell you the truth, it never worked once. There was one girl, came up to the stall and asked me out, proper little stunner as well."

"Oh yeah?" Bernie had a mock, hurt look on her face.

"You can imagine me all dressed in yellow, with a bright red face. I looked a right bloody picture. Turns out that she did for a bet. Her mates bet her twenty quid that she wouldn't ask me out."

"They still haven't paid me that twenty pounds," Bernie laughed.

****

I arrived around six and the lower school hall was already half full. The Saratoga Roadshow was in residence and the music was blasting, well as much as it could be in a school disco. Elvis and me had arrived together, not the most fashionable lads in the hall by a long way. I had on my Christmas clothes, a pair of baggy, tapered Geordie Jeans, a checked blue shirt and light blue, slip on shoes with white socks. Elvis wore a pair of light grey trousers that resembled Farah slacks but, as all the fashion victims would tell you, they weren't the real thing as the pocket was in the wrong place and they were missing the crucial 'f' tag. He had a pair of dark grey slip-ons and wore a navy body warmer over a Madness T-shirt that he had owned since he was thirteen. It was starting to get a little tight on him but he liked it and that was what mattered.

We bought a cup of orange squash each and headed into the hall. There were a handful of girls on the dance floor, swaying gently to some poppy, soul number. The lads were dotted around the edge of the hall, attempting to look cool but not sure whether to dance yet. Bumper had on a cool, red, Michael Jackson style, leather jacket. It might have been plastic but the effect was great. He also had on the tight, black sta-press and black slip-ons with white socks. He stopped short of wearing a hat but was still by far the sharpest dresser in there. The lads in their Pringle jumpers may have disagreed but Bumper wasn't a label guy, he had style. He practised his moon walking by the side of the dance floor. The girls stopped dancing for a while to watch him but only because he was about to bump into Mr Burns.

I looked about and as yet, Kev and his mates hadn't turned up. They had made noises that they were too old for school discos but we knew they would be here. A Christmas Disco was a Christmas disco after all and nobody wanted to miss out. Claire had just arrived with Karen and looked fantastic. She wore a white A-line skirt and turquoise blouse. I could just make out the pattern of he bra under the thin material. I said hello as she walked past but blushed when I thought about her underwear. I also thought about what my chances of getting a Christmas kiss off her were but decided I was wasting my time despite it being a well-known fact that the girls were more up for it at Christmas. Just asking for a Christmas kiss was likely to be successful, unless you were a complete cheb like me.

The wallflowers were soon sprung into action when Every little thing she does is magic by the Police came on. There was a surge onto the dance floor while everyone pogoed and tried to emulate the dance that Sting performed in the video. I looked over to Claire who was now dancing with Karen. Her breasts jiggled ever so slightly under her blouse and I smiled over. I'm sure she smiled back. Spirits were high; it was going to be a good night.

****

"You selfish Bastard," Elvis was furious.

"I'm the selfish one? He only has to say no if he doesn't want to get involved."

"He's just got married and you're planning to get him killed."

"Nobody's going to get killed," I argued, "you opted out remember. I just thought I would be polite and let you know what I was doing." Elvis was beginning to annoy me.

"Well you're still a selfish prick."

"What are you two arguing about?" Marie returned from the toilets.

163

"Nothing, I was just saying I was tired and wanted to go home. Elvis was trying to persuade me to stop."

"Surely you can stop for one more."

"Let him go if he wants. It's a free country."

I grabbed my jacket and said my goodbyes. I left my car in the car park and got the girl from reception to phone me a taxi. I needed Elvis on my side but I didn't know how to persuade him.

****

After the Police had been on we all had an excuse to stay on the dance floor. Despite her smile, I had already decided that I would have no chance of a Christmas kiss from Claire so I looked about for a victim with lesser morals. There was a commotion at the door and a couple of the teachers headed for the entrance hall. Sara Nesbitt had downed the best part of a bottle of Strongbow before she arrived and had now thrown up in the entrance hall. They left her in the staff room until her parents came to collect her and somebody went to find some sand to cover the pile of vomit. By Monday the story would have been exaggerated to the level where she had drunk a litre of vodka and two bottles of whisky.

Everyone went back to dancing just as we saw Davison and friends arrive. After Sara's entrance they were now checking everyone's breath to see if they had been drinking. To a man, every one of Kev's gang's breaths stunk of extra strong mints. It did little to hide the smell of cider but it did enough to gain them entrance. This was mainly because the teachers gave up after smelling Tomma's breath that stunk more of halitosis than cheap cider. They all lined up against the back wall looking edgy.

We danced, jumped about and pretty much enjoyed ourselves for the rest of the evening. It was getting towards the end of the night when the Thompson Twins 'Hold me now' came on. It was one of my favourites at the time and became one of my all time favourites when Karen Walker asked me to dance. I had spent all evening wondering how to ask someone to dance and she had saved me the bother. I hadn't really taken that much notice of her before apart from her being Claire's best mate but I couldn't hide my grin, I really liked her. She was about an inch taller than me and had brown, bobbed shoulder length hair. She had a pretty, slightly up turned nose and a beautiful smile. She looked cool in her pink and grey, diamond-patterned sweater. I realised that as I was taking all of this in, I hadn't actually replied.

"Come on then, are you going to dance or not?"

Taking my hand Karen led me away from my friends. She placed her arms around my neck and, as was the custom, I placed mine round her waist. We shuffled around. I'm not much of a dancer so I doubt we were in time to the music. Her head was on my shoulder as we danced. Elvis, Bumper and Gilbert had now stopped dancing and were stood behind Karen with their thumbs up. All apart from Bumper who had formed a circle with the thumb and forefinger of his left hand and was poking the index finger of his right hand through it repeatedly. I mouthed "Fuck Off," as I shuffled round so that Karen was facing them. I wish I hadn't. I was now looking straight at Claire Pearson who was dancing with Kevin Davison. The earlier feelings of elation now sunk to the bottom of my stomach. I felt sick. I knew I shouldn't be feeling like this, I was with Karen after all. I shuffled round again so that I couldn't see Claire and Kev. The record had now changed. It was the last one of the evening. 'It must be love' Madness' cover of the Labbe Siffre classic.

"Am I going to get my Christmas kiss then?" Karen shook me out of my thoughts.

"What? Yeah. Certainly."

Whilst this was my first kiss, I knew what to do; I'd been practising on my pillow for long enough. We snogged for the length of the record. To be honest I didn't know when to stop but Karen didn't seem to mind so we carried on. We left the hall hand in hand and kissed again as we left. Her dad was waiting in the car park for her. Bumper, Elvis and Gilbert were waiting for me outside.

"Well done mate, what was it like?" Elvis shook my hand.

"Well, you know," I said dismissively.

166

"I don't. That's why I'm asking," said Elvis. They all slapped me on the back and congratulated me on the way home but I wasn't as happy as I should have been. I hadn't seen Claire kiss Kev but she had been dancing with him. That was bad enough.

I went straight to bed when I got home, not sure how I should be feeling. My tears soaked the pillow as I cried myself to sleep.

****

I was quite surprised to find Bumper working the day after his nuptials. He explained that he couldn't afford to lose the business by going away on honeymoon, which was understandable. I was even more surprised at how readily he agreed to my plan.

"You do realise how dangerous this could be, don't you?"

"Fuck dangerous. I spend all day dressed as a great big banana and it begins to wear you down after a while. It's about time I had some excitement in my life. Count me in."

"If you're sure?"

"Never been more sure in my life," Bumper's big yellow hand slapped me on the back.

"We'll meet up for a drink tomorrow night then?"

I felt a little guilty asking him to go out with me the day after his wedding but if it bothered him, he didn't show it.

"Yeah. Who else has volunteered so far?"

"There's a couple who have put their names forward but I'd rather keep the names to myself for now." I knew that I only really had Gilbert on board at the moment but I didn't want to scare Bumper off straight away.

"Need to know basis and all that. I like it. Very Secret Squirrel."

Bumper was getting into the spirit of things. Hopefully his involvement might encourage Elvis. A young girl approached the stall.

"All right, Bumper? I'll have a dozen bananas and a pound of grapes please."

"Jesus pet. You'll shite yourself away with all that," Bumper got a snigger out of his customer and I wondered how he got away with it.

"See you tomorrow then?"

"Yeah, good to see you again mate"

I headed back to the car, pleased that I'd got Bumper to agree but I really needed Elvis' help. I knew I was going to have to go and see him.

****

"Mr Burns wants to see you," Sara Nesbitt approached me in the yard.

"What for, I haven't done anything?"

"How would I know? He was giving me a bollocking for Friday night then said that you had to meet him in the entrance hall."

I headed off to meet Burns, unsure what I was meant to have done. I passed Claire and Karen on the way. Karen smiled over but I pretended not to see her.

Burns wasn't there and I had to wait ten minutes until he arrived.

"I've been picking the football team," he explained, "and you will be playing at right back. I hope you can be bothered to turn up this time."

I had to admit that I was surprised at my inclusion. Not that I was the worst player in the school but I certainly wasn't the best. I was usually overlooked because of my size. What was all the more surprising was that Mr Burns was picking the team and we had a history after I refused to play for his chess team. When you are being bullied at school it's best to keep a low profile and being on the chess team was the last thing I needed to do but Burns hadn't understood. This had been four years ago but I think he still held a grudge. I tried to act cool but inwardly I was really chuffed, I'd never been picked for anything before, except the chess team of course, and that hardly counted.

****

"I don't give a toss about the law. What do you think is paying for this house, your poxy job at the hairdressers? I don't think so. Where do you think your car came from? Do you think the garage was giving them away? No? Exactly. I paid for them and how I earn my money is nobody's business but mine. It certainly isn't yours. Now go and be a nice little housewife and make me some tea you stupid bitch."

Kev slammed the door behind him. A tear formed in Claire's eye. She wandered into the kitchen and started to make the tea. As she opened the fridge she noticed the bottle of Chardonnay. She removed it and poured herself a glass. It was times like this that she wished she had friends of her own. Since she left school she had become cut off from everybody else. Now the only people she knew were friends of Kev and she couldn't speak to them.

The invitation to the school reunion was lying on the kitchen bench. She was definitely going to go now, with or without Kev. *The people he's mixing with now, I'm going to be on my own anyway. It's about time I started making friends again.* Her mind was made up. Now she had to find a way of telling Kev. His mood had changed since Pete first suggested the reunion. It wasn't going to be easy he hated everybody he went to school with. She tried to cover up the damage as much as she could. It wasn't the first time that Kev had hit her but it was going to be the last. She tried to remember what happened to that ambitious young girl from school. Yes, she had the nice house, the nice car and plenty of money but there was something missing. The face looking back at her from the mirror was not one of a happy successful woman but that of a battered, bruised and beaten wife. She knew she was going to have to leave him, she just didn't know how or where she was going to go.

****

None of the lads seemed that surprised that I had been picked for the football team. By the time the game came along I had begun to become accepted as part of the team. I hadn't been able to resist telling everybody that I had been picked and today was my big day. I couldn't wait for the end of school so the match could start. Mr Burns knew this and he had me exactly where he wanted me, in the palm of his hand. When I was boarding the bus Burns pulled me to one side.

"Where do you think you are going?"

"On the bus Sir," I replied

"No you're not, we don't need you."

The words cut into me like a knife. The bastard had stitched me up. Now I had to walk home on my own, in my football gear. I forced back the tears as I trudged home and hung around for over an hour before I went in for my tea.

"How was the match?" asked my mother.

"Not bad."

"Will you be playing in the next one?"

"I doubt it. Most of the other players were much better than me."

"You don't know that. I'm sure you'll be picked. Why haven't you come home with your dad?"

"What?"

"They let him finish work early so he could go and see you make your debut. Didn't you see him?"

****

Claire picked up the invite for the school reunion. That's when she would do it, they met at school, and it was fitting that they would part at the school reunion. She had been happy, once. She remembered school; she was popular, especially with the boys and people used to take an interest in what she said. Now she just seems to be ignored both at home and when she's out. She half expected it from Kev, he always was an ignorant bastard but it was the way she was ignored by everyone else that really hurt. Yes, everybody would say hello; they would then always make their excuses and carry on with their lives. She knew why, it was Kev. She was guilty by association. She wasn't stupid. She knew what type of business he was in and she also knew that he was always going to attract enemies. It was the people from school who ignored her that hurt the most. They knew the real Claire. Why wouldn't they accept her?

There's always Gilbert I suppose, she thought. He never treated her any differently. This also upset her. She knew that Gilbert had suffered more than most at the hands of Kev, both physically and mentally. She always used Gilbert as a sounding block for her moans and groans. He knew some of her deepest feelings but he never divulged them to anyone as far as she knew and she would love to repay him for his loyalty. Maybe at the reunion she would be able to put things right. By leaving Kev she might be able to gain back the trust of the people she really cared about.

****

"Bless you my child."

"Fuck off you freak."

David Brodie didn't bat an eyelid and continued on his path. Followed by half a dozen would be disciples he approached his next convert.

"Arise my son. You can now walk."

He removed his hands from the head of the teenager who had been sat on the step outside the school.

"I could already walk you bloody Pillock."

The Messiah was only one of the many guises that David had used. Until very recently he had been Elvis Presley and before that a very convincing Bruce Forsyth. A brief stint as Van Gogh came to an abrupt end when an over enthusiastic Kevin Davison took it all too literally and tried to remove his ear with a pair of safety scissors. A career on the stage surely beckoned, either that or a spell in a mental institution. The disciples each carried a bible and took turns reading from it. I can't quite remember whether they used to sing a few lines from their favourite Elvis number during Brodie's previous incarnation but they seemed happy.

The teachers must have taken a joint decision to ignore Brodie's antics. Being the second coming of the Lord in a Catholic school should have been worthy of some response however Jesus Christ the second only appeared at lunch time and the teachers were all too busy drinking coffee and smoking tabs. Strangely enough the disciples only discipled during their lunch break as well. Bible recitals were all well and good whilst following the good lord but try getting them to read in class and it was a totally different story.

173

Claire looked at Pete's phone number. It was his return more than anything else that made her realise that she had to leave Kev. Pete coming home had reminded her of how she used to be. She had missed him and wished that he had never left. If he had stayed fifteen years ago, maybe things would have been different. Claire knew that he had always wanted to be part of her life. Maybe if she had given him the chance, he wouldn't have gone away. Now wasn't the time for reminiscing about chances missed. Now was a time to get organised. She was about to make the biggest step of her life and she had some planning to do. She swept her hair into a ponytail and put on some sunglasses to hide her black eye. It was time to go to work. She started, albeit briefly, to feel good about herself again.

****

The rain had started lashing against the windows. Why was it always grey in Sunderland? The storm did bring some relief from the normal misty dampness that seemed to hang over the school. They talk about the smog in L.A. and London but it was nothing compared to Sunderland's. Pollutants from car exhausts or chimneys didn't cause it, merely shite weather. The rain was welcome break and at least it kept the shagging dogs off the school field.

'RUSHELO'. The graffiti on the desk had bothered Kev for a while. Who was 'Rushelo' and why hadn't Kev heard of him? If he was going to learn one thing whilst he was at school it was the identity of 'Rushelo'. Kev pondered this during his Religious Studies lesson. He sat at the same desk each week and each week he wondered who this mystery person was. Perhaps it was an anagram. He started writing down the names of people in his class and working out what anagrams he could make out of their names. He was quite pleased that his own name could be rearranged to spell 'vikin inavadors'. Peter Wood was 'weerd poo' whilst Billy Lockswood was amusingly 'old willy bolocks'. He looked forward to sharing this with his mates but it still bothered him that he didn't know who 'Rushelo' was.

It barely kept him awake and he started nodding off. I was also drifting into a daydream. Religious Studies was a joke. Try and be like a good catholic boy, try and be nice to people, and don't forget to fill the collection box on the way out. That's the only religious education I've ever had. Somebody told me that the Catholic Church is the richest organisation in the world. It doesn't surprise me. If you think about it, if the first person in church puts a pound in the collection tray then everybody else has to try and beat it, get well in with the priest. They all think that the more money they put in, the further up the queue they'll go for getting into heaven. It's the oldest con trick in the book and it's not as if you can ask for your money back once you're dead! I think I'll try it one day, make myself a few bob.

"Davison, are you awake?"

Mr Burn's shout brought me out of my slumber. What? Shit, I forgot Religious studies. Reading out of the Bible, Jesus Christ can you think of anything more boring? Kev was nearly fast asleep at his desk.

"Well are you going to read for us then Kevin? Today if possible."

Sarcastic twat, I thought

"Yes Sir," Kev mumbled.

****

I headed up the cold, damp stairwell to Elvis's flat, it was a depressing walk. I wasn't sure what I was going to say but knew I had to make amends for last night. I possibly shouldn't have told Elvis that I was going to approach Bumper but I thought he needed convincing. Marie answered the door.

"He's in there," she said pointing to the living room, "nursing a very big hangover I hope."

"We didn't have that much last night."

Whilst we had been at the hotel all day we had paced ourselves. Elvis hadn't seemed drunk when I left. Angry, maybe, but certainly not drunk.

"You might not have but he certainly did when he came home. He got through best part of a bottle of whisky. I don't know what you were talking about but you certainly got him wound up. I've never seen him like that." Marie looked worried.

"Do you think he's up to visitors? I can go away if you like."

She shook her head and frowned.

"No, fifteen years is long enough. You're not going to disappear again that easily. Whatever it is you two need to sort out, you'd better get it done. I'm away down the shops," she removed her glasses and rubbed her eyes. "I'll be back in about half an hour and you can tell him I'll expect him to be gone by the time I get back."

"You can't throw him out for getting drunk once," I protested, "it was my fault."

"Thank you for your concern but I meant I expect him to go to work. He should have been there an hour ago."

"Sorry, bit of an over-reaction there. I'll see how he is. See you later," I said sheepishly.

"You're a right pair. One's as bad as the other. Don't forget, I don't want to see either of you when I get back."

"Message received and understood."

I walked into the sitting room as Marie left for the shops. Elvis was sat on the couch with a blanket wrapped round him. He hadn't been shaved and his eyes were bloodshot. In fact they looked that bad I thought he had been punched. He looked rough.

"In the dog house then?" I tried the direct approach.

"Looks that way. I suppose I did go a bit over the top last night."

"About last night. I'm sorry to have pushed you. I should never have asked you to get involved in the first place. I realise that now. I didn't take into consideration what you had to lose. Marie and Declan, the flat, you were right to turn me down."

I sat down in the armchair opposite Elvis.

"Yeah, well I did a lot of thinking last night. Maybe you were right. Maybe I should start sticking up for myself. I don't want my child to be brought up in this stinking little flat."

"It's quite a nice flat..."

"Don't patronise me, I deserve better. It's time I fought back. Give Davison a taste of his own medicine."

"Quite a bit has changed since I spoke to you last night. I've got a couple more willing parties. There's no need for you to get involved if you don't want to. We'll manage."

I desperately wanted him on board but I wanted it to be his decision.

"Has anybody else been stupid enough to agree to your mad plan?"

"A couple."

"Bumper?"

"Yeah....and Gilbert."

"Gilbert? Fucking Hell, now you are scraping the barrel. Jesus, you can definitely count me in now. If I don't come along you are bound to get killed. How did you agree to him coming along?"

"It just sort of happened. I saw Gilbert on the way home the other night. He'd had a bit of a run in with Kev, we got talking and then we headed back to his house for a coffee."

"Very cosy, I must say. He's probably forgotten by now. He's not the brightest bulb on the Christmas tree you know."

"I know, I know but he is going to come in very handy. Gilbert has hidden depths."

"Hidden depths, Gilbert? I'll take your word for it. What about banana boy, how did you persuade him to get involved?"

"Strange one Bumper. He didn't take any persuading at all. Agreed straight away. I think you're forgetting how many people hold grudges against our Mr Davison."

"I see your point. Anyway I suppose we'll be the last people he'll be expecting trouble from."

"Exactly. So I can count you in then?"

"I suppose so. It's not like I've got anything better to do with my sad miserable life."

"I'll see you tomorrow night then. Half seven at the Ivy House."

"I don't think Marie will let me out again after last night."

"I'll tell her I'm going to have a serious word with you about your drinking. How could she refuse me? You haven't seen me for fifteen years. She'll understand."

"I hope so because if she doesn't, we'll have to worry about more than Kevin Davison!"

****

Mr Burns had woken me briefly but I found myself drifting again. Burns had decided that Kevin Davison, the least Christian lad in the school, should read out of the Bible. This should have had some strange ironic charm but I couldn't see it. Instead we had to sit and listen to him drone on in his dull, monotone voice. The sky had gone grey again; it looked like rain.

God I really don't want to be here.

I thought about far away places, Australia, Florida, anywhere warm and away from Kevin Davison. I contemplated what I had been doing with my life and realised that it didn't amount to much. I was bored, unhappy and generally depressed. The raindrops started forming on the windowpane. I watched two race to the bottom, silently betting with myself as to which one would get there first. I lost. I needed to start taking some risks, start making a life for myself.

And still Kevin Davison droned on.

"... and Jesus said to the blind man...."

"PISS OFF YOU BLIND BASTARD!"

****

By the time Elvis got to the Ivy House, Gilbert and me were already there. I was worried that he might have changed his mind again and not turned up. He ordered a pint of Guinness and sat down with us in the corner of the bar.

"Alright, Gilbert?"

"Fine mate, yourself?"

"Not too bad. Bumper not here yet?" Elvis pulled up a chair.

"No, he said he might be a little late. Peak time for his stall after office hours," replied Gilbert.

"So what's the big plan then?" Elvis looked me straight in the eye.

180

"I think we should wait till Bumper gets here but you'll be impressed, I guarantee it. You should see what Gilbert has come up with, outstanding it is."

"I'm sure it is. So what have you been up to recently then, Gilbert? I haven't seen you around much."

"A bit of gardening. I've been working down the park. I've also been getting a bit fiddle work here and there. Cash in hand. I was working for Kev until the other day. I used to get four pound an hour and I pretty much could do what I wanted with the garden. I quite enjoyed it really. He started to get on my nerves recently though. Constantly criticising. I mean, what does he know about gardening? He was always having a go, calling me stupid."

"I can see how you were offended."

Elvis's sarcasm wasn't well hidden but it went unnoticed. I shot him an angry stare.

Gilbert continued, "I know people have always called me stupid, even when I was at school. Especially when I was at school in fact. You probably thought I was as well."

Elvis said nothing but his scarlet face told it's own story.

"I'd been left school for about five years when I heard about dyslexia. It wasn't something that people really mentioned back then. It all started to make sense, the problems I was having at school. Know what I mean?"

We were now transfixed.

"I looked into it a bit further, then I went for some tests."

"So that was it then?" I asked. "You suffer from dyslexia?"

"No, it turns out I was just thick after all."

Gilbert looked deflated. Elvis and me were lost for words so I decided to change the subject.

"You never said what happened the other day at Kev's. How did you lose your job?"

"He'd been arguing with Claire," explained Gilbert. "Not one of their normal spats either, this was all out war. I normally try and ignore it when they shout at each other; I'm just there to do the garden. This time was different though, I was thinking about going in and stepping in between them."

"You stood up to Kev?" Elvis was surprised.

"No, I thought about it but once again the coward in me came out, too many years of beatings. I've learnt my lesson, learnt to keep my head down. I'm not proud of myself, you probably think I'm pathetic." His eyes were welling up.

"Nobody would expect you to intervene in one of their arguments," I tried to reassure Gilbert, "in fact I'm not sure I would intervene either."

"And you would just stand back and let him hit Claire then would you?"

"He hit her?" My mood changed, I could feel the anger building up inside of me. I was going to explode. "I should go round and kill the Bastard now."

****

Now I'd been in trouble at school, not doing homework and that sort of thing but nothing like the trouble I was about to experience. What do you do when you've been thrown out of class? Burns hadn't given me any instructions. Did I go straight to the Headmaster's office? Did I go home? Did I go to confession and say a couple of Bloody Marys and a few How's your Fathers? I wish he'd said.

Then Kev appeared. Fucking Hell he'd sent Kevin Davison to beat the shit out of me, I never expected that. Surely that's not allowed. Swear in Religious and they send the school bully to stick a crucifix up your arse. Now I was off. There was no fucking way I was staying to see what he was going to do to me. I knew the Catholic Church was corrupt but I didn't know they sent out punishment squads.

"Oi, Pete, where are you going?"

Shit too late.

"Fucking hilarious that, Pete. I was pissing myself."

"Well, I was a bit bored," I said, thinking on the spot.

"Aye, me too. Probably get detention."

"I just hope he doesn't tell our Dads."

"Well he's not likely to tell mine is he?"

Oh shit, I'm a dead man.'

"I mean he only gets to talk to them that went upstairs, not down below where my dad is."

****

"Cool it. We are meant to be keeping a low profile," Elvis tried to calm me down.

"I knew he was an arsehole but hitting women, hitting Claire, it makes me more sure than ever now." I turned to Gilbert. "What happened? Is Claire alright?"

"Yeah. I mean it was a pretty hard punch, second one in a week, but then he turned his attentions to me. I was pleased in a way, if he's hitting me at least I know he's not hitting her."

The tears were now falling down Gilbert's cheeks.

"Very admirable." Elvis didn't mean to sound sarcastic this time but that's how it came out. "I'm sorry, I didn't mean it to come out like that. I should never have doubted you. Believe me, you've been far braver than most men. You should be proud of yourself."

"Well I'm not. Hopefully though, with Pete's plan I might be able to do something, actually stand up for myself for once. Give Kev what he really deserves."

"Too fucking right," Elvis agreed. "Let's give this Bastard something he'll never forget."

All eyes turned to the door as a six-foot banana came bounding through it.

"Evening lads, sorry I'm late. Have I missed much?"

"Jesus, I thought we were meant to be keeping a low profile."

After the seriousness of Gilbert's story, the three of us fell about in fits of laughter. Gilbert's tears now turned to tears of laughter.

"What's the joke?"

184

Bumper was the distraction we needed.

"Sit yourself down mate. I'll get them in."

I headed to the bar, chuckling to myself. Elvis was right; these are the last people on earth Davison would expect trouble from. He was in for one big surprise.

****

"They say that everybody has their fifteen minutes of fame, well Pete's lasted all of about ten seconds until Burnsy got hold of him." Kev had his usual audience grouped around the radiator in the toilet. They were hanging on every word. Seeming genuinely interested rather than scared for a change.

"He was dragged out by his hair, the little prick was even laughing. I mean, I don't like the dickhead but you have to admit he was funny," Kev was howling as he relived the tale. "Uproar, complete and utter mayhem. Everybody was in hysterics, except Mr Burns of course."

"Tell them what you said, Kev."

Tomma was beside him at the radiator, lighting his second tab of the day.

"I wasn't going to be upstaged by Pete Wood so I decided to join in."

"Sir, my Bible seems to have a misprint. That's what he said" Tomma had enthusiastically picked up the story. "What? Said Burns. Well, in mine Sir, it says, "Fuck off you blind bastard!" Can you believe that? Kev was funnier than Wood although Burns didn't think so."

Kev continued. "Get out Davison before I bounce this sodding Bible off that brainless little head of yours. You bloody little heathen. Now I don't even know what a heathen is but he didn't sound happy. The blood vessels in his temples had swelled to ten times their normal size and he gripped the back of the chair to keep balance. "You're going straight to hell you little..." Kev grabbed his chest and slumped backwards against the wall "...Bastards!"

****

"Why is Why?" the most frequently asked question in Britain?" I asked

"Eh?"

"Well, possibly not in your case, Gilbert but everyone else in this country. When you ask someone to do something, the reply is never how are we going to do this? or what will we need to achieve this? It's always why do we have to do the bloody thing in the first place?"

"You've lost me, Pete."

"What I'm trying to say, Bumper is that when we are asked to do something we never just agree. We're a bunch of cynical Bastards. We question everything. I'm asking for support now. You have to trust me. We've all agreed we're in this together. Now is the time for us to show it, without question. Are you in or not? This is your final chance to back out."

"I'm in."

"Thanks, Gilbert."

"Me as well, " said Bumper.

"That just leaves you, Elvis. In or out?"

Elvis looked down into his pint of Guinness. This was his chance to stand up and take control of his life. He could also lose what he already had. This was the biggest decision of his life.

"Why do I feel like I'm in this whether I like it or not?"

"Because."

"That's as good an answer as any. Count me in. I'd rather live like a lion for one day than a lamb for the rest of my life."

"Good man. What are you drinking?" I stood up to go to the bar.

"Why is that the least asked question around here?" laughed Bumper.

****

"See you tomorrow, gorgeous."

Dominic gave Tracy one last kiss on the cheek and let his hand slip out of her's as he headed down the path. He waved from the garden gate and then strolled down to the back lane which was the shortcut to his home.

Dominic Ledger had been seeing Tracy Cole for just over a week now and life was good. She went to Southwick Comp and was a bit of a stunner. All of his friends were jealous.

He swaggered down the back lane laughing to himself, not noticing the figure hiding in the shadows behind the dustbins. The blow to the back of his head knocked him clean off his feet. He wasn't getting up again.

****

The jukebox was now drowning out the conversation. It was Fresher's week and the students in the pub with their newly found freedom and student loans had just discovered the late 70's and a wave of nostalgia swept over the four lads sat in the corner of the bar. Jilted John blasted out accompanied by a six-foot banana, an Elvis Costello look-alike, an illiterate, unemployed gardener and a thirty-one-year-old man who for probably the first time in his life felt like he belonged.

"I WAS GOING OUT WITH A GIRL..." sang the quartet of misfits.

".... AND HER NAME WAS JULIE..."

The students looked on in disbelief. This was their week to get pissed and make fools of themselves and it was being hijacked by a bunch of old farts.

"...GORDON THINKS HE'S BETTER THAN ME, JUST BECAUSE HE'S COOL AND TRENDYYYYY..."

A pissed, looking lad of about eighteen approached us. He was wearing standard black jeans, DM's and a baggy jumper.

"Do you mind? I didn't put money in the juke box to listen to you four arseholes."

He tried to sound threatening but his Home Counties accent didn't help him.

".... GORDON IS A MORON, GORDON IS A MORON..." Elvis sang, his face inches away from the student's.

A couple of his friends ambled over.

"Are you going to shut up are am I going to have to make you?"

Three pints of snakebite had turned the student into a one-man fighting machine and he moved towards us.

".... I DON'T CARE, YEAH, YEAH, I DON'T CARE, YEAH, YEAH..."

Bumper stood up and belted out the line. The student considered his options but obviously thought better of fighting a six-foot banana with a questionable taste in music and decided to back off taking his friends with him.

"So much for a low profile," laughed Elvis.

****

After the religious incident I had been allowed into Kev's gang but I still didn't feel entirely welcome. I still felt that it was temporary and needed to prove myself. It didn't take long for me to get the opportunity. For years a rivalry had been building up between the pupils of St Patrick's and Southwick Comprehensive. It followed the same pattern each year and had almost become tradition. There wasn't much of an explanation for it other than young men wanting to mark their territory. Lads from both schools lived on the same estates, sometimes even next door to each other but when rival estates started fighting, the school divisions soon came to the fore. This year was no different.

It had all started quite innocently with Dominic Ledger, one of the quieter lads in our year, going out with a girl called Tracy Cole from Southwick Comp. Unluckily for Dominic he was completely unaware of who Tracy's ex boyfriend was. Joe Ingham, Southwick Comp's equivalent of Kevin Davison, wasn't a happy man.

After Dominic had walked Tracy home one evening he headed down the back lane that was a short cut to his home. When he was halfway down the lane he felt a blow to the back of his head. He felt nothing else until he woke up in hospital the next morning with a fractured jaw, severe bruising and a number of broken ribs. He had been knocked out with the first blow but his assailants had continued to beat him whilst he was unconscious.

The playground was buzzing the next day with tales of his injuries, which had been ridiculously exaggerated and this year's feud had officially started. The headmaster didn't help by having a special assembly for Dominic, leaving most to think he was at death's door. It didn't take long before two and two were put together and revenge was called for. We were going to war and Joe Ingham was our enemy.

I'm not a violent person, never have been and I had deep reservations about this. This was all going to escalate out of control and somebody was going to get seriously hurt. I didn't want any part of it but I was now part of Kev's gang. I had no choice.

190

"The subject is now entering the building, over."

"We're not in the secret service, Bumper. Keep it plain and simple."

I checked along the road one last time, it was remarkably quiet.

"Alright, keep your hair on. Davison has just gone into the Gym. You should have at least an hour before he comes out."

"Thanks, Bumper. Keep us informed of his movements."

"No problem mate. Be careful."

"We will. See you soon."

I ended the call.

"Right lads, time to go to work."

"It's now or never." Elvis was visibly shaking.

"Lets do it."

Gilbert was first out of the car. He opened the gate into Kev's garden and strode down the path, a man on a mission.

"You alright?" I was worried about Elvis. I had pretty much forced him into this. "You can always back out now if you want."

"And who's going to hack into the computer then? Gilbert?"

"If you're sure?"

"As sure as I'll ever be, come on."

We followed Gilbert down the path and round the side of the house.

"How did you manage to get hold of a set of keys then, Gilbert?" asked Elvis.

"I was the gardener, wasn't I? I needed the keys for the garage to get the tools. Kev also trusted me to look after the house when they were away. He knew I wouldn't dare take anything, he would kill me."

Gilbert opened the side door and went in. We followed as he went to switch off the alarm.

"Shit! I forgot it was a keypad alarm."

"What do you mean."?

"It's a four digit combination, not a key that switches it off," Gilbert looked worried.

"Well I'd gathered that much. Put the combination in then."

The beeping of the alarm seemed to be getting louder.

"That's just it. I can't remember it."

Our plan was going to fail at the first hurdle.

"You c c c can't remember it?" Elvis' voice was getting as high pitched as the beeps of the alarm.

"Well I've never been that good with numbers have I?

The beeping got louder, faster.

"I thought it was words you had problems with."

"Both really."

"I don't think n n n now is the time to t t t tell us, do you?" Elvis was becoming hysterical.

The alarm was going to go off any second.

****

Plans were hatched that lunchtime. Retribution was going to be swift and painful. A message was going to be sent to Joe Ingham that nobody messes with lads from St Pat's. Kev, luckily, let me know that he didn't need everybody to be involved at this stage. It would be a two-man job. I struggled to hide my relief. I didn't know what would be worse, going along with one of Kev's plans or letting him know I couldn't go as I was grounded after the Religious episode. He didn't tell anybody except Tomma what the plan was. I suspected that he was going with him.

Next morning the school was buzzing again as everybody turned up early to see what had happened. We didn't have to wait long. Stephen Ford lived near to Ingham's right-hand man Junior Carling and he had seen the ambulance. Carling had been hanging around the shops at the far end of Southwick Green with Ingham's gang. They were on a high after the attack on Dominic and up until now nobody had tried to retaliate. He set off for home about eleven thirty and crossed the road by the bingo hall and walked home past St Hilda's church. What happened next was unclear but one thing that was certain was that he had turned into a ball of flames before he got to his front door.

****

"Who originally put in the combination?" I was now at the keypad. Faster, louder.

"What's that got to do with anything?" asked Gilbert.

The sweat was clinging to my forehead.

Louder, faster, louder, faster.

"Who?" I had to raise my voice over the noise of the alarm.

Faster and faster. Louder and louder.

"I don't .... Kev, it was Kev," Gilbert blurted out.

Beepbeepbeepbeep...... Faster and faster........ Beepbeepbeep......
Louder and louder.... Beepbeepbeep.......

Silence.

None of us breathed for what seemed like an eternity.

"What happened?" Elvis was the first to speak.

"One, two, three, four."

"What?"

"The combination. One, two, three, four. What other sequence could Kevin Davison remember?" I laughed.

"Gilbert couldn't fucking remember it," Elvis had a point. "I could do without any more surprises like that. I've only brought one pair of underpants with me and I think they are already full."

"Well we're in now. Let's not waste any more time. Good work, Gilbert."

"Thanks. His office is down here."

We headed down the passage. Obviously, Claire had more influence over the interior design. Everything was simplistic, with just a few black and white photos breaking up the walls.

"Any of these yours, Gilbert?"

"Yeah. Kev doesn't know though. I gave them to Claire. He thinks she paid a lot of money for them. Thinks they were done by Lord Lichfield or something."

"You took these photos?" Elvis was surprised. "You never fail to amaze me, Gilbert."

I tried the door to the office.

"Shit, It's locked. He's obviously got something to hide."

"Let's kick it in." Elvis took a running kick at it and fell flat on his arse. The door didn't budge.

"Not very subtle, Elvis. The idea is to get in and out without him knowing we've been here."

"Have you got any brighter ideas? Unless The Artful Dodger here knows how to pick locks."

"We could always use the key," Gilbert unlocked the door.

"Oh very security conscious, I must say. What the fuck has he given you a key to his office for?" Elvis shook his head in disbelief.

"I told you, he trusts me. I used to water the plants in here every day. He knows I wouldn't be able to even switch the computer on, never mind discover it's hidden secrets."

"Come on, Elvis. Let your fingers do the walking. Find out what you can." I led Elvis to the desk.

"Expensive bit of kit this. Must have cost a packet," observed Elvis. "Mind you, I could have built it for half the price if he had come to me."

"A quarter, by the time he took his cut," I laughed as Elvis switched on the computer.

Gilbert had already lost interest in the conversation. He was checking the plant in the corner.

"See what happens when I leave. This plant is nearly dead. I'm going to have to water it."

"Leave it, Gilbert. He's not meant to know we've been here. Not yet."

"But...."

"No buts. Trust me on this. Come on you can show me the rest of the house. You'll be all right on your own won't you, Elvis?"

"Yeah, I'll work a lot quicker without you two rabbiting in my ear."

Gilbert took me through to the back lounge that led onto the conservatory and the indoor swimming pool.

"Fancy a dip?" I asked.

"Can't swim."

"Me neither. Remember swimming lessons at school. I used to fucking hate them."

"Me too," Gilbert laughed.

I realised it was the first time he had really seen Gilbert smile since I came home. He had been laughing in the pub the other night but that was through the tears he had already shed so I didn't think it counted.

"Have you never fancied learning to swim since you left school?"

"I struggle enough to keep my head above water when I'm on dry land."

I thought I knew what Gilbert meant.

****

The police spent most of that day at our school and interviewed the usual suspects. Everyone knew who the fire starter was but nobody was going to say a word, they didn't want to be next. I'm sure that the police also knew the culprit but couldn't prove it. Carling was unwilling or unable to speak and DC Carter was keen to nip this in the bud.

"Come on, Davison. You're telling me you know nothing about this?"

They were sat in an interview room at Southwick Police station. Kev had one of the carers from the home with him.

"I was at home all night. If Junior Carling wants to spontaneously combust on his way home that's up to him."

"That's not funny, Davison. The poor lad could have died."

Carter thought back to when he had been the investigating officer for Kev's father's death. He had a certain amount of sympathy for the lad after he had sat with his father's body through out the night but he was rapidly losing patience with him now. The lad was cocky, aggressive and almost definitely guilty. He just couldn't prove it.

"We know there's a dispute between you and Ingham. We don't want this to get out of control."

Carter went to light a cigarette. He almost offered Kev one but remembered his age.

"I'll tell you what I know," Kev sat forward, elbows on the table and stared Carter in the eye. "That gang, Ingham and all his mates. They all sniff gas behind the shops on the Green. I think you should put a stop to it. Anyway, I bet that's what they were doing and Carling, the thick bastard that he is, probably lit a tab and blew himself up with the fumes."

Kev slumped back into his chair with a satisfied grin on his face.

"This is a waste of my fucking time! Get out of my face." Carter was furious.

"Don't be a stranger."

"Don't push your luck, Davison. I've got my eye on you."

Kev laughed as the carer forced him out of the door.

None of the carers were going to dispute Kev's story, he knew too much. He was in the clear for now but the police let him know in no uncertain terms what the consequences would be if anything like this happened again.

Kev returned to class a hero, much to the distaste of the teachers. I have to admit that I was no more comfortable with it than they were. It was attempted murder after all but I chose to say nothing.

Nothing had happened for a couple of days and it looked like the severity of the attack on Carling had scared off Southwick Comp for good. We were wrong. Ingham's revenge was just as vicious but a lot more risky.

****

I looked out over the garden.

"This all your work?"

"Yeah."

"You've definitely got a skill there, Gilbert."

"Can I ask you something, Pete?"

"Fire away."

"It's just that ...... it doesn't matter, it's not important."

"No, go on."

"Well, you've been away for fifteen years."

"Yeah?"

"You've just come home and you've got me, Elvis and Bumper breaking into houses for you. Getting into some pretty heavy shit."

"I gave you the choice."

"I know. I wasn't having a go. Look at it from my point of view though. You've obviously done quite well since you left school, made a bit of money. What I'm trying to say is that if this goes wrong, you could walk away. Disappear again. Nobody would know where you had gone. We would still be here though. We've nowhere else to go. Elvis has a family. Bumper has his business. Admittedly I don't have much to lose but Kev is a killer. How do we know that you're not using us to get what you want? Planning to disappear into the night. Leaving us to pick up the pieces."

I was hurt but I could see where he was coming from.

"You don't, Gilbert. You'll just have to trust me. Is this all you want for yourself? Gardening for someone you've hated since the age of twelve? You're better than that, Gilbert. I know I couldn't have done this without you but it doesn't mean I've used you. We're in it together all of us. We're all doing this for the same reason. We owe it to Davison. We owe it to ourselves and he'll get what's coming to him. You'll see. Just imagine the satisfaction in being the one who brought his empire crashing in around his ears."

****

I was sat in the yard having my lunch with Gilbert. I didn't want to be seen with him as it might have affected my relationship with Kev so we sat slightly round the corner near to the woodwork block. Kev and the rest of the gang were smoking near to the bike shed that backed on to the old garage. We were facing the lower

200

schoolyard where the younger kids played. It rang alongside the main road towards the heart of Southwick.

There were three lads walking across the yard but I didn't take much notice. A lot of lads went down to Sweaty Val's chip shop for their lunch and walked back through the lower schoolyard. It was only when they got within a few feet of me that I noticed they weren't St Pat's pupils. The badges from their blazers were missing, as were the ties, but they were wearing white shirts that nobody wore in our school. I suddenly recognised a face, Ingham. He looked straight at me and then must have decided that we posed no threat so walked straight past us. He was heading towards Kev who had his back to us.

Everyone was watching the fifth year girls in netball practice and nobody noticed who was coming. I wanted to shout as I saw Ingham pull a black football sock from his pocket but something stopped me. He raised the battery filled sock and swung it towards Tomma's head. There was a crunch like a heavy ceramic pot being dropped and Tomma fell to the floor instantly. Everything appeared to be in slow motion. Ingham replaced the sock in his pocket and, along with his two accomplices, walked straight out of the far gate and away.

Nobody reacted for a few seconds, not even Kev. A large pool of blood had now formed around Tomma's head. Everyone stood and stared.

Until he started shaking.

****

The monitor reflected in Elvis' glasses. He tapped away with a satisfied grin on his face.
This'll teach the Bastard.

****

Nobody knew what to do as Tomma's arms and legs flailed.

"What's happening?" Shrieked one of the girls.

"He's swallowed his fucking tongue. He's having a heppa!"

Bumper pushed through the crowd and elbowed Kev out of the way; a move that would normally have resulted in a hiding but Kev was just staring in disbelief. He had gone white. Tomma had now turned blue and was choking. Bumper knelt beside Tomma and steadied his head as he removed his tongue from his throat.

"Get a fucking ambulance," shouted Bumper as he cradled Tomma's head.

By now the teachers had come streaming out of the staff room to see what the commotion was about. Miss Shipp came running over with a cushion in her hand.

"Here use this," she said as she handed it to Bumper.

"Can't we put it in a carrier bag or something?" Mr Gutteridge the Headmaster was right behind her. "We don't want him to bleed on it."

"Fuck Off," Bumper screamed as he snatched the cushion from Miss Shipp. "Can't you see that he's fucking dying?"

Gutteridge tried to protest but he was ushered away by Miss Shipp.

Whilst all of this was going on virtually nobody had moved. Bumper stayed with Tomma until the ambulance came and eventually the teachers restored some semblance of order. I went back inside with everyone else and went to the toilet to splash my face. Whilst I was drying my hands I heard somebody throwing up in one of the cubicles.

"Are you alright in there?" I said as I knocked on the door.

"Yeah, I'm ok."

I waited until Kevin Davison came out to make sure he was really ok. He was as white as a sheet.

"Ok, mate?" I asked again.

"You won't tell anybody about that will you?" It wasn't a request.

"Don't worry, I won't say a word. Come on, let's get back to class before somebody misses us."

"I'm going to have to finish this." Kev wiped his mouth with the sleeve of his blazer.

"How do you mean?"

"That was a challenge. He could have taken me out easily if he had wanted to but he chose to take out Tomma instead. He wants to see how I will react."

"And?"

"It's going to have to be a one on one. It's the only way, Ingham and me. I'm going to need some back up though."

I knew, by the tone of his voice, that there was no way out of this one.

****

"When people tell you that you can't or shouldn't do something, what they really mean is that they don't want you to do it. Think back to every time that someone has told you that you can't do something. You can guarantee that they will have been looking after their own self interests."

Gilbert nodded as if he understood what I meant.

"What I'm saying is that when Kevin Davison tells you that you will never be a successful gardener or a famous photographer it is because he doesn't want you to be. He wants to be the only successful one around here. If you were successful he would lose you as a gardener and wouldn't be able to pay you buttons anymore."

I was on a bit of a roll now so I continued.

"When someone tells you that you can not or you should not remember this. If you unravel a knot, what have you got?" I didn't wait for him to answer. "A piece of string. And how long is a piece of string? It's as long as you want it to be. You're the master of your own destiny. You can become whatever you want to. It's your choice."

"Pete?" interrupted Gilbert.

"Yeah?"

"I haven't got a bloody clue what you're talking about."

"Yeah, sorry. I seem to have rambled on a bit. I think what I mean is don't let people walk all over you. Make sure you get paid what you are worth."

"Shame you don't have a garden at the lighthouse. I could have done it for you and charged you a fortune."

"I could always get a window box."

****

All of the arrangements were made through Brian Hathaway. He was a pleasant lad who I'm sure wouldn't have wanted to get involved but he was unfortunate enough to live next door to Ingham. He wouldn't get any trouble, as he was just the messenger that's how it worked.

The fight was to take place out the Tasty Bake takeaway on Friday lunchtime. The Tasty Bake was at the top of my street and was definitely our turf. I felt a little bit better about this as I had a guaranteed escape route and, as it was on our patch, the turn out from our school would be substantial. We would have plenty of back up if it got out of hand. I was even happier when Kev had told me that they had agreed not to use weapons. They were going to settle it fair and square.

****

"Can I ask you something, Gilbert?"

I looked past the swimming pool and out over the garden.

"Course you can, as long as it's not maths."

"Do you ever think about your dad, ever wonder where he is?"

"Sometimes, I used to think about him a lot when I was a kid. Thought that things might have been different if I had a father. Then gradually, after a while, I started thinking about him less and less; it became less of an issue. When I was twenty-one I toyed with the idea of trying to find him. You always hold out hope that they are going to be some multi-millionaire who hadn't known about you. You hope that they will come and find you one day but then I woke up to myself."

"Have you never asked your mother?"

"How could I? If she wanted me to know she would have told me. There must be some reason why she didn't tell me."

"I'm sure your father was a good man, I'm sure he loved you in his own way."

"Whatever, all I know is that he was never there for me when I needed him. I'm just glad I have friends like you I can rely on."

The phone rang and both of us jumped.

"Fucking Hell Pete. He's left early. He hasn't had his usual work out," Bumper was frantic.

"Where's he going?"

"I don't fucking know, I'm not Mystic bleeding Meg you know."

"Alright. Follow him. Keep us up to date." I tried to stay calm.

****

I didn't concentrate much in my lessons on Friday morning and I had thought about bunking off for the morning and coming back at lunchtime but decided it was too dangerous. The morning flew by and we all congregated in the yard. The fight wasn't until one so Kev sent out some scouts and the rest of us went for lunch. We didn't want to all go at the same time as it would arouse suspicion.

When we finished lunch, we walked over the lower schoolyard, jumped the fence and headed to the Tasty Bake. I couldn't believe the crowd that had gathered. There must have been at least one hundred and fifty. There was a splattering of girls but it was mainly lads. Admittedly a lot of them were younger than us but it still looked impressive. They cheered as we approached and I thought that maybe it wouldn't be as bad as I thought.

We all chatted and exchanged pleasantries as we waited for Ingham. It was now five past one, Ingham was late but nobody was particularly concerned. Whilst his gang could come from one of four directions we were fairly certain that they would come along the main road. In any case we would see them from miles off, there wouldn't be any surprise attacks.

Sam Newcombe who lived a few doors up from me came walking up the street. I knew him to say hello to but he didn't mix with us much as he went to Southwick Comp. He had his uniform on and the mood turned ugly. I thought he was a little stupid to walk into this crowd but Sam wasn't the one we were here to fight. Nick stepped in front of him and blocked his path.

"He's ok, Nick, I know him," I said.

Nick didn't move and stared Sam straight in the eyes although Sam didn't appear to be intimidated.

"Come on, Nick, just leave it," I said.

He still didn't move.

"Nick, if Pete says he's ok then he's ok," Kev spoke up and Nick moved aside.

"Alright, Pete? Waiting for Ingham?" said Sam.

"Yeah, he's cutting it a bit fine."

"I think you're going to have a long wait. He's not coming."

"Have you heard this, Kev? Ingham's bottled it," I said.

"He wouldn't bottle it. We'll wait," Kev gave Sam an unconcerned glance and carried on chatting to someone else.

"Your choice Pete, I'm only telling you what I know."

"Yeah cheers, Sam. I'll think we'll hang on a little longer though."

We waited another ten minutes and still nobody showed.

"What do you think, Kev?" asked Nick.

"I don't know. I can't believe he would walk into our yard and take out Tomma but won't come down here to fight me. He's up to something. Where could he surprise us on the way back to school?"

"The only place they could hide in any numbers is the industrial estate. Do you think they're waiting there?"

"Could be. Take a couple of others and go on a recce. We'll wait here for you"

"I'll go."

This was a chance to prove myself. I was fairly good at making myself invisible and I knew the area like the back of my hand so I was sure I was the best man for the job.

"No you're ok, Pete. They can manage. You stay here."

Nick and a couple others headed off towards the Industrial Estate. Everyone was a bit edgy now. We thought that they weren't coming but weren't sure. We were confident on our own turf but the walk back could be dangerous. We needed to know what was happening?

We didn't have to wait for Nick to get our answer.

****

A woman in her forties, trying to look twenty, approached Bumper. Slightly overweight, she had her died blonde hair tied back in a ponytail and wore an expensive looking, white Nike tracksuit. Her face was brown, part sun-bed tan and part make up. It did little to hide her wrinkles.

"I'll have half a dozen bananas please."

"We haven't got any."

He didn't look at her as he slammed the sides up on the stall.

"You've got no bananas?" The woman grabbed Bumper's arm.

"YES, WE HAVE NO BANANAS!"

Bumper ran to the van and threw the shocked woman a bag of prunes.

"Here, have these. They'll match your face."

He jumped into the van and set off in chase of Kev, his wheels spinning and leaving black rubber scorched onto the concrete.

Gilbert and me headed back to the office.

"How are we doing?" I asked. "Have you got what we wanted?"

"It wasn't as easy as I thought. He's got pretty tight security on here," Elvis replied.

"Not too tight for our Elvis though?"

"Here," Elvis threw me a box of floppy disks, "all of his protection rackets, drug deals and other shady business practices. Everything you or our friendly local Bobbies would like to know about Mr Kevin Davison. He must have thought he had the most secure passwords as none of the information is encrypted; it has names, dates, the lot. Not all of the local police force would be too happy though. Some of their names seem to pop up quite a lot."

"Well I don't want to worry you but there is one thing you might not have discovered about our Mr Davison yet." I studied the box of disks.

"What's that?"

"It's that he has left the gym and he's on his way home."

"I'm not finished yet," Elvis protested.

"I thought we had everything we needed to get him banged up."

"We have but we don't want his stay inside to be pleasant do we."

"How do you mean?" I was confused.

"Nobody inside likes a nonce, do they? What do you think will happen when the police raid the house and find files from Mr Burn's favourite website on Kev's hard drive? They're not going to keep it quiet are they?"

"You mean...?"

"Downloading it now."

"How long?"

"Five, ten minutes at the most," Elvis replied.

"He'll be back in less than five."

I looked nervously towards the door.

"Too late to back out now. He'll definitely know we've been here. You'll have to delay him."

"How?"

"Bumper. He's watching him isn't he?"

****

The un-silenced exhaust of a motor cross bike roared behind us. The rider, who wasn't wearing a helmet, was hurtling along the pavement at some speed, sending the old women at the bus stop into a panic. The bike was heading straight for the crowd and everybody parted as it screeched to a halt in front of Kev. It was Dave Lennox. He was in the same home as Kev and was another thug. He went to Southwick Comp but still got on with Kev as he didn't take sides in the war with Ingham. Too many problems of his own to deal with he said.

"He's not coming Kev, " said Lennox.

"You sure?" Kev knew that he was a fairly reliable source.

"He's still there at the moment. Said he's definitely not coming down."

"You better not be taking the piss. If he's lying in wait for me somewhere I'll come after you."

"Swear on it mate. He's not coming."

A ripple of excitement spread around the crowd. Nick arrived a couple of minutes later.

"They're not there, Kev. He's bottled it."

"Looks like you're right. He's fucking bottled it!"

Kev punched Nick on the arm and, as the bike roared of into the distance, we headed back to school.

****

"Fucking stupid thing." Bumper dropped the phone when it rang.

"That's not a very pleasant greeting for your friends," I laughed.

"Are you out yet? He's nearly home," Bumper sounded hassled.

"You're going to have to delay him."

"How?"

"I don't know. Use your initiative."

I heard a screech of brakes and then the verbal onslaught.

"YOU FUCKING STUPID...NUN BASTARD!"

A car had halted suddenly on the roundabout, Bumper slammed the brakes on and narrowly missed crashing into the back of the silver Metro that had stopped in front of him. He automatically started his own brand of Road Rage. Admittedly he didn't expect a sixty-year-old nun to get out of the car. On the other hand, she could hardly have expected to be abused by a six-foot banana.

"What's happening, Bumper?"

"Divine, bastard intervention, that's what. If she doesn't get out of the fucking way I'll be sending her straight back upstairs to see her boss."

Bumper floored the accelerator of his bright yellow transit and started to overtake the startled nun. Luckily Kev's Shogun hadn't got very far. It was stuck at the road works and Bumper started to catch him up. Kev's 4-wheel drive started to pull away and Bumper slipped in behind him. He beeped his horn and waved at Kev but as was normally the case Kev was playing hardcore garage in his car and couldn't hear a thing. As they speeded up, Bumper realised he was going to have to attempt to overtake him. He dropped down to third and pulled out knowing that it's never a good idea to cut Kev up, even if you are pretending to help him. Bumper waved desperately as he swerved alongside Kev's motor. The Mondeo coming in the opposite direction flashed his lights frantically. Bumper was trying to hide his fear, which wasn't easy to do, driving at sixty miles an hour, in a thirty zone with only one hand on the wheel! He pulled in front of the Shogun and slammed on the brakes. Kev broke sharply behind him, narrowly avoiding skidding into the side of the van.

****

The walk back to school was jubilant. We were the conquering heroes without even having to fight. I had stood side by side with Kev and Ingham had bottled it. We were all late back for school

215

after lunch but nobody gave a toss. With it being Friday afternoon, the teachers didn't seem to care either and nobody got into any trouble.

The jubilation lasted all weekend but came to an abrupt end on Monday morning. Brian Hathaway came to school sporting a black eye. He walked straight up to Kev.

"He'll have you today, at Marley Potts field. One o'clock."

I slumped against the wall.

Oh Fuck, I thought.

Kev spent all morning trying to drum up support but nobody was biting. Everyone knew about Marley Potts field; it was definitely their turf and was where some of the most legendary battles of the last few years had taken place. The place was notorious.

"Come on Pete, you have to come. You're one of us now."

I felt like I had no choice. There was no way that we were going to muster the same numbers that we had on Friday. Aside from the location our numbers were going to be depleted by the fact that Jamie and Martin had been suspended this morning. They had celebrated Friday's victory by going into Woolworth's in the town centre, emptying the display basket full of footballs and kicking

216

them all over the store creating havoc. The police had been called and they were now in serious trouble.

Much to Kev's disgust, Nick had also refused to go. He tried to warn Kev that it was too dangerous and he didn't want any part of it. The top men in the gang were all missing; perhaps I could prove my loyalty now.

"Yeah I'll be there, Kev." I noticed Elvis shake his head in the background. He hadn't spoken to me much recently.

From the hundred and fifty that had turned up on Friday, our number had now been whittled down to thirteen. This number included many like myself, there to prove their loyalty to Kev but hoping desperately that it didn't turn violent. I hadn't eaten lunch, as I felt sick. My stomach was churning and the mood of the group was sombre.

"Keep hold of this for me Pete," Kev handed me a short metal bar.

"I thought there were no weapons."

"There shouldn't be but just in case. If it gets nasty just lash out with it, take as many out as you can."

"Shouldn't you keep it?" I said, "You're in more danger than me."

"Once I'm down I'm finished. If you see anybody jump in just hit out as hard as you can."

Nobody expected Ingham to bottle it this time.

****

"Fucking stupid twat!" Kev jumped out of the car, he reached for his automatic but chose the car jack instead. "What the fuck do you think you're doing?"

He dragged the driver's door of the Transit open and brandished the car jack in his right hand.

"Phone call for you," Bumper didn't know why he said it but he knew that he was going to die as soon as the words left his mouth. It was the best he could think off at such short notice. "At the gym. Somebody phoned for you just after you left."

"You nearly ran me off the road to tell me that?"

"It might have been important."

"Have you never heard of mobiles?" Kev took his phone from the car and threw the car jack back onto the passenger seat. "If it was that important they would have contacted me on this. As they haven't, I think we can safely assume that it wasn't that important you fucking moron."

"Nice phone."

"What?" Kev was going a bright shade of scarlet and there was now a crowd of onlookers

"I've got one just like it."

Bumper picked up his mobile. As it happened it was the mobile that had been bought specifically for today and he really didn't have the faintest idea how it worked.

"What the fuck have you got one for? Why would a six foot banana need a mobile phone?"

"Oh you know, running my own business and that."

"You couldn't run a bath. Look, you don't even know how to use it."

"Eh?" Bumper looked at the phone and realised he hadn't ended the call.

"Who are you talking to?"

Elvis, Gilbert and me were listening to every word on the other end.

"Hello, earth calling Bumper the Banana boy. Beam me up Scotty. ET phone home."

Kev was now beginning to enjoy ridiculing Bumper in front of the small crowd that had started growing. He switched the phone off and handed it back to Bumper.

"Here, have it back. And be careful, you could have somebody's eye out with that." Kev laughed and got back into his car.

Bumper thought he had shit himself but he wasn't sure. He didn't care.

****

We headed onto the field. To the left of us were allotments and to the right was the football field and then more grass that sloped up steeply towards the changing rooms. Ahead of us was the main road that led to Southwick Comp, behind us were a line of bushes. We had come in through the gate separating the bushes from the allotments. There was nobody on the field when we got there.

"Which way do you think they will come?" I asked.

"Probably come straight from school up the main road. No need to surprise us."

We waited for about ten minutes and still nobody showed.

"Do you think he's bottled again?"

"No. I'm not happy about this," Kev eyed the field anxiously. "He shouldn't be late on his own patch. What's he up to?"

We waited nervously for another five minutes then we heard the rumble of Lennox's exhaust again. He came racing up the pavement again from the direction of the school.

"He's on his way, Kev. Good luck mate, you're going to need it."

He sped off up the slope towards the changing rooms. As I watched him disappear over the brow of the hill a crowd started forming at the top of it. We were well outnumbered by about ten to one.

"Stand your ground lads!" Shouted Kev.

I looked behind me to check my escape route.

Oh Fuck.

We were surrounded. About one hundred lads were spilling through the gate that we had emerged through fifteen minutes ago. On the roadside an even bigger crowd emerged. This was the crowd that would include Ingham. I fingered the metal bar inside my pocket. I didn't want to get it out as I didn't want to provoke anyone. Then I realised that they were all tooled up. Metal bars, pool cues, and baseball bats, basically whatever they could get their hands on. I'm sure that Stephen Ford had started to sob behind me. The crowd started heading down the hill.

"It's just like fucking Zulu," said Paul Loftus.

They converged on us from all sides but there was still no sign of Ingham. A few lads brushed past me and they started surrounding Kev. I edged towards the back of the crowd and noticed a few others had done the same. Everyone was concentrating on Kev. The crowd on the far side parted and Ingham emerged from it, launching his assault. There were no pleasantries exchanged as Kev landed a right hook on his jaw and rocked him on his feet. He followed it with a left, right combination.

"Go on!"

"Kill him!"

This was it. The adrenaline was pumping. I tried to force myself forward so that I could get a better view. Ingham tried to swing a few punches but didn't connect properly, Kev followed with another combination and blood was now spilling out of Ingham's nose. He kicked Ingham in the balls and he staggered backwards into the crowd. Kev followed him.

That's when the mallet hit him.

****

"Finished?" I asked as I stuck my head round the door.
"All done and dusted, " said Elvis with a self satisfied look on his face.
"Let's get out of here then. Thanks again lads. You've done yourselves proud."
We were safely out of sight when Kev's car pulled into the drive.
"A job well done, I must say."
I noticed the front of Bumper's yellow transit van at the end of the road and we walked towards it.
"Come on lads, I think we've all earned a drink."
As we climbed into Bumper's van a red BMW pulled into Kev's drive. A sun tanned blonde stepped out.
"Who's that?" asked Bumper.
"Mrs Elizabeth Ingham," replied Gilbert.

"Who?" Bumper was confused.

"You'll see."

A smug grin spread across my face as I opened the side door of the van deliberately letting Gilbert have the front passenger seat.

****

Someone had been carrying a woodwork mallet and as soon as Kev had started getting the upper hand, they intervened. His nose had shattered and he collapsed. They swarmed around him like ants, swinging bats and metal bars and systematically dismantling his face. I tried to get near him but it was impossible, there were hundreds of them. I pulled the bar from my pocket but it was useless against such a crowd. If I took one out there would be another hundred to take his place.

"Get them," somebody shouted.

Then the crowd turned. They were facing me. I turned to run and realised the rest of my school friends already had a head start on me. I felt a thud on the back of my neck but didn't go down. I couldn't go down. I ran as fast as I could but I was never that good a runner. I felt another bat narrowly miss me. I threw the metal bar behind me and heard a crunch and a thud.

"Bastard."

I saw Stephen Ford desperately trying to climb the fence into the allotments but he wasn't going to make it. Somebody grabbed his leg and he fell back to the floor. The bats started swinging. I couldn't help him. I had to keep moving. It was chaos, there were people running everywhere. People who were meant to be chasing me were ahead of me; bodies were lying on the ground surrounded by swarms of people after their blood. I got through the gate in time to see Paul Loftus hurdle the fence into the Junior School. He was away. He had been the school athletics champion and knew the fence was no problem. I wasn't so sure. I was even less sure when I saw David Stoker try and hurdle it and stumble. They were onto him and he was taking a hiding. I decided against it and turned right and ran towards the school.

The adrenaline was pumping and I don't think I was even afraid at that stage; I just had to keep on running. Then I saw the bus. It was pulling away but the doors were still open. This was my only chance. I ran along side it while it was indicating to pull out. I got to the doors just as they were closing. I dived and grabbed the metal pole as I dragged myself aboard.

"What the fuck are you doing?" shouted the driver.

"Just fucking drive," I shouted to the obvious disgust of the elderly lady in the front seats.

The driver agreed when an angry mob started attacking the bus with baseball bats. He put his foot down and sped away. I turned to the bus where everybody was staring at me. Apart from the elderly lady, the bus driver and me, everybody was wearing Southwick Comp uniforms.

****

"It's sad the way he's turned out?"

Elvis and myself were sat in the Bungalow Café having a coffee. I looked out over the harbour and towards the lighthouse. The sea was quite choppy but inside the harbour walls it remained calm. Tim was stood outside taking photos of the sea.   He   had changed since I went away. It was rumoured that he had spent some time in Cherry Knowles mental home.

"What happened to him?" I asked. "He was great when we were kids, always looking out for us."

"I'm not sure. He lost his job down the shipyards and just seemed to decline from there. He went silent on us, barely ever speaks."

It really was sad to see someone we all looked up to as kids turn out like this.

"Do you remember this?" I said as I removed a ticket from my wallet.

"Newcastle City Hall, Eleventh March Nineteen Eighty One, " replied Elvis. "Still the best concert I've ever seen. Why have you kept the ticket?"

"Memento I suppose, a reminder of how things used to be." I replaced the ticket in my wallet.

"In the years before Kevin Davison you mean?"

"Maybe. Anyway, is there nothing we can do to help Tim? It hurts me to see him like this."

"I tried a few years ago. I offered him a job in the shop, lugging boxes and stuff. I could barely afford it but I think I owed him that much. He turned it down. Although he's gone silent, he hasn't lost his marbles, far from it. He's just decided not to bother with anyone, decided to opt out. Don't let anyone tell you that he's been in Cherry Knocker, it's not true."

"If that's how he wants it I suppose there's nothing we can do but keep an eye out for him."

I watched Tim adjust the camera lens and take a photo of the lighthouse.

"Do you want another coffee mate?"

I nodded as Elvis headed to the counter. There was a fishing boat returning into the harbour, riding the waves like some giant bucking bronco.

"He drinks in the Whistle if you want to see him," Elvis had returned with the coffees, "I try to avoid it because Davison's gang drink there."

"I might pop in to see him, I'm sure there must be something I can do for him."

"You could help him with his dress sense, look at him."

We watched Tim for a few seconds.

"Do you think he's under the impression that he looks smart or is he just taking the piss?" I was glad that Elvis had lightened the mood a little.

"I think he has it sussed. Shirt and tie, v-neck jumper, suit jacket, different coloured trousers and a pair of trainers. Fucking trainers. I ask you," I laughed.

"Looking forward to tonight?" Elvis asked.

"Which part?"

"The reunion."

"Yeah, should be a good laugh."

"We'll see. I've got to get home for my tea and then I'm going to have a look for my old sta-press. I'm sure I'll still fit into them."

"Can't wait to see it. Catch you later."

I watched Elvis leave, Tim was still snapping away. I sat back, looked out towards the lighthouse and contemplated what I was about to do.

****

Luckily the passengers on the bus didn't care much that I had been in a battle with their classmates. As it appeared that half their school were at the fight I could only assume that this was the half that were non-violent and were possibly more scared of me than I was of them.

I got off the bus after two stops and I was now half way in between St Pat's and Southwick Comp. I removed my tie, ripped off my badge and headed back to school.

When I got back to the school everybody wanted to know what had happened. Paul Loftus was already back and had been filling them in. A couple others returned bruised and battered but generally ok. Stephen Ford didn't return that day, or for the next six weeks as he was too scared to come out of the house. A special assembly was held that afternoon to warn us of the dangers of violence. I wasn't listening as I had my eyes planted firmly on the police officers in the entrance hall and the van outside. They were taking this seriously. Kev took a right beating he could even be dead. We were in real trouble. After the assembly a number of names were read out and told to stop behind. Mine wasn't amongst them. Most of the names had been the usual suspects who were called upon when this sort of thing happened. On this occasion they were innocent.

"Why didn't you help him? Why did you run?" Sara grabbed me by the arm.

There was no point explaining that I was the last to run and there was nothing I could have done. I shrugged my shoulders and walked away.

While I was walking out of the assembly I noticed a face I recognised talking to the police in the entrance hall. The face was swollen ridiculously and he resembled a cabbage patch doll but it was definitely Kev. He was alive.

****

"For years, all I ever wanted to be was popular. Then I realised that it would never happen," I explained, "nobody can be truly popular."

The sun was reflecting off the ripples on the sea. The downpour had gone as quickly as it had arrived. Seagulls circled above us as Claire and me sat on the balcony of the lighthouse. She had popped round to make sure I was still going to the reunion tonight.

"In your lifetime you'll have two, three if you're lucky, people who really like you, people who genuinely think the world of you," I continued. "Everybody else will just treat you with varying degrees of contempt. There maybe some who say they like you but nine times out of ten, they don't know the real you. It's just a superficial show that's put on for the crowd."

"That's a very cynical view of life," said Claire.

She had covered her bruising slightly with make up but you could still make out where Kev had smacked her. She seemed slightly on edge.

"Life gets you like that. You can be respected, that's one thing. Unlikely but it is an option. Then you can be feared. Fear can be dressed up however you like it. Fear can look like respect and it is

229

often passed off as popularity but it is only when you know the difference that you can control it. I've decided, popularity is unobtainable, it's time to be feared."

"So is this just you, or have you written off the whole human race?"

"Everyone. Go on see if you can name one person who is popular. Someone who isn't despised by as many people as those who claim to love him."

"Santa Claus, "Claire had a satisfied grin on her face, "everyone loves good, old Father Christmas."

"Too easy. The Catholic Church hates him. They think he's the Devil."

"All right then, The Pope. The Catholic Church can't hate him."

"He is the Devil, head of the biggest criminal organisation in the world. Do as I say or go to hell. I think that one qualifies as fear."

"Fair enough, you have a point. It doesn't mean that you should give up. I still like you," Claire tried to lighten the conversation.

"You haven't seen me for fifteen years."

"Well that means that you haven't done anything in the last fifteen years for me to stop liking you," Claire grinned. She knew she was beginning to get the upper hand.

"Give it time."

"That's no way to treat an old friend."

"Best to know now to avoid disappointment later."

"I'll take my chances. Come on you grumpy old bugger. Walk me home?"

Claire took my hand and led me to the spiral staircase.

"You can try all you like, Peter Wood. You're not going to be feared. You're too likeable," Claire laughed.

"Can I ask you something?" She looked straight into my eyes. "Why did you come home, Pete?"

"Come on, let's get you home before your incredibly popular husband notices you're missing and decides to spread some fear around."

****

Apart from the damage from the initial blow, Kev had survived quite well. The beating had been so frantic, nobody had connected properly and he had just curled into a ball. He suffered a broken nose, bruising to his face, arms and legs but very little else and returned to school a week later a hero. Everyone knew he would have won the fight if nobody had jumped in and he said nothing to the police. Ingham wouldn't be back and the war was over until next year.

I wasn't so lucky. It turned out that the only casualty from the comp apart from Ingham was the lad I managed to hit in the face with the metal bar. I had assumed this would have given me some credibility with the gang.

I was wrong.

"You ran Wood and you could have helped me," Kev was unforgiving.

"Everyone ran. There's nothing I could have done. Half of your mates didn't even turn up."

"At least they had the decency to say they weren't going to fight. You said you would then bottled it."

"I didn't bottle, I was there, I was hit with a baseball bat."
"I'm going to make you pay for this, Wood."
I fought back the tears as somebody smacked me on the back of the head.

****

A light breeze put a slight chill in the air and it had started to become overcast again, the night was beginning to draw in. We watched the seagulls swirl in the air above the white patches in the waves. A cargo ship had left the harbour and was now turning left for the trip towards Norway. Claire seemed reluctant to leave.
"I had a dream last night," I said as I put on my coat, "I'm not sure what to make of it."
"Mmmm?"
Claire had sat back down in the armchair. She was wearing a camel coloured, woollen coat to protect her from the wind.
"When we are sat here, we can watch the birds flying, soaring into the sky without a care in the world. Occasionally when they are

232

swirling around the top of the lighthouse, they don't see the glass. They try and fly straight through it. There's a thud and they fall to the ground. It's quite unnerving the first time you see it."

"That's terrible. Do they survive?"

"Most of the time they're just stunned and fly off, until this morning that is. I was in that dozing state just before you wake up. They say that's when most dreams occur. Anyway while I was sleeping this seagull flew straight into the glass. The noise must have woken me but that's when the dream happened. In the split second before I woke, it wasn't a bird banging on the glass; it was the hand of the Grim Reaper I saw, the hand of Death. It was a bony, slender claw protruding out of a black sleeve. It shook me up a little bit."

"What do you think it meant?" she asked.

"I don't know. It could mean nothing, it could mean everything."

"You've had a rough time since you came home. Maybe it's the stress of everything getting on top of you. You should relax more, you're really uptight," Claire walked behind me and started massaging my shoulders through my jumper. "You're in knots."

"You could be right." I placed my left hand on hers and smiled. "When I got out of bed I came out onto the balcony. There was a seagull lying here, it's neck was broken. Maybe that's what it was all about. Maybe Death had come to take away the bird. Who knows?"

I looked up at Claire and thought about kissing her but it somehow didn't seem like the right moment. She gave my shoulder one last squeeze and sat back down.

We sat there for another hour, not really saying anything. Eventually Claire decided that she had to leave. "Don't worry about the dream. You're not going to die. I'm not going to let you get away that easily. She kissed me gently on top of the head and ran her hand through my hair. "See you later, Pete. Don't go anywhere."

I stood up and took her hand in mine. I looked straight into her emerald eyes and gave her hand a squeeze.

"I won't."

As we walked back along the pier I noticed a lone fisherman. The pier was now private property and fishing was prohibited. I thought about asking him to move on but he had possibly been fishing there for years. Who was I to take that away from him?

****

From the day Kev returned to school my life was made a living hell. I was spat on, punched, kicked and generally abused at every turn. Tomma and the rest of the gang eventually returned and when they were at full strength they were formidable.

"You can keep away from me as well." I was disappointed at Elvis' response.

234

"Come on, Elvis. You're my best mate."

"Was your best mate. You soon abandoned me when you thought you were part of Davison's gang. Look where it got you. If I start mixing with you again I'm going to end up getting it as well. It's hassle I could do without."

I sloped off to the canteen, wondering if I could make a plate of chips last the whole lunchtime. At least there was some sort of protection in the canteen.

When I eventually left the restaurant Elvis was waiting for me.

"Look, I still stand by what I said earlier but there's something I think you should know." He had been in one of the cubicles in the toilets and had heard Kev and his mates talking."They're going to be waiting for you after school. You're going to have to go home a different way."

"I'm going to have to walk miles if I'm going to avoid them."

The only other route home was by walking around the top of Marley Potts estate. Something I wasn't particularly keen on.

"It's the only way if you want to avoid a kicking, " replied Elvis. "And if they find out it was me who told you, I'll be the one getting the kicking." He was right, unless I set off early.

"How are you going to get out of school early? It's Geography last lesson, there's no way Dunny will let you out."

"Can't do anything about it if I'm not there," I said.

"What do you mean?"

"See you later mate. I'm away home."

"You can't what about registration?"

He had a point. I went to registration and as soon as it was over I headed for the front gate and walked out. Nobody saw me. Nobody was expecting it. Suddenly I felt an overwhelming sense of relief sweep over me.

****

Claire placed her arm around me. The orange glow of the streetlights and the fret coming in from the sea combined to form a luminous haze.

"Do you never miss seeing the stars?" I asked her. "Do you not wish that you could lie back in the grass and stare up into the evening sky without this orangeness? I used to do that quite a lot, completely lose myself in my thoughts. Better than any drugs, better than any religion."

"And you would know, would you?" she challenged.

236

"Surely the point of religion, the chief selling point, is freedom. To be alone with your thoughts with no distractions is the greatest freedom. That's why people are never happy when they are together. You can only be truly happy when you are alone. The happy couple is a myth."

"God, you can be a miserable bugger at times. I thought we were having a good time. These last two weeks have been really special to me. Obviously you don't feel the same. Someone must have really hurt you once for you to be so bitter."

"I'm not bitter, just realistic. Why build yourself up to be knocked back down again." I put my hands in my pockets.

"That's it isn't it? You don't really believe any of that crap. It's just another one of your little self-defence mechanisms. Don't let anyone get close because you'll only get hurt. That's bollocks and you know it." Claire was surprised at how angry she had become.

"I think you've just proved my point. If you were alone you wouldn't be having this argument. Unless you were schizophrenic and then I suppose you wouldn't be truly alone."

"Ok I give in. You win we're all going to lead miserable unproductive lives and die unhappy. Now can we just try and enjoy this walk along the seafront before the rain comes and spoils it."

"I quite like the rain."

"That doesn't surprise me," Claire smiled.

We walked for about ten minutes in complete silence, quietly enjoying each other's company.

"I've got to go. His Majesty will be expecting his tea by now. See you tonight."

Claire headed across the road, past the concrete lions and up the garden path. I checked my watch, not long now.

****

I didn't know what to do with the rest of my day. I hadn't felt this relaxed in ages. I went home and had a few games of snooker, equalling my record break of thirty. I then went upstairs and had a wank, it would be rude not to. I played my Depeché Mode tapes at full blast and generally enjoyed myself. This was definitely the way forward. For the next couple of weeks I did the same every day. I would go in for registration and then walk straight out of the gate, only returning for afternoon registration. Elvis and Bumper soon joined me. It hadn't taken Kev long to work out who had tipped me off and he administered a sound to beating to Elvis.

Elvis saw the benefits of my new found freedom but Bumper wasn't really sure why he was there. He just said that the idea of playing snooker and listening to tapes appealed to him.

We started playing games on the computer. They were normally banned in my house, the computer was an educational tool but Elvis' parents were a little more liberal. He had stacks.

Like all good things, it had to come to an end. A letter to my parents soon put a stop to it.

****

Tomma knew it was all going to come on top sooner or later. He'd had a good innings and now was the time to get out. He'd planned it from the start and now he had enough money to move to Oz and disappear. Not as much as he had hoped but that was unavoidable. He had managed to skim that money from Ingham but that meant his need to get away all the more urgent. There were just a couple of loose ends to tie up and then he'd be away.

Tomma didn't feel sorry for Kev; he's had it coming. He did murder Nick Couzens after all. Whether he had the right motive is irrelevant. He was still the man with the knife. A little phone call just before he boarded the plane would have Carter and the wooden tops pissing themselves with excitement.

Fuck Davison, Fuck Ingham, Fuck everyone.

Tomma knew that disappearing would make him look like a bad person but he didn't really care. All he wanted was to be liked, to be popular. Then life got in the way, people got in the way so they had to be removed. He was thirty one years old and this was the first time he had actually done something that was for him alone. He'd been living Davison's pocket for the last twenty years, it was time to move on. This would be his last time in the Whistle with the lads. He fingered the wrap of Charlie in his hand. Yes, tonight was going to be a good one and he was determined to enjoy it.

****

"Straighten your tie."

My mother tried to strangle me with my neckpiece then tried to reinforce the side parting she had combed into my hair that morning. Taking a tissue from her pocket, she spat on it and started wiping an imaginary mark from my face.

"For Christ's sake, Mam. I'm fifteen, I can manage to wash myself."

"Well you should try and act your age sometimes. And don't take the Lord's name in vain. No the wonder you're in so much trouble with an attitude like that. I don't know where we went wrong with you."

I was tempted to tell her, when I saw Bumper forcing back a grin at the other side of the entrance hall.

"I don't know what you're smirking at," said his mother.

"I don't smirk. Stunts your growth apparently."

This was too much for Elvis who burst out laughing. Mrs Morris hit him so hard that his glasses flew across the floor.

The humour kept our minds off what was coming; we were all due in Gutteridge's office to get our punishment. We had been bunking off for about three weeks now thinking that nobody had seen us. The funny thing was that the teachers had watched us from the staff room window as we walked out of the gate. They hadn't bothered to say anything at the time as they were probably thinking we would set a trend that would take the likes of Kevin Davison out of their lessons giving them an easy ride. When they eventually realised that we were never going to be trend setters they decided to pull us in. I'm not sure how they explained to Gutteridge that they had quite happily watched pupils walk out of the school and not done anything about it. I would loved to have seen them try and explain it to my mother but I was never going to get the chance.

****

I could sense that something was going to go off. I also knew that when it did I would have to move quickly. I realised that none of the lads really trusted me but as I was on good terms with Ingham they decided to tolerate me. Tomma remembered me from school and I think he had noticed how close me and Claire had become, even if Kev hadn't. When it did go off I wasn't expecting it but believe me, I moved quicker than I ever have before.

I'd only gone into the Whistle for a quiet pint before the reunion. Hopefully I would get to have a word with Tim. He was at the bar and nodded in acknowledgement as I came in. I suddenly found myself without anything to say to him. He carried a camera around his neck but everybody knew that it had no film in it. At worst the lads saw him as a minor irritation when he was pretending to take photos but most of the time he was seen as comical character, someone to take the piss out of.

This particular Friday had started like any other for them, most of the lads meeting up in the whistle after work for a few beers before hitting the Town. Kev was missing but that wasn't unusual, he was probably sorting some business. The lads always had a reputation as trouble but everyone has to have a local and the whistle was theirs, a few high jinks but nothing over the top. Big Dave the landlord used to work with my dad and I was surprised that he tolerated them. He explained that business was business and he couldn't afford to kick them out. Especially as he didn't want the repercussions. He also expressed surprise that I would mix with the likes of Ingham. I explained but I'm not sure he believed me.

I took my pint and sat in the corner under the window. A few of the lads nodded in my direction but none really made the effort to speak. I watched them perform their usual antics. Levis copies were sold out of a large holdall, tales of female conquests were relived, loud enough for everyone to hear. Everything appeared normal, except for Tomma. I thought about giving him an invite for tonight then thought again. If he wanted one he could ask. He seemed to be on edge. Tim was taking a few snaps, all the lads were posing, a few of them with spliff in hand others lining up the Charlie in the back room. I don't know whether Tomma suspected something was up but he took too much of an interest in Tim's camera.

Everybody thinks that Tim is a gentle giant but if you've had the piss taken out of you for the past ten years and haven't said a word in all that time then you're going to have some anger building up inside of you. This was the night it was going to come out and boy did it come out!

"What's that fat cunt taking pictures of?" Tomma knew he should leave it alone, tonight of all nights, but the coke was taking over.

"We're only having a laugh, Tomma. It's got no film in it."

"What are you taking pictures of retard?"

Tomma poked Tim in the stomach. Tim ignored him.

"I'm talking to you shit for brains," Tomma tried to grab Tim's camera from round his neck. "Give us a look at your camera fatty."

Tim pushed him aside. Nothing nasty but to a wannabe hard man being given the brush off by the local fruitcake is a bit of an embarrassment.

"Who do you think you are pushing you fat cunt?"

Tomma tried to take a swing but Tim knocked him flat on his arse. His broken nose produced a stream of scarlet.

"You're a fucking dead man."

Tomma produced a knife. I was shocked to see it but I guess that most of the lads are tooled up these days. By now most of them were up and were going to lay in to Tim. I couldn't stand by and watch it happen. He always looked out for us. This wasn't in my plans but what the hell? I headed over to the bar, picking up a bottle of Becks from the table and smashed it straight over Tomma's head. He went down in a heap and I knew he wasn't going to get up. I saw someone coming for me out of the corner of my eye. I didn't wait to find out who it was and slammed the remainder of the bottle straight in his face. The adrenaline was pumping now, this is what it was all about, and this is why they all loved fighting. I was rushing! I landed a swift kick in the bollocks to the nearest man to me. I had been like a firework waiting to go off. They all wanted a piece of me but not half as much as I wanted a piece of them. I caught a glimpse of the knife just before I saw the body collapse in front of me, Tim's huge frame towering above it with a broken stool in his hand, the knife lying hopelessly in the limp hand on the floor.

Big Dave came racing in and stood between me and Tim and the rest of the crowd. The baseball bat in his hand and the damage we had already inflicted deterred anyone from having another go.

"You two get out now, I'll take care of these little shits."

We didn't need a second invitation. Dave had bought us some time and we needed to hit the ground running. Dave dished out one last blow to the image of the Davison's gang.

"You, pick up the rest of your face and get this fucking mess tidied up before you even think of leaving this pub."

****

There was an uneasy tension in the entrance hall. The three mothers eyeing each other with suspicion, not speaking. Eventually my Mam broke the silence.

"If you're looking for who's to blame in all of this, look no further than this one here."

I felt it a little unfair to lay the blame solely on Elvis or Bumper; I thought it was even more unfair when I realised that she meant me. Usually in these sorts of situations the Mothers argue amongst themselves about who was the bad influence on their children. In this case my mother left Elvis and Bumper's mothers in no doubt that I was the ringleader and I would be suitably punished. They seemed happy enough with this.

My Mam had obviously been on the phone earlier to agree my punishment with Gutteridge. As soon as I sat down his office, he dished it out. I was to be on report for my remaining time at school. After each lesson I would have to get the relevant teacher to fill in a report about how I had behaved in class, turning up was a good start. They also had to comment on my homework and anything else they saw fit. I was then to present it to the deputy head at the end of each day where he would review it and then sign it and keep it on my file. It was going to be a nightmare for me. Not only was I going to have to turn up for each lesson, I was going to have to do homework as well. Add this to the grounding I was going to get and the daily beatings from Kevin Davison and it was quite a punishment.

"We'd like you to sign this," Gutteridge shoved a sheet of A4 paper in front of me.

"What is it?"

"Just do as you are told and sign it." My mother had no time for questions.

I glanced at the head of the paper. It was a behavioural contract. I'm not sure if this was Gutteridge's invention or whether it was common practice in most schools. Basically I was signing this form to say that I agreed to abide by all school rules, attend school when expected to do so and most important of all, treat teachers with the respect they deserve. It was a joke but I had no choice. The paper was worthless anyway so I had nothing to lose.

"Where do I sign?"

I signed the paper and Mr Gutteridge called through for his secretary to photocopy it. We waited in silence for her to return. My mother thanked Mr Gutteridge as we left and assured him of my future good behaviour. I wasn't so sure.

****

"Ignore it," Elizabeth grabbed Kev's arm.
"What if it's important?"

He reached over to get to the phone. Elizabeth dragged him back, kissing his shoulder gently.

"They'll ring back. I thought you didn't use your home phone for business anyway."

She climbed on top of Kev, pinning his shoulders to the bed. He liked it when she was in control.

Kev and Elizabeth had been having an affair for nearly two years now. They both knew how dangerous it was. If Joe, her husband, ever found out they would both be dead. Kev suspected that his wife knew but she had never said anything, he could take care of her anyway. He had been a bit wary when Elizabeth and him first got together; thinking that she might have been spying on him for her old man. For this reason he kept pillow talk to a minimum, except when he wanted to know something about Joe's business. No matter how hard she tried, Elizabeth just couldn't help talking. Kev had acted on the information sometimes, leading her husband to think he had a mole in his organisation; not for one moment thinking it was his wife.

Kev looked at the tattoo on her back; Joe was convinced that the Chinese writing was his name; Elizabeth swore that it was Kev's. He thought he loved her.

Kev climbed out of bed and headed for the bathroom, he left the door open as he urinated. He knew they had been taking more risks recently. Once they would never have dreamed of meeting at Kev's house but Claire was out shopping for something to wear to the reunion. Joe was always busy on a Friday night in the club. He came back to the bedroom without washing his hands.

"Joe got much on tonight?"

"He wouldn't say. It's all very hush-hush."

"Must be something big going down."

The phone rang again as he was about to get back into bed. He unplugged it from the wall.

"Come on, we've got another hour before Claire gets back."

He jumped onto the bed and crawled under the covers as he went down on her.

****

Elvis and Bumper got away with being on report for two weeks and they were grounded for the same period. I soon came to realise that it took quite a while for the teachers to fill in the report after each lesson and it took even longer for us to wait for Mr Swinbank after school. This meant less time for Davison and his gang to wreak revenge on us. Lunchtime, however, was always a problem and there was no way we could avoid them all day.

Football hooliganism was becoming the big thing now and Kev and his mates wanted to be part of it. Every Monday morning was awash with tales of beatings handed out on a Saturday. Whether they were an active part of it or just eager onlookers was unsure but it certainly guaranteed them an audience. They had moved up a level now and if any of the stories were true, which I'm sure some of them were, they were now capable of levels of unbelievable violence against complete strangers; a worrying development.

"When we got to Middlesborough Station they were all waiting for us."

Kev had a crowd around his desk and they were lapping up every word. While Elvis and me were disgusted by his stories we were still as interested as everybody else and listened from a distance.

"It all kicked off and we were right in the middle of it. I took a couple of them out and then I saw Tomma go down."

Tomma was sitting beside him proudly sporting a particularly painful looking black eye.

"I waded into them with my Stanley," continued Kev, "nearly took some cunt's ear off."

Claire walked away from his desk in disgust.

"You're an animal."

"They soon fucked off after that. We walked down to Ayresome Park and nobody touched us. They knew who we were and they were scared shitless." He then went into his pocket and produced a red handled Stanley knife. "Look, it's still got the blood on it."

Everybody was in awe of him. I turned away and started to talk to Elvis. We tried to ignore him but he seemed to get louder.

"Look how sharp it is."

Everybody started laughing, except Claire who screamed at him.

"Pack it in, Kev. You're not funny."

I turned round to see what was happening and realised he was stood right behind me. I didn't hear him come up behind me and hadn't felt a thing as he had sliced straight through my blazer with his knife. It was indeed as sharp as he had said. Not only had it sliced through my blazer but it gone through my jumper as well. A couple more centimetres and I would have been sporting a twelve-inch gash across my back. As it was I was now going to have to think of an excuse to tell my mother as to why my uniform was ruined.

****

I don't think I've ever seen so many photos in one place, on the walls, on the coffee table, even on the chairs, piles of them everywhere. So much for him having no film. Black and white photos are somehow so much more revealing than colour, more dramatic.

"Bit of a hobby you have here Tim," I shouted through to the kitchen.

It was more than a hobby it was an obsession. This was the second house I'd been in this week that was full of photos. Maybe this was the new craze in Sunderland. It's funny but even the most familiar places look completely different when presented like this. The school, the pub, even the bus stop at the end of the street. He must have photographed nearly every spot in the city. There were some familiar faces as well, Big Dave, Kev, all of the lads in fact. Ingham was even in the pictures, he wouldn't be happy about that. Then I saw it, Nick Couzens, lying dying on the floor with Kev stood above him with a knife.

Jesus Christ, Tim has known all along who killed Nick and he hasn't said a word.

"They make interesting viewing don't they?"

I jumped. I hadn't realised that Tim was in the doorway.

"Christ you gave me a fright there. I read about this in the paper the other night. They said it was a pub brawl but they had no leads. How come you haven't handed these into the Police?"

"Because I know of your involvement with Davison and Ingham. I know all about you, every move you've made since you moved away. I thought I'd keep an eye on you and you're beginning to get out of your depth aren't you?"

"You don't say anything for years. When you do decide to open your mouth it's to tell me you've been stalking me for the past fifteen years. What sort of a freak are you?"

"Take a look at this."

Tim threw a photo on to the table. It was a picture of me carrying Ingham's kids out of the burning house, very dramatic.

"I didn't know you were there. How come I never saw you?"

"Take a look at this, five minutes earlier."

There I was staring straight into the camera, lighter fuel in hand. I never saw him. Shit if these ever end up in the hands of the police, or worse still, Ingham, I might as well kiss my arse goodbye.

"What do you want Tim? Is it money? I'll give you money, buy as many cameras as you like."

****

Over the next few days it began to dawn on me exactly how far behind I had become. Years of not doing any homework and not paying attention in class, coupled with my weeks of bunking off had left me with absolutely no idea what any of the teachers were talking about.

I had been moved into the bottom stream for most subjects but was still, inexplicably, in the top stream for English. English Language would be a doddle; you just made it up as you went along. English Literature, on the other hand was a completely different matter; they at least expected you to have read the books you were being tested on.

****

"Leave, Pete. Take your money, take Claire and disappear. I'll make sure these photos end up in the right hands. I'm sure that D.I. Carter will be very interested. Of course I'll make sure your involvement is omitted. When he has the evidence in front of him he's not going to dig any deeper is he?"

"Don't you see? I've already run away once and look what happened. Nothing changed, it never does."

I flicked through the photos on Tim's coffee table and lingered over one of Claire in her dark glasses.

"I have to end this once and for all. I have to end it now before it's too late."

"It already is too late, Pete. Things are getting out of hand, they probably would have anyway but you haven't helped matters."

"I never meant all of this to happen you know. Davison pushed me into it. I don't expect you to understand."

"Why does Davison need to be punished, because he's a bully? Who's going to punish you, Pete?"

Tim placed a photo of Elvis, Gilbert and Bumper in front of me. The three were in suits, laughing.

"That was Bumper's thirtieth birthday. Look how happy they are. You have it in your head that they are permanently miserable and you can save them from all of it but you're wrong. They're no happier and no more miserable than anyone else. They're just trying to get through life as best they can. If it wasn't Davison it would be somebody else."

"Surely getting rid of Davison would help them."

"It wouldn't. You would just be getting them into more trouble than they can handle."

"I can't just walk away."

"Like you said, you've done it before. Davison's empire is beginning to crumble around him. Leave and leave him to rot."

"It's something I have to deal with, Tim. It's personal."

"You think I don't understand. Do you think I've never been bullied? We slogged our guts out at the yards and then we were dumped. Look what it did to me."

"That's different."

"Fine, if that's what you think but remember if you get the other lads involved in your vendetta you'll be turning into exactly the type of person you claim to despise. You've got a chance to put this right. Disappear now before it all caves in around your ears. This is your only chance, Pete. Take it."

"I can't do it, Tim. I know exactly what you mean but I can't just up and leave. I have things I need to take care of."

****

"I'm never going to be able to read all of the books in time," I was sat in the computer room with Bumper and Elvis. "If I get the Penguin Passbooks for each one at least I will be in with a fighting chance."

"But why do you need to raise the money? Can't you ask your parents?"

"What, and risk telling them that I haven't got a clue what the first line is in Macbeth? I don't think so. I tried to get my pocket money backdated. It was stopped months ago. My Mam just said that it served me right for lying."

"When shall we three meet again?" asked Bumper.

"What?"

"In thunder, lightning, or in rain?"

"What are you on about, Bumper?" I said. "We're not going anywhere."

"It's the first line in Macbeth, you know, the three witches?"

"You worry me sometimes."

"You worry me. The exam is in a few weeks and you have no idea about Macbeth, Chaucer or anything else."

"Let me worry about that. Are you going to help me?"

"It seems like a good idea but what if we get caught?"

"We won't. None of the teachers know the first thing about computers. They'll never realise."

"Let's give it a go, we've got nothing to lose."

****

"Can't you see, Tim? It's not just me; it's Elvis, Bumper and Gilbert. They had to be involved."

"They didn't need to be involved, you know your way around a computer system; you're forgetting what I know about you. Why did you have to get Elvis involved when you could do it yourself?"

"I'm not the only one who needs to exorcise the ghosts of the past. I wasn't the only one put through hell by Davison; he has affected each and every one of them." I thumbed through the photos of my friends. "Look at the state Elvis and Bumper's businesses are in because of him. And then there's Gilbert, he's never going to make anything of himself and he has the talent to do so. People like Kev need to be put in their place but more importantly than that people like us need to do it. If we don't, the next Kevin Davison will just come along and take it all away from us."

"There's nobody who looks out for Gilbert more than me. That's why I don't want you to go through with it. I understand everything you have said but what if it doesn't work?"

"It has to, we have no choice," I replied.

"If it doesn't, Davison will kill you; you do know that don't you?"

"It had crossed my mind. His friends already know something is up and after the performance in the Whistle tonight we're hardly going to be winning any popularity competitions. I think you should start looking after yourself. It's not safe to stay here tonight; they know where you live. I've got the old lighthouse now, nobody knows about it apart from Gilbert and Claire, you'll be safe there."

"Thanks, you're probably right but I'll take my chances here."

"The offer's always there if you want to change your mind. Make sure you lock up properly. Anyway, what did you mean when you said that nobody looks out for Gilbert more than you, I didn't realise you kept in touch?"

Tim fidgeted nervously with the lens of his camera, not looking me in the eye.

"Pete, I think there is something I should tell you."

We approached David Stoker who was tapping away on his keyboard at the corner of the room.

"Alright Pete?"

"Fine mate. How's the programming going?"

"Nightmare. I haven't got a clue what I'm doing and it counts for twenty percent of the final mark. I've got no chance. How about you?"

"Did mine ages ago. In fact it's a bit of a hobby of mine, I do it in my spare time. I could help you out if you wanted," I suggested.

"What, coaching?"

"Sort of. Have a look at this."

I placed a disk in the drive and ran the program. It was fairly easy for me to produce but the bright colours impressed David.

"What do you think?"

"It's great but wouldn't that be cheating?"

"Not really. I've written down how it all works, in case anybody questions you. Like you said, it's just like I've been coaching you."

"I'm not sure. What's in it for you?"

"Three pounds if you have it. But if you don't want it, I'll not be offended. I can sell it elsewhere."

I closed down the program and went to remove the disk.

"No, you're ok, just leave it there." He fished into his pocket and handed me three, pound coins. "You sure it will work?"

"Of course it will. You have my money back guarantee."

Pleased with our first sale we headed for our next customer. Tony Evans had never quite forgiven me for beating him into second place in the end of year exams at St Christopher's. Throughout his time at St Pat's he had been top of the class in everything, except computers. Elvis was always the star of the show and I'm sure I would have been up there with him if I had bothered to apply myself.

"How dare you?" Tony was furious.

"What?"

"How dare you suggest that you are more qualified to program a computer than me? I should report you right now."

He was visibly upset at the accusation.

"We weren't trying to offend anyone, just trying to help," Elvis explained. "We know you're going to be top in the theory we just thought you would like to be top in programming as well."

"I will be top and without your help as well. Now if you don't go away, I'm going straight to the headmaster."

Dejected, we left the room.

"Who else can we try?" I asked Elvis.

"No one."

"What do you mean no one?"

"That's it. There are only four people in the whole school who are taking the exam and two of them are us. Everyone else was crap at computers."

"Why didn't you tell me this earlier? I'm never going to get the money now."

"What are you going to do then? How are you going to afford the books?"

"There's only one thing I can do."

Bumper and Elvis looked at each other.

"No way," they said in unison.

****

"I'm his father, Pete."

"How come, I thought he never knew his Dad?"

"He didn't, in fact he still doesn't know the truth." Tim told me the whole story.

"It's not something I'm proud of, you have to understand how lonely I was. I had friends, mostly down the shipyards, your Dad included. I always had problems chatting up women though, I was shy and it was killing me. I heard the lads talking in the shipyards, you know how they do, don't leave anything to the imagination. They were talking about a lass a few of them had slept with who lived in Southwick.

"Gilbert's Mam, Eileen?" Tim nodded.

"They were mainly married men as well. At first I was disgusted at the thought, then I met her. She was in the Torrens when we went for a pint after work. She wasn't the slapper everyone had made out, she was just lonely like me. We only did it the once, upstairs while the two brothers played in the sitting room. Didn't last long but she was quite sweet, didn't force me out of the door as soon as I was finished, didn't make me feel too bad. I decided then that I would never go back."

There was sadness in his voice. He continued.

"A few week's later I heard the lad's talking again, Eileen was pregnant. None of them knew that I had been there but somehow I knew it was my baby. Don't ask me to explain it; it was just a feeling I had. I went round to see Eileen and she said it was definitely mine but she didn't want anything from me. I offered to marry her but she turned me down, said that it would only confuse the kids. It tore me up inside knowing that I had a baby son and couldn't see him but there was nothing I could do"

"Could you not have fought for custody?"

"I would never have won. When would I have been able to look after him, I was at work all day? It was for the best."

Why have you never told Gilbert? It must have been chewing him up thinking he had no father and all the time you were a couple of streets away."

"I know what you think but I couldn't; his mother didn't want me to. As the years went by it got harder; how do you tell someone that for the last thirty years his father has been living round the corner but hasn't been round to see him. It would crucify him, he would end up hating me."

"You don't know that, he's a forgiving person, he could welcome you with open arms."

"If your plan doesn't work I may never get the chance to tell him."

I felt guilty; while I thought that the other lads all wanted to be involved I hadn't bothered to stop and ask their families.

"I've struck up a bit of a friendship with him over the last couple of years through the photography. I've always been into it, as you can see. A few years ago I saw him in the park and he was taking photos of a flowerbed he had laid, really good work it was. You could tell he was proud of it and I struck up a conversation with him, gave him a few tips on lighting etc. I think he was a bit wary at first, he's had a lot of cruelty in his life so strange men approaching you in the park is bound to set alarm bells ringing. I saw him most days and after a couple of weeks we'd built up some trust between us. He invited me round for tea and showed me some of his work, far better than his old man's."

"Possibly not as incriminating. He's never mentioned you, how come he never told me about any friends?" I asked.

"We sort of drifted apart. He started working more for Kev and he didn't like me going round there. I've still kept an eye on Gilbert; don't think for one moment that I've deserted him. It kills me to see the way that bastard Davison treats him; I'd like to rip his head off with my bare hands."

"Now you see how I feel."

"The difference is that I haven't. When I found out you were back I knew there would be trouble. I know what you have been doing and I didn't want you to get my son mixed up in your vendettas. I also know how persuasive you can be so I can see how he was convinced."

"He needs this as much as me."

"Maybe, but I need you to promise me one thing."

"Go on."

"You've got to make it work, this plan of yours. I don't want any comeback on Gilbert; he's not big enough or clever enough to look after himself, especially against the likes of Davison. I'll still look out for him but I'm not sure that I can deal with Davison. Make it work Pete, put an end to it all, for everybody's sake."

He handed me a brown envelope.

"Make sure these end up in the right hands."

They were photographs, incriminating photographs. Every one of them incriminated Kevin Davison and his gang in one way or another.

"Don't worry, they'll definitely end up with the right people. I promise I'll take care of Gilbert. This time Kevin Davison is not coming out on top."

****

As soon as the bell went for lunch we were out of the gate and ran all of the way to Southwick Library. We had come prepared with notebooks, pens and stern looks. We shuffled about for a few minutes before we found what we were looking for. For some reason, schoolchildren are always unfairly treated with suspicion.

Admittedly we were planning to steal on this occasion but it wasn't really the point.

The caretaker at Southwick Library, Mr Wright, was notorious. The slightest bit of misbehaviour and he was onto you. A lifetime ban would be placed on you and your name put in the window. As we approached Mr Wright, Michael Baker walked through the door. Baker was an unknown quantity; he was in Gilbert's class at school and had a reputation for violence. On the other hand, whenever we had come across him he had been nothing but friendly. He didn't look pleased to see us; perhaps he was up to something similar. He nodded at us as he went up to the counter and we nodded back sheepishly, deciding it wasn't wise to stare and turned away. We knew it was unwise to laugh when we heard the assistant say "This is overdue isn't it? Don't you think you're a bit old for Noddy and Big Ears?" He told us later that he was returning it for his little brother. We chose to believe him.

Mr Wright was a tall, balding man in his early sixties. He wore one of those brown overalls, the type that only caretakers and woodwork teachers had access to. True to form he eyed us with suspicion. Then Bumper spoke up.

"I wonder if you could help. We are doing a project on the decline of morals in the youth of today. We wondered if you had any views."

We had hit the jackpot, he had views and boy did he want to share them.

"Where the fuck is he?" Tomma was desperately trying to ring Kev on his mobile. "He's not answering his home phone and his mobile is on voicemail. We have to find him."

"I thought we weren't meant to phone him on his home phone."

"We're not but this is a fucking emergency!"

"Why don't we just go and do the business? We don't need Kev's permission to sort out a retard like Tim."

Jamie was pacing the floor in the flat he shared with Tomma. A large Union Jack hung on one wall, a painting of the Queen on another. The rest of the gang was there, nursing their wounds from the battle in the Whistle.

"You know the rules, we don't move without his say. He'll turn up, we'll just have to wait."

"Why can't it be like the olden days? We used to go and sort out anybody who gave us grief, we didn't need a fucking board meeting."

"We're not a bunch of teenage football hooligans anymore, anything we do attracts attention and therefore effects the business. Sit your arse down and wait for Kev's call, I've left him a message."

"This is our fucking reputation at stake not Kevin bloody Davison's. In case you have forgotten, it was me who got a bar stool smashed off his head." Jamie was furious.

"Our reputation is Kev's reputation. If someone makes a move on his business then he calls the shots. I'll not tell you again, sit the fuck down."

Jamie petulantly swung his baseball bat at the coffee table and knocked a number of Budweiser cans and an ashtray onto the far wall.

"Fucking Bastards," he screamed.

"I was drinking that," moaned Ian Whelan, one of the younger members of the gang. He'd only been with them a couple of months and he was pushing his luck speaking up against Jamie.

"It'll be your fucking head next time. Anyway, where were you when it kicked off? I can't remember you doing your bit when it was needed."

"I was in the toilets with some Colombian marching powder. When I came out it was all over."

"Very convenient. I've got my eye on you son, if you step out of line I'll fucking have you."

"Where the fuck are you Kev?" Tomma tried the mobile again.

****

"Do you ever get children misbehaving in here?" asked Bumper.

"All the time. They're all on glue these days. Those that aren't on drugs."

We were sat at a table in the annexe of the library where the educational books were. Mr Wright sat on one side of the table, the three of us on the other. One of the assistants popped her head round the door but soon disappeared when she realised that Mr Wright was on one of his rants about how things were better in his day.

"That's Wright, W, R, I, G, H, T. Are you sure you're getting all of this?"

"Every word," said Bumper sincerely.

I stood up and moved over to the bookshelf.

"So you're telling us that while there are all these marvellous books here," I picked up one of the books I was looking for and thumbed through it's pages, "they don't read them, they just misbehave?" I shook my head in disgust as I replaced the book on the shelf.

"Disgraceful it is." We all nodded.

"Do you have a list of the children who are banned that we could look at?"

I looked at Elvis and Bumper admiringly. Whilst they had been reluctant to get involved, they were both fully into it now. Mr Wright was eating out of their hands.

"Better than that, I've got them all up here," he said pointing to his temple.

We had hoped he would disappear to get the list, giving me time to rifle the books I needed. It was a change to the plan but we would see how it went.

"Thompson, Gelder…" he started to reel of the names. It was the usual suspects. "…Kevin Davison, right little toe rag that one, he's the ring leader." This was our chance and Bumper dangled the line in front of him.

"Did you hear the story of how his dad died?"

"No, what happened?"

He took the bait and Bumper started to tell the whole Kevin Davison story. Mr Wright was all ears. While Bumper went through the tale, I took the books I needed and placed them inside a carefully constructed slit in the lining of my blazer. When I had got what I needed I returned to the table.

"We're going to have to get back. Lunch time is nearly over."

"You mean that you are doing this work in your own time?" said Mr Wright. "I wish there were more kids like you. I should contact the school and tell them what good lads you are."

We looked a bit shocked.

"There's no need for that," Bumper laughed, "you don't want to embarrass us and make us look like swots."

Mr Wright waved us off from the entrance to the library, my blazer now sagging from the extra weight. He straightened his lapels and headed back indoors. We had got away with it.

"Don't ever ask me to do anything like that again," Elvis was annoyed. "I nearly did a Gilbert in there."

****

It had been two hours since the fight in the whistle and there was still no word from Kev.

"Come on Tomma. We can't leave it any longer, we're going to have to make the decision without Kev."

He knew that if he didn't do something they would know something was up. He didn't want to rouse their suspicions.

"I'm not happy about this, I wish he was here. Right, everyone get tooled up we're going to sort out this Tim fella. Nobody touches Wood though, there's something about him I don't like, Kev's going to have to call the shots on that one."

Everyone started gathering up the weapons, baseball bats, knives and various other tools of the trade.

"Ian, bring the petrol, in case we need to smoke this fucker out."

"Anything you say boss."

"Don't call me boss."

This was the last thing that Tomma wanted to be involved in, tonight of all nights.

They packed into two cars and drove the mile to Tim's flat.

"Right everybody knows what they are doing. This is a quick operation, in and out; send a message that nobody fucks with us. Ian, you're on look out," Tomma opened the driver's door.

"But I want to be involved."

"You should have got fucking involved when you had the chance then shouldn't you?"

Tomma looked up and down the street and when he was satisfied it was clear they all got out of the cars.

"Come on let's do it."

They jogged across the road. There were no lights on in the house but that didn't deter the gang.

"We know you're in there retard," Tomma shouted through the letterbox. Jamie threw a half-brick through the upstairs window.

"We're coming to get you." They all whooped and cheered. Another brick went though the downstairs window.

Tim sat in the far corner of the bedroom, knees tucked into his chest. He was sobbing; on his lap were photos of Gilbert growing up. He knew he could have run but what was the point? He couldn't run forever. He had no fight left in him and curled up tighter as he heard the front door being kicked in.

The mob streamed into the hall swinging their bats wildly at anything they could see, the telephone table, the mirror, the framed photographs on the wall. They spread out amongst the downstairs rooms, systematically tearing them apart. Tim could hear the bangs and crashes from upstairs and knew it would be his turn next. Tomma took his baseball bat and smashed Tim's camera into tiny fragments.

"He's not down here, come on Jamie." They headed upstairs.

"We're coming to get you," shrieked Jamie. "Come to Daddy."

Tim heard them as they crashed through the door of the first bedroom and then the bathroom. The footsteps moved along the landing towards his room. The door edged open.

"Come on Timmy baby, there's a good boy." A flash of orange light lit up the room. Flames licked up the curtains and leapt towards the bed.

"What the fuck was that?" shouted Tomma.

The fierce heat drove them back.

"I know he's in there. I'm going to do the bastard," Jamie went for the door again.

"Don't be fucking stupid, we'll get burned alive. There's no way he'll get out of there in one piece. Let's leave it."

"What the fuck was that? The whole place just went up." Jamie and Tomma headed down the stairs towards the front door.

"Petrol bomb, whoever threw it is in serious trouble." Tomma was seething.

"Come on, everybody out, playtimes over," he shouted to the rest of the gang as he walked out of the door.

The flames leapt out of the window above him, the shadowy shape of Ian flickered in the garden.

"What the fuck are you doing here? I thought I told you to stay in the car."

"Burning him out, somebody had to do the business."

Tomma threw his whole weight into the punch. Ian's nose split open as he fell backwards onto the grass.

"Let's get out of here."

As they headed for the gate they heard the sirens, then the blue flashing lights of the police van mixed with the orange flames to light up the night sky. The lights cast dark eerie shadows across the faces of the gang. They couldn't escape. Another van approached from the far end of the street. Tomma leaned on his bat, resigned to defeat.

"I knew we should have waited for Kev."

I slumped to the ground with my back to the wall as the flames spread to the downstairs window. Tears welled up in my eyes. This was my fault, when was it going to stop?

It has to end tonight. I thought as I picked myself up.

I was heading back to the lighthouse when the thought hit me.

What the hell am I going to tell Gilbert?

****

After being on report for two weeks, the teacher's attitudes began to change. I realised that whilst I was quite happy to delay my breaks as long as possible, they weren't. They wanted to get off for a cup of coffee and a cigarette. The last thing they wanted was to waste time on someone like me who didn't care what they thought. They started putting standard phrases on my reports before they even checked my homework. They always said it was very good so nobody questioned them. My mother soon stopped checking my homework, assuming the teachers were doing their job. Some teachers, Mr Bramble in particular, would sign it at the beginning of the lesson. I'm not sure he even knew who I was. I decided to put this to the test. It wasn't long before Mr Swinbank got bored with me as well. This had obviously been my mother's idea and they were all sick of it. He decided that instead of waiting for him at the end of school I could just put the report in his pigeonhole at the end of the day. This led to an opportunity.

We had double English with Mr Bramble for the last two periods on a Thursday. I handed my report to Bumper and went home. It worked a treat. Bramble signed the form as usual, not even noticing the change in personnel and Bumper popped it into Mr Swinbank's pigeonhole on his way home. I had an early finish and my mother was none the wiser. I wasn't stupid enough to try it on in every lesson. I still went to the ones where I knew I would be missed but I managed to whittle it down to half days for most of the week. It wasn't long before Bumper and Elvis joined me again.

"Who's got my report then, Bumper? You're meant to be getting it signed for me."

"It's ok. Karen Walker said she would do it for you."

"Karen Walker? Haven't you noticed? She's a girl for Christ's sake."

"They'll never notice," replied Bumper.

"Never notice? She's wearing a skirt!"

"That's not what I meant. They never check the name on the report. They'll just think it's hers. Don't worry you know I'm right."

He potted the black and went into a three nil lead.

"Ok then. If you say so."

I removed my tie as I started racking the balls up for another frame. He had been right, we got away with it. We were on easy street. We played plenty of snooker, nudging my highest break up to forty-five, Bumper's was sixty. My tape collection was growing and Elvis and me, deciding that the games that he brought round were getting boring, started designing our own. We were good, even if I do say so myself and between us we became pretty proficient programmers. I was learning more by not being at school.

****

"Come on Elvis, we're going to be late," Marie was getting annoyed.

"I don't get it," Elvis was crouched over his computer "all this money is in our account and it shouldn't be there."

"It's an internet bank, they're always making mistakes. It'll not be there tomorrow."

"But it's a million pounds, Marie. Imagine if we just get one day's interest, we'll be rich."

"Well we won't so get your head out of the clouds and get a move on."

Elvis took one last look at the screen, shook his head and closed down his computer.

"Very strange."

****

We were doing quite well at avoiding Kevin Davison. Most days we managed to escape to my house and with his new found career as football hooligan he had become less interested in us. That was, until I fell ill.

"I don't feel well."

"I don't care. You're going to school."

After my past performance I could understand why my mother didn't believe me but I really was ill. I was sitting in the kitchen as my Mam was making toast under the grill. My dad must have had bacon sandwiches before he went to work this morning as the smell of fat was overpowering. I'd managed to eat my sugar puffs but was really struggling to keep them down. I belched and had to force the sick back down. Sweat was now pouring out of my forehead and I felt faint. I wanted my mother to see how ill I was but she was late for work as it was, she took no notice.

"Come on get a move on. Don't think you can skive here all day either. I'm going to make sure Bernice up the road keeps an eye on the house. She has a spare key so she'll be coming in to check that you're not here," she put her coat on and headed for the door. "Get to school. The fresh air will do you good."

It did for a while. When I walked out of the door the breeze hit me and it immediately cooled the sweat on my forehead. I swung my bag over my shoulder and headed shakily up the street. I didn't really care about Bernice. I was going in for registration and I was coming straight home. I'd do well to get that far.

When I got to class the usual Monday morning crowd had gathered around Kev's desk. He was telling yet another of his now monotonous tales.

"He was on the platform at Seaburn Station. You could tell he was a cockney by the way he dressed. They have no style these southerners." Everyone nodded in agreement as if they had a clue what he was talking about. "We had to be sure so Tomma went and asked him the time. Fucking class it was. Five thirty Guvnor he replied. Fucking Guvnor. Cockney wanker. Tomma laid the head on him and we all steamed in. Took his watch, his gold chain and his wallet. Even took his jacket, cool as fuck it was."

"I thought you said they had no style?" Claire spoke up.

"What?"

"Cockneys. You said they had no style then you said you stole his jacket because it was cool. Which one was it?"

"Fuck off, Claire. What would you know about anything?" He was riled.

"How many of you were there, ten, eleven, on to one? You're so hard aren't you?" A few of the girls laughed.

"He was a cockney. He deserved it."

Kev was going red. On a normal day I would have enjoyed this exchange but I wasn't feeling well. In fact I wasn't feeling very well at all. I didn't think I would even make registration.

"Well I'm really proud of you. I'm sure he'll have rushed home to London to tell all of his friends just how hard you all are. You're pathetic."

Claire had won and headed back to her desk. The crowd started to disperse. A couple of lads hung back to see if Kev had any more tales but he didn't seem to be in the mood anymore. I wasn't doing very well and was trying to compose myself. It didn't help when Sara Nesbitt started eating a bag of Cheesy Puffs. She was an animal. Who eats Cheesy Puffs for breakfast? The stench of artificial cheese wafted over and my stomach started churning again. What happened next was completely out of my control. Kev, obviously still pissed off at being shown up by Claire, reverted to form and decided to come and hassle me. I really wasn't in the mood.

"Get into any fights at the weekend, Wood?" he sneered.

Please go away I kept my head down and stared at my desk.

"Not speaking? You'd have bottled it wouldn't you, even if it was ten on to one? You'd have shat your pants and ran away wouldn't you?" He poked me in the side.

"Leave me alone."

The smell was getting stronger.

"Who do you think you're talking to?"

He pushed my head into the desk. Everything started to blur in front of my eyes. The stench of cheese stuck to my nostrils.

"Come and have a go if you want to. I'm ready."

He shoved me again. He obviously wasn't ready for what I had in store. Streams of vomit shot out of my mouth and covered his trousers and Nike Trainers. It stunk of sugar Puffs and everyone started howling with laughter. He was going to murder me but I started to smile. Just then Mr Burns walked into the room.

"What's happening?" he shouted. "Davison, get back to your desk"

"I can't sir. He's been sick on me. He did it deliberately."

"Wood. Go outside and get some fresh air. Barry go out with him and check he's alright. As for you Davison, err, go and clean yourself up."

"How can I clean myself up? It stinks."

I headed out of the door and sat on the step outside. I had to admit that I felt a lot better for it. Both Bumper and me started laughing. We were there for about five minutes when Mr Burns came out.

"You did that deliberately didn't you, Wood?"

"Good shot wasn't it sir?" said Bumper.

Mr Burns smiled but didn't reply.

"Ok. You better get yourself off home to bed."

"Can you phone my Mam and tell her? She'll never believe me."

"Off you go. I'm going to have to try and sort Davison out now."

I went home and went straight to bed. Whilst I felt a lot better, I was still a little weak. I tried not to think about what Kev would do as I drifted off to sleep.

****

"Leave it." Claire said. The phone was ringing again.

"It might be important." Argued Kev.

"I don't care, we're going to this reunion tonight and you promised me that you wouldn't let business get in the way for once. Everybody's going to be there already, come on." Claire was adamant. She put in her earring and straightened her dress.

"How do I look?"

"Great."

He wished that she made this type of effort for him. The phone stopped ringing.

"How's the phone ringing downstairs and not in here?" Claire picked up the phone from the bedside cabinet and noticed it wasn't connected.

"Like you said, we're not going to let business get in the way this evening. I unplugged it so we weren't disturbed."

"Bit drastic isn't it. Come on, I don't want to miss anyone." She ushered Kev out of the bedroom and switched out the light. "You don't have to drive tonight, Kev. We can easily get a taxi if you want a drink."

"Drinking at a school disco is a bit old fashioned don't you think?" He didn't want to go, he had a business to run and Friday was his busiest night.

"Let your hair down for once, you never know, you might enjoy yourself!"

****

My head was thumping and there was a ringing in my ears. It was getting louder as I started to wake. Then I realised it was the door. Somebody was banging on the door and ringing the bell. They weren't giving in. I went to the window to see who it was. I peeled back the curtains slightly so they wouldn't notice me looking. It was Kev. Mr Burns must have let him out to go home and get changed. As he couldn't go home stinking of vomit, Mr Burns had loaned him

279

the only spare pair of trousers in the school, a pair of cricket whites. He looked ridiculous and it appeared that he wanted to take it out on someone. Well it wasn't going to be me. I went back to bed and pulled the pillow over my head. I would take my punishment at a later date thanks very much.

The banging and ringing eventually stopped and he must have given up. Then I heard the lock turn.

Christ, he's breaking in.

The phone was by the front door; there was no way I was going to reach it before he got in.

Shit.

I looked around frantically for something to protect myself with. I noticed the two-part snooker cue I had got for Christmas a couple of years ago. Strangely it was purple with black stripes, a weird combination in anyone's eyes. I hadn't used it much as it wasn't really any better than the one-piece cues that came with the table, that's why it was still lying in the bedroom. I took the heavier bottom end and held it in my right hand. What were the instructions he had given me when he had the fight?

"Just swing it and take out as many as you can."

That was what I was going to have to do. I edged out of the bedroom door and stood on the landing at the top of the stairs. I peeked though the banister rails and saw his distinctive cricket whites at the bottom of the stairs. I backed into the doorway of my parent's room and waited for him to come up the stairs. I would have more chance if I waited for him to get up to the top. A voice called up from the bottom of the stairs.

"Are you there, Pete?" It was Bernice. Of course, she had let him in. Maybe he had forced her at knifepoint. I decided not to answer.

"One of your friends is here. He wants to know if he can borrow some trousers. He's had an accident in his."

I stifled a laugh.

"He must be asleep love," she said to Kev, "best leave him if he's not well. I don't know what you're worried about anyway those trousers look really smart."

I heard her close the door behind her and I headed back to bed. I knew I would suffer when I got back to school but I was beginning to think it was worth it.

Cockneys have no style? I bet even cockneys aren't walking about wearing school blazers with a pair of cricket whites.

It hadn't helped that when Kev had been walking home, he bumped into Joe Ingham and his mates. Nobody had said anything but as he was trying to build his reputation as a football casual it was a humiliation he could have done without.

****

"What do you want to go and do that for?" Elvis was looking worried again

"I have to do it. He has to know who is responsible for his downfall. That's the whole point," I replied.

"It's far too risky. He'll kill you."

"If I don't tell him he'll just think it was bad luck or, at worst, one of his competitors muscling in. He has to know it was us, the ones he tormented all those years ago."

"I'm not sure."

"He has to feel the guilt, feel remorse," I explained. "There would be no point otherwise. This will all have been worthless."

"Isn't it enough to know you are responsible?" Bumper was also concerned.

"No. I want to see his face. I want him to say he is sorry."

"I don't get it," said Elvis.

"I do." Gilbert had been sitting quietly for some time now.

"So you want to come with me then?" I asked.

"You must be fucking joking. We still don't know what he has up his sleeve. I don't want to be there but you can send him my regards. Let him know I was part of it."

"Me too," said Bumper.

"That just leaves you, Elvis. Are you sure?"

"I can see your point, I'm just a bit worried that..."

"A bit worried that what?"

"...that he's not finished. That this will all come back to haunt us later."

"Believe me, he's finished. There will be no repercussions."

"Fuck it. Count me in. Let him know. Don't forget to tell him who's idea it was to download the pictures from Burns' files."

"You've got a deal. Sure none of you want to come and see it for yourselves?"

"No. He's all yours."

"Any chance of that dance now?" Claire had sneaked up behind me. None of us had noticed.

"Not at the moment. I've got a little bit of business to attend to."

"Well don't take too long. Gilbert here might have swept me off my feet by then."

She grabbed Gilbert by the hand and led him to the dance-floor. His grin went from ear to ear.

****

My Mam had made me go back to school on the Tuesday even though I still didn't feel right. It was possibly more the thought of seeing Kev that was making me sick now. Every time I was anywhere near him I tensed up, expecting a punch or worse but it never came.

"I hate swimming," I said to Elvis as we changed.

I could barely swim which left me in the shallow end with Gilbert and the rest of the strugglers. This was the only time Gilbert and me were in the same class as he was in the bottom stream but there was no discrimination in sports. I felt sorry for Gilbert. My life was hell but I got to see what he had to put up with. He was regularly pushed in to the deep end, struggling to get out only to be pushed straight back in.

"There is Miss Shipp though." Miss Shipp was one of the younger teachers in the school.

"You have a good point there, Elvis."

"She's got a couple."

She always dressed in a blue tracksuit that hid her swimsuit. It did little to hide the shape of her giant breasts.

"Did you hear about her being caught having sex in the showers with Mr Armstrong?"

"Yeah, lucky bastard. Did you hear the one about Miss Mortimer and the nun in the lift on a school trip to Italy?"

Both were great stories but unconfirmed. Then again we wouldn't let anything as insignificant as the truth get in the way of a good story. I liked Miss Shipp; she always gave us encouragement and stuck up for us when the competent swimmers tried to laugh at us. I have to admit I sometimes pictured Miss Shipp and me in the showers when I was masturbating.

Swimming was one of the lessons I couldn't get out of, Miss Shipp would notice I was missing. Anyway I would quite miss her as well if I didn't go. She had been looking particularly nice recently and whilst I was always wary of Kev throwing my towel and underwear into the foot pool I still quite enjoyed the lessons. Mr Armstrong had now started coming into the changing rooms after the lessons to make sure there was no misbehaving. I think there had been a complaint after Chris Miskell had left.

I was in the shallow end as usual and I had just swum a width without aid for the first time.

"Well done, Pete," Miss Shipp was wearing her blue tracksuit again with a green swimsuit underneath. "What are you boys doing?" She shouted just before there was a huge splash in the deep end. It was Gilbert. They had dragged him up to the deep end and thrown him in.

"Miss, it's Gilbert. He can't swim," shouted Tomma.

Miss Shipp stripped off her tracksuit and ran along the side of the pool. She dived in, barely breaking the water. She swam straight over to Gilbert and dragged him out. Although I was in the shallow end I could still make out the nipples protruding through her swimsuit. With her hair soaked back and the water dripping of her, Miss Shipp looked gorgeous. I fought to keep down a boner, Gilbert didn't fight to keep down his. What I hadn't noticed while all this was going on was Kevin Davison sneaking into the changing rooms.

****

Ingham sat at his desk surveying the photos in front of him. Gilbert had done a really good job with them.

"How could she? The little slag." He threw them across his desk.

"Where did the photos come from?" Junior had seen Ingham like this before and he wasn't sure which way it was going to go.

"I don't fucking know, I don't bleeding care. These two have been having a right laugh at my expense. You're probably all in on it, aren't you? I'm just one big joke. Think it's funny do you? Seeing the boss' wife being shafted behind his back,"

Ingham lunged out from behind the desk, pointing the gun hard into Junior's cheek. "Dare you to laugh now. Go on. Think I'm funny now do you?"

He had his left hand gripping Junior's neck as he forced him backwards over the desk.

"Take it easy, I'm on your side," Junior had begun to panic. "Do you think if I knew I would have let it go on? It would have been nipped in the bud a long time ago."

Ingham released his grip; Junior rubbed his throat.

"Point taken," Ingham slumped back into his leather swivel armchair. "What now? I suppose I'm going to have to kill him, aren't I?" He didn't like killing people, it was his job, and it had become a chore.

"It would be rude not to," Junior was excited.

"I don't know what's going on anymore. Let's do it then. Got your shooter?"

"Do bears shit in the woods?"

Ingham picked up the handgun from the desk, cradling it like a child.

"Come on my little beauty. Let's go to work."

"Ready when you are Boss."

286

Junior picked up the shotgun that was behind the chair. He looked out of the window of Ingham's office. The nightclub was in the centre of town and overlooked High street.

"Fucking typical. It's started to rain. Why do we never get a nice day for it?"

He watched as revellers ran for cover, their little dresses and short-sleeved shirts getting soaked in the rain.

"The sun shines on the righteousness my friend. We're destined to be pissing wet for a long time yet."

They went out of the back door and into the car park. They took a couple of the doormen from the front of the club. They wouldn't be missed for a couple of hours, it was early and was likely to be a quiet night due to the weather. Junior put the shotgun in the boot alongside the Uzi that was already there. Ingham climbed into the driver's seat and placed his automatic in his inside pocket. Junior climbed in the passenger seat. The two doormen were already in the back.

"You do realise the implications don't you?" asked Ingham. "If we take out Davison, we've got a turf war on our hands. He supplies the whole of North Sunderland. We'll have a lot of people to answer to."

"It's a matter of principle boss, it's been coming for a long time. This is the straw that broke the camel's back."

"Let's go and get this over with," Ingham pulled out and headed over the bridge. "We're off to the seaside."

The swimming lesson finished early and we were all sent to get changed. Miss Shipp and Mr Armstrong stayed with Gilbert to make sure he was alright. He was fine but he milked it for as long as he could whilst Miss Shipp was cradling him in her arms. He wasn't as stupid as he made out. I headed back to the changing rooms and started drying myself off. I didn't use the shower and took off my trunks whilst keeping the towel wrapped around me. I went into my bag to get my underpants. They weren't there. Neither were my trousers, or any of my uniform for that matter. I could hear giggling coming from the girls changing room and everybody climbed onto the bench to see if they could find out what they were laughing about. It didn't take me long to realise. The girls were due to do swimming for their next lesson and on the windows of the girl's changing rooms were my underpants, trousers and the rest of my uniform.

"Elvis. Any chance you could get them for me, mate?"

"I would mate but I've been told I can't."

"Who by?" Then I saw Kev.

"Looks like you're going to have to get them yourself, Wood. Not so funny now is it, not having any trousers?"

Everyone crowded round me and pushed me out of the door wearing just a towel. Kev came out behind me. All of the girls were standing looking out of the window, cheering. Luckily I was mostly shielded from the main school. I was going to have to make a run for it. Just as I set off, Kev grabbed my towel.

"You'll not be needing this," he laughed as he closed the door behind him.

****

Elvis and me sat at the top of the stairs outside the science blocks. We had gone for a look around the old school; it had changed. The school was now a college and, as you would expect after fifteen years, most of the classrooms had been refurbished. It had been a funny night seeing all the old faces, making small talk and exchanging pleasantries. I knew the night was far from over but thought it was only right that I took some time out to talk to Elvis. Everything had happened so quickly since I had come home and I think it was fair to say that I had turned his world upside down. I owed him an explanation.

"You never did tell me what you had been up to for the last fifteen years," Elvis flicked his foot at an imaginary object on the stairs, "and after the last couple of weeks I'm not sure I want to know."

"Come on, I want to show you something." I helped Elvis up from the stairs.

He was a little unsure on his feet, as he had drunk quite a lot of Stones despite being under strict instructions from Marie not to get too drunk. He had been doing a lot of that lately. We headed back down towards the hall and walked into the middle of the Pogues' Irish Rover. Everyone was swirling round and whooping, not least

Claire and Gilbert. Everyone was enjoying themselves; whatever my motives, the reunion had been a success. We walked down the side of the hall to where the Chapel used to be. The pale blue, plastic sliding doors were still there and I was surprised to find the chapel intact when I slid them back. I ushered Elvis inside and closed the door behind us. The doors slightly muffled the sound of the opening bars to Madness' Baggy Trousers, which was now blasting out of the speakers. We both grinned. The heating duct was still there and I told Elvis the whole story from beginning to end, trying not to leave anything out.

"That's sick," Elvis was disgusted.

"I hated Riley but for Burnsy to do that to him was a bit below the belt."

"Funny all the same," laughed Elvis. "I take it you saw the paper the other night?" Elvis now turned serious.

"Yeah, I did. What did you feel when you saw it?"

"Guilty I suppose. He was a sick mother fucker all right, as your story has just proved but did he deserve to die like that?"

I had no answer and just shrugged.

"Look outside," I said. "everyone's enjoying them selves and they are all carrying pictures of a dead man, probably the same picture that killed him. This place is fucked up; we're fucked up."

Elvis nodded.

"Have you ever considered killing yourself?" I asked.

Elvis was shocked at the question.

"What?"

"I have, briefly. The difference between Burnsy and me is that I didn't go through with it. Call me a coward if you like, everybody says that people who kill themselves are very brave but I don't believe that. They are the real cowards. Everybody has a choice in life, you can check out like Burnsy or you can stand up and face the music."

"Or you could run away," Elvis suggested.

"Fair point. What I am trying to say is, that if you make a decision you have to stand by it. If Burnsy didn't want people to see him dressed in a black rubber mask and briefs then he shouldn't have taken pictures of himself and posted them on the Net. I feel sorry for his wife but not for him. She's the one who has to live with it."

I'm not sure whether Elvis agreed with me but he didn't say.

"Come on, finish the story. What happened after Burns did that to Riley?"

I continued and told him the rest of the story.

"Now do you understand why I had to leave? Davison was going to come back at some point and he was going to come after me."

"He hasn't yet. Maybe he doesn't know."

"He does, I'm sure of it. I don't know why he hasn't acted yet, maybe he is just biding his time."

"So why did you come back? You must have known he would want revenge. You're taking one hell of a risk."

We were now both sat on the altar with our feet swinging below.

"I hold all the aces now. I can hurt him more than he can hurt me, he just doesn't know it yet."

"I'm not sure, " said Elvis examining one of the candlesticks. "I don't think you should go there tonight, it's too dangerous."

"I have to, I have to finish it."

"This is all fascinating but you've still avoided the main question. What have you been doing for the past fifteen years?"

****

"But everybody wears trainers Mam," I protested.

"I don't care what everybody else does, I'm only bothered what you do. The school rules say that you wear sensible shoes to and from school and trainers when you get there. That's exactly what you are going to do," My mother didn't care that this would make me even more of a target than I was already, "and you can take those white socks off as well."

"Jesus Christ."

"Don't take the Lord's name in vain."

I trudged upstairs knowing exactly what the day was going to bring.

Everywhere I looked, the pupils of St Patrick's were wearing trainers. Boys, Girls, Adidas, Nike, everybody was wearing them but me. I tried not to make eye contact with anyone and scoured the ground hoping to see another pair of sensible shoes. I didn't. Even if everybody else was wearing shoes, my pale blue slip-ons were bound to stand out. Especially with grey socks. My Mam wouldn't let me have Kickers or Pods; they were far too expensive, a waste of money.

"Nice shoes," Sara Nesbitt spotted them and let everybody in her crowd know. "Get dressed by Mammy this morning?"

I felt a small thud against the back of my head. I didn't look round but waited until I was out of sight before I pulled the chewing gum from my hair. I tried the door in the hope that it would be open and I would be able to get into class early.

Normally, getting into class before nine is to be avoided as you don't want to look like a swot but I needed to change into my trainers even if they were Dunlops. As per usual the door was locked, the teachers enjoying a lie in or an extra cup of coffee before they saw fit to let us in. I slumped down on the step and waited for the abuse.

Shit. I thought as I sat down.

I stood straight back up again and removed the chewing gum from the seat of my pants. It was the same piece that I had thrown to the floor moments earlier. I put up with the usual abuse for the next ten minutes. The doorway had now become crowded with people waiting to get in from the cold. I felt a slap on the back of my head and turned round. Martin Gelder was standing there, hands in pockets, trying to look innocent. His friends tried to suppress giggles. I turned back round again and tried to ignore them. Another slap, this time I didn't look round. They would get bored…eventually.

I looked at my watch when Mr Burns came to open the door. It was 8.59.

"Slowly now, form a queue."

He placed his hand in front of me and let everybody pass. I was going to protest that I had been there first but what was the point?

****

I think the story of my past came as a bit of a disappointment to Elvis. I'm sure he was expecting stories of espionage and near death experiences. The true story was far duller.

"Remember when we did our Computer Studies 'O' Level? Well the programming side of it only went towards twenty per cent of the final result but I got the full twenty marks," I explained. "There was a software company that wanted to break into the games market. They had some friends on the examining board that tipped them off about anybody with potential. It wasn't strictly legal but they had the money so they could pretty much do as they liked. They contacted me and asked me to go for an interview."

"Landmark Software?" asked Elvis.

"How did you know?"

"They asked me to go down as well. I thought it was a wind up and ignored it."

Elvis put the candlestick back on the altar. I wasn't sure whether to continue with the rest of the story.

"And that's where I've been," I ended it there.

"Surely that's not all of it. You haven't been sat in a little office down south for the past fifteen years. Landmark is one of the biggest software companies in the world, admittedly it isn't Microsoft but it's big enough. You must be on a fair wage."

"When I joined the company they had just started in the games market. It was beginning to really take off with the likes of the Spectrum and Commodore 64 so I was coming in at just the right time. I became one of their brightest games programmers and I got all the benefits that came with it. The fast car, the penthouse flat, I was doing really well but I wasn't happy."

"How couldn't you be happy, all that money and flash cars?"

"I had no friends, not like the old days. The lads at work were ok but they were all computer geeks mainly. Sometimes you want to talk about something other than Bits and Bytes. I occasionally thought about getting in touch but there was always the spectre of Davison in the back of my mind."

"You're home now. What changed your mind?"

"When a company is paying you that amount of money, they expect you to put the hours in. I was working the clock round; it wasn't as if I had a social life. My life was computers and I had no time to enjoy the little luxuries I had bought. I spent most nights asleep in the office."

"It must have been tough."

I'm not sure whether Elvis was being sarcastic.

"I decided to go it alone, set up my own business. We left on good terms and I left with a large pay off on the understanding that we worked at opposite ends of the games market. You don't argue with a company like that so I set up on my own and went from strength to strength. You've even got some of my posters up in your shop."

"I can't see you as the big businessman. It must be a cut-throat world, how did you deal with it?"

"The games companies pretty much leave each other alone. There's a certain amount of spying, people infiltrating the company and selling their secrets. You accept it as part of the business. It's a bit cat and mouse but it makes life more interesting, you expect a certain amount of gamesmanship, if you excuse the pun but it never got rough."

"How do you deal with people like Kev? Did nobody try and muscle in? You can't move in Sunderland without Davison or Ingham taking a slice. It must be the same down south."

"They tried but we were a new type of business. They didn't quite know how to deal with us. I got a visit one day from a gentleman named Charlie Grenaco. He was well known in the area, a different league altogether from Kev. Despite the name I don't think he was connected to the Mafia but he was still someone you didn't mess with. He offered me an insurance policy for one thousand pounds a week. In the large scheme of things, it wasn't a great deal of money but I wasn't going to stand for it."

"One thousand pounds not a great deal of money? You haven't been living at the other end of the country, you've been on another planet."

"One thing that Landmark taught me was that although money buys you a certain amount of power, knowledge is where the real power is. I'd become quite a proficient hacker in my time at Landmark and I had employed two of the best computer brains in the country. We froze his bank accounts, had his mobile phone, electricity and gas switched off. We even set up a phantom account with a home protection scheme where they call the police on your behalf whenever your burglar alarm goes off. We set off the imaginary alarm every night for a week. Having the police at the door wasn't good for business so he withdrew his offer of insurance. We put everything back to normal for him and he left us alone after that."

"He could have killed you. People like that don't take kindly to people taking the piss."

"I realised that. It was a calculated risk. I told him that I had tapped into his computers and if anything happened to me or any of my associates, the files would mysteriously end up on the computer systems of Kent CID. We had an uneasy alliance. I occasionally did some work for him, information gathering, that sort of thing. Whilst we had the upper hand and I didn't like breaking the law, I didn't want to push my luck."

"Amazing, I didn't think you had it in you. It's good to see you are doing well. Any jobs going for an old school friend?"

"I'm out of the business now mate. I sold up just over a year ago, got out just before the dot com bubble burst. It didn't affect the gaming market that much but we had gambled on moving onto the internet, thought there would be a huge market for multi player games. I was wrong; it was the first big mistake I made. Luckily the City had thought it was a great idea at the time and bought me out. I got out by the skin of my teeth. I sold up and went travelling. I've only spent three months of the last eighteen in this country."

"This is all fascinating but there is one thing that is bothering me. You obviously have a fortune and you've already said that both money and knowledge get you power. You've tapped into computer systems of mobile phone companies and the electricity board. Why did you need Bumper, Gilbert and me to help you break into Davison's? You could have done it yourself."

"You're right I could have. I could have sat at home in the South of England and ruined him. I could have paid someone to bump him off and it would never come back to me but that isn't the point. He has to know it was us, he has to know that the people who he had made suffer for all those years had come back to haunt him. How did you feel after we had got out of the house?"

"Excited, scared, ecstatic."

"Exactly, you needed the satisfaction of turning him over as much as I did. It all ends tonight, Elvis. There will be no comeback, he's finished."

****

When I eventually got to class it was full. The usual suspects were there, Kev, Gelder, and Tomma. All of them ready for a laugh at my expense. Elvis was already there and I sat down next to him.

"Alright mate?" he said.

"The usual," I replied.

I took my trainers from my bag and removed the slip-on from my right foot. As I did, Kev snatched it from my hand.

"Lovely shade of blue, Wood," he shouted waving my shoe in the air. Nearly everybody laughed. I bowed my head and tried to ignore him. "What do you think, Tomma?" He threw the shoe across the classroom.

"Give us it back," I pleaded.

"Come and get it," goaded Tomma.

I hobbled over to him, one shoe on and one shoe off. As I got to him, he threw it to Martin Gelder.

"Want to look at it, Mugs?"

I knew it was pointless trying to chase the shoe around the room and shuffled back to my desk. I put on my right trainer and went to get my left one.

"Looking for this?" Davison was now waving my left trainer in the air.

"Come on, give us it back. Burns will be here soon."

"What do you say?"

"Please?" The word nearly stuck in my throat.

"No," he laughed as he threw the trainer towards Tomma.

"Give him it back Kev," shouted Claire.

"I haven't got it." He opened his arms wide with an innocent look on his face.

Claire wasn't impressed.

"Then get it from your imbecilic friends and give it back to Pete."

"Ooh. Give it back to Pete? Upset your little boyfriend have I?"

"Jealous are you?"

The smile was wiped from his face and I couldn't help smirking. I soon stopped when he punched me and knocked me off my chair.

"Grow up Kev."

Claire's face was now bright red and everybody was watching. The door opened and Mr Burns walked in. The crowd slowly moved back to their seats, all except Claire and Kev who stood staring at each other. I climbed back onto my chair.

"Come on, everybody back to your desks."

He waited until everybody was seated and started walking up the aisle, looking at the ground as he went.

"Where's your trainers, Curtis?" He was wearing a pair of Kickers.

"Forgot them Sir."

"Detention."

Of all days why did he have to choose today to do a shoe inspection?

"You all know the rules. You can wear your normal shoed to and from school and then change into to your trainers when you get here."

The school had some bizarre rules but none quite as stupid as the shoe rule.

"I take it that you're quite happy to wear down our beautiful parquet floors with your clumpy shoes are you, Curtis?"

"But they've got rubber soles just like trainers, Sir."

"Don't argue, it was a rhetorical question."

Mr Burns moved round the class dishing out detentions as he saw fit. I was at the front of the class and the route he chose which meant that I would be the last person he saw. I heard the clicking of his segged brogues on the wooden floor behind me.

"Get dressed in the dark, Wood?"

"Sorry Sir?"

"Are you trying to be funny? Where's your other trainer?"

I looked across at Tomma. He glared back.

"Don't know Sir."

"We'll see if you can remember when you are in detention tonight then."

I looked round the class for a friendly face to help me out. Perhaps Claire would say something; she had stood up to Kev after all. I looked at her hopefully; she smiled back sadly and shrugged her shoulders. Why should she bother?

****

I checked my watch as I stood at the fire exit. *Not long now.* Claire had followed me out.

"You hate Kev don't you?" She said.

"In a way."

"I can't say that I blame you, I hate him myself sometimes. Is that why you came home?"

I didn't answer

"Is Kev the unfinished business you were talking about?"

I moved onto the fire escape and looked out over the school yard. The rain had now stopped but there was still dampness in the air. Claire followed.

"I should have known really. It's just that somewhere in the back of my mind I'd hoped that it was me that you'd come back for."

"Perhaps you should go."

"No, I'm sorry. Just promise me that you won't do anything stupid. Kev's a dangerous man. I don't want you to get hurt."

"A little late for that. You should go back inside before he misses you."

"You're right," said Claire, "I just don't want to leave you here. I don't want you to disappear again. Promise me you'll still be here when I get back."

"I can't do that."

"Well at least promise that you'll be careful. I've really missed you Pete."

"Take care of yourself Claire."

****

The rest of the day was hell as Kev made me beg and perform numerous demeaning tasks before they decided to return my footwear. I got it back just in time for detention.

"Nice to see you've found your trainer, Wood. Where was it?" said Burns sarcastically.

"Don't know, Sir."

"I thought you would have learnt your lesson by now. I want a five hundred word essay on the inside of a ping pong ball before you go home tonight."

I sat down and got out my pen. I had done this essay a thousand times before and virtually knew it word for word.

****

"What do you think, Elvis?"

"What?" Elvis, his eyes transfixed on the couple in the corner, obviously not listening.

"Pete and Claire. Do you think they'll get together? That Kevin Davison is a complete bastard, she would be much better off with Pete."

"God that's Tracy Lough and John Marriner. She wouldn't have touched him when they were at school. Now look at them."

"People change you know. Not everyone obviously, look at us but people do. It's human nature. Good luck to them."

"I think Tracy's turned desperate, worried she'll be left on the shelf."

"Listen to the Lady Killer there, since when were you the expert?"

"Yeah, I suppose you've got a point. We're happy though aren't we?" Elvis took Marie's hand." I'm sorry if I went a bit strange when Pete came home. It just brought up a lot of memories, a lot of old feelings. I suppose I went off the rails a bit."

"Well if that's as far as you're going to stray I suppose I can live with it. It was as much a shock for me to see Pete. He seems like the same person, I still love him to bits but there's something different, something harder about him."

"Maybe I should have taken a leaf out of his book. Stood up to a few people a long time ago."

"I love you the way you are." Marie kissed Elvis softly on the cheek. "People like Kev will get what's coming to them eventually. You can bank on it."

"I already have," Elvis muttered with a grin on his face as he led Marie to the dance floor. Spandau Ballet were never one of his favourites but it seemed appropriate now. Gold'played out from the speakers and Elvis thought again about the money in his account.

****

"Where have you been? Your tea is ruined," my Mam was furious.

"Nowhere."

"You've been in detention haven't you?"

"No."

"Don't lie. What have you been in for this time?"

"Nothing. I didn't do anything."

This was the truth but I could hardly explain.

"Maybe I should go up to the school then. Find out why my son was in detention when he had done nothing wrong."

I hoped this was an empty threat because if there was one thing that would give Kev a field day, it would be my Mam coming to the school.

"Go and do your homework."

"Haven't got any."

"What have I just told you about lying? Get your backside upstairs and get your homework done. I want to see it when you're finished."

I knew I wasn't coming downstairs that evening. Kevin Davison had pissed in my bag, ruining all of my exercise books, how was I going to explain that?

****

"Hi Pete, long time no see."

I'd just walked back in from the fire escape.

"Karen?"

This was definitely a blast from the past.

"How are you? You're looking well."

"You as well, you look great."

Karen Walker barely looked different from when she was at school.

"I'm ok. I'm working in a call centre at Doxford, doing quite well. I've got a little boy Cameron, he's two."

"Great, I'm really pleased for you."

I don't know why but my response was tinged with a little sadness. I think Karen picked up on it.

"I'm not with the father if that's what you're thinking, he doesn't know about Cam. It was a one off, stupid mistake. I didn't think he deserved to know. Not that I would swap Cam for the world mind. How about you, are you married yet?"

"No, still as hopeless as ever."

"Still running away then?"

"Yeah, sorry about that."

We were virtually on the same spot as where we had that first kiss.

"It's only taken me best part of sixteen years to get over it," she laughed. "I knew you liked Claire, it was obvious. She's a nice girl. It's funny how things work out though isn't it. Who'd have thought that they would be together now?"

"I have to admit that it came as a bit of a shock," I said.

"What are you doing now then? You've obviously been away for a while. Surely you haven't been hiding from me for all this time."

For a moment I thought she was serious. I realised that since I had come home, this had been the first conversation I had entered into without wanting something from the person involved.

"Do you want a drink? Orange squash?"

306

"Yes please as long as it has vodka in it. You have to promise to come back though."

I looked over her shoulder to see Bumper and Elvis. Bumper was making the same sign with his thumb and forefinger that he had sixteen years ago. I laughed and went for the drinks. Claire was dancing with Gilbert when I came back from the bar. I smiled over but I think something had changed between us. I returned to Karen and handed her the drink.

"Welcome back Pete," she said as she pecked me on the cheek. "Fancy going for a walk?"

I agreed and we headed out of the fire escape. Karen linked my arm and we walked around the perimeter of the school, past the swimming baths and towards the upper school. We talked. We talked about everything. Her career, she was doing very well as an Operations Manager for a Mobile Phone company. I talked briefly about my career, missing out the bits about gangsters and blackmail. She told me about her drunken fling with one of the Directors at a conference, Cameron's father. I didn't think any worse of her for it. She hadn't been very lucky with her relationships but was getting to like the life of a single mother. I tried to think of a relationship story of my own but couldn't. I considered lying but it didn't feel right. Karen smiled and leant in closer to me. Her smile was exactly the same as I remembered. She told me as much as she knew about the people we had gone to school with. We had been in different classes for a lot of subjects but knew a lot of the same people.

"Do you ever think about that night?" she said.

"Which one?"

"The Christmas Disco. Have you any idea what you did to me?" She pushed me away and looked me in the eye. "That was my first kiss and you were thinking of somebody else all the time. Imagine what that has done to me."

I was shocked and tried to mumble an apology. She hit me on the arm.

"I'm joking you idiot. I got over you, eventually. What sort of twisted screw up do you think I am?"

I relaxed again.

"I've always been a little jealous of Claire mind, not that I would swap what I have for what she's got. Is that why you came home, Claire?"

"I'm not sure. I thought I had for a while but now I'm confused. I'm not sure what I want anymore but I don't think it's Claire. I came back to finish business, erase some ghosts from the past but everywhere I turn I seem be turning up more."

"So that's what I am, a ghost from the past that you want to eliminate?" She faked a shocked look.

"No not at all. It's been great to see you. This is the first real conversation I've had since I have come home. Come on, tell me more about Cam."

She showed me a photo that she had in her purse. He was the double of his mother and shared the same smile.

"You should come and see him sometime. If you hang about long enough."

"I'd love to." I meant it.

We started heading back to the school hall.

"Can I ask you something?" She took my hand in hers.

"Go ahead."

"What are you thinking about?"

"I don't know. Just stuff, you know."

"Not Claire then?"

"No, not at all."

Karen looked me in the eyes.

"Sure?"

"Positive."

Then she kissed me. Her lips were warm and I could taste the orange from the vodka we had just drunk. She stroked the back of my head and I hugged her closer to me. We could hear the music from the hall, it wasn't Madness but I didn't care. This was definitely the happiest I had been since I'd come home.

"We'd better get back before anybody misses us." She gave my hand a squeeze and we walked back without speaking.

When we got back to the party it was in full swing. Nobody appeared to have noticed we were missing, except Elvis, who just smiled as we came back in through the fire escape.

"What are your plans for the rest of the night?" She asked.

"Got to meet up with a few old friends. I've got a lot of catching up to do."

I couldn't tell her the truth. I couldn't back out of the plan now but I was less sure of my motives.

"Well try and save the last dance for me. I'll understand if you don't but here's my number anyway. Give me a ring sometime. Preferably within the next sixteen years." She handed me her business card and smiled.

"I promise, the last dance is yours."

I gave her a peck on the cheek and headed for the door. I had business to attend to.

****

I threw my bag on the floor and slumped on the bed. I placed my hand on the radiator and as expected, the heating was turned off. My mother thought it was a waste. I took the sopping books from my bag spread them out across the floor. I mopped each page with an old T-shirt to take away the worst of the dampness. I then placed them across the radiator hoping that they would somehow dry out by morning. I wrapped my quilt around me and switched on my BBC computer to work on my latest program. My parents had bought it as an educational tool so didn't allow me to have any games. I spent my time learning how to program so I could create my own games and had already managed a couple of basic ones.

I didn't show my Mam my exercise books the next morning. Whilst the radiators hadn't been switched on, they did eventually dry out but they were ruined. The pages were crumpled, the words all blurred. I considered saying I had dropped them in a puddle but there was no disguising the unmistakable stench of urine.

"I don't believe you sometimes," my mother was exasperated. "Why didn't you tell me last night that you had lost them again? There's no television for you for the rest of the week and you're going to do the washing up every night after tea."

I shrugged resignedly and headed off for school. The rest of the week would follow a familiar pattern. I would have my tea, wash up and go upstairs to go on my computer, waiting for the shout from my mother telling me I hadn't washed the pans properly and to come down and do them again.

The days weren't any different.

"I've lost it Sir."

"What again?"

"Yes Sir."

I had to go into each lesson and explain to the increasingly exasperated teachers that I hadn't done my homework as I had lost my exercise book. I had seen Paul Loftus use this excuse and he got away with it. I never did. Each teacher made me pay for a new book and also gave me detention.

"What do you mean you've been in detention again?" My Mam was now screaming at me.

"You know that I've lost my books. I've already told you that."

I was wasting my time.

"I'm phoning the school. This is getting ridiculous."

I thought that she might have tried to find the root of the problem but true to form, my mother and the teachers agreed that I was a hopeless case. I was put on permanent washing up duties and placed on a one-month TV embargo. It was around this time that I became a compulsive masturbator. Along with my computer it was the only form of entertainment left open to me.

****

It had started to drizzle when I left the hall. It had been about an hour since Kev had taken the phone call and left the reunion suddenly. I parked at the Seaburn centre and took the short walk down to the seafront and along to Kev's house. As I approached the front gate a woman was leaving the house. She looked vaguely familiar but I couldn't quite place her. She wore a black leather mini skirt and stiletto heels. I waited on the corner until she left the garden and headed down the road.

A light was on in the study and as I got to the front door it was already ajar. I edged it open a little further and walked in. There were no signs of life so I turned right and headed down the passage towards the study. A stream of light was coming from beneath the door. I stood outside for a moment, realising that I'd started to sweat, and tried to compose myself. I had worked this out in my head a thousand times but now; now that I was actually here, I started to shake. My heart started to race.

It's now or never.

I opened the door quickly and walked in. I wasn't sure what I was expecting; I certainly hadn't expected to see Kev sat behind his desk with an automatic pistol in his hand.

****

I explained my situation to Elvis as we walked to school.

"The one good thing to come out of this is that I don't have to leave school at the same time as Kevin Davison and his mates."

"Not a bad thing, unless they've been in detention as well."

"The teachers have become sick of giving me essays on Ping Pong balls and other pointless exercises so at least I'm able to do my homework before I go home," I said. "I get to spend the whole night on the computer. I'm getting quite good these days."

"Me as well. With you not being out much I've been doing quite a bit myself."

"Stop here a second." I darted down the back lane.

"What are you doing?" Elvis had followed me.

"Changing my shoes."

"Why didn't you change them in the house?"

"You wouldn't understand."

I had my trainers in my bag and was wearing my white socks under my grey ones. This way, my mother was satisfied that I was leaving the house in the correct shoes and socks and I would also arrive at school in my trainers saving me from more humiliation.

"God, you're weird sometimes."

****

"Pete. Come in. I've been expecting you," Kev waved me in with his gun.

"You have?"

This wasn't how I'd planned it.

"How long did you say it's been? Ten, twelve...."

"Fifteen. It's been fifteen years since we left school."

"Fifteen years? Long time. So where did you go? No, actually, why did you come back?"

"Unfinished business."

"Claire?"

"There were other, more pressing matters."

I noticed the half empty bottle of Jack Daniels on Kev's desk.

"I've known all along you know, about you and Claire. I knew she always held a torch for you. That's ok though. I didn't hold it against you. Not until you came back anyway. Now it's different. I've always known she didn't really love me. She may have thought she did at one time but that's all changed now. Now that little Peter Wood is back."

Kev took a mouthful of bourbon and pointed at the chair with his gun. I chose to stand.

"I should kill you," he said.

314

"Why haven't you? I've been here for five minutes now; you've got a gun in your hand. I'm sure a man of your means and contacts could have taken care of the business as soon as I arrived back."

"I could have killed you years ago, I should have killed you years ago. I knew it was you who stitched me up. The trouble is Pete. I've always admired you. Feared you in a way. Not in a physical way obviously. That would be ridiculous. When you decided that you had had enough you just walked way. Left it all behind. I couldn't do that I get too excited."

"I wouldn't have had you down as one of the most emotional people in the world."

"Anger Pete, anger," Kev slammed the tumbler down on the desk. "That's my biggest enemy. I can't control it, like now for instance. I know someone else has stitched me up and really I should kill them. I certainly feel like it. It wouldn't be the first time but when does it stop?"

"When you want it to I suppose."

"Well it's going to stop now. Right here in this room. With just me and you."

He took a large swig from the bottle. I looked round the room. The clock on the wall showed it was ten past ten, I had already been there longer than expected.

"You know the truth don't you, Pete? I'm grateful that you kept it a secret for so long but it had to come out sooner or later."

I wasn't sure what he meant but I decided not to interrupt.

315

"He used to beat us you know, my sister and me? He used to get pissed up on whisky then beat the shit out of us. Belt sometimes even a table leg when he was particularly angry. I used to think it was my fault. Remember how I was always in trouble at school? I thought I was the cause of his drinking and the beatings. I didn't for one minute think it was the other way round."

His eyes were bloodshot, possibly tears, more likely just the drink.

"Go on."

"When Rowcroft used to beat me at school I used to laugh at him, get him to hit me harder. I knew that no matter what he threw at me, it wouldn't be half as bad as what my father did to me when I got home."

Kev took another swig of whisky.

"How did you cope with it? Did you never want to fight back?"

"Thing is, I was so used to it, I stopped being bothered. I used to take the beatings and get on with my life."

Kev offered me the bottle. I shook my head.

"It was only when I realised what he was really doing to my sister that it started to affect me."

****

Elvis showed me his broken glasses, the sellotape barely keeping the frames together. The damage came courtesy of Kevin Davison. Elvis explained that he and Gilbert had been getting hassled by Kev after school when I wasn't there. I felt a little guilty but was quite happy that somebody else was taking it for a

316

change. I was therefore bitterly disappointed when Kevin Davison came to see me that morning.

"Have you done your maths homework, Pete?" He wasn't threatening; in fact he was quite polite.

"Yeah, I did it last night in detention."

"I didn't get a chance to do mine. I had some business to take care of. Any chance I can copy yours mate?"

Fuck off you moron, do your own homework. See how you like detention.

"Yeah, no problem. As long as I get it back after registration, we've got maths first period."

"I'll get it done now."

I knew I wouldn't get it back but I was becoming used to detention now so I was resigned to it. I handed over my book reluctantly.

"Might be worth changing a couple of answers, we don't them to know you've copied."

I was sure that I had got mine one hundred percent right and didn't want to make it obvious.

"Yeah, you're probably right. Don't want them thinking I've turned into some type of swot."

****

Kev drained his glass, "After he had beaten us, he always apologised, said it was due to the stress he was under since Mum died. He seemed to make a special effort with my sister. Like any child I was jealous, I wanted to know why she was getting more attention than me. One night he came in after the pubs had closed, drunk as usual. We had waited up for him as we always did, waiting to see what type of mood he would be in. It was a bad one. As soon as he came through the door he removed his belt and attacked me. I tried to protect Elaine but she got it as well. She ran upstairs and eventually my Dad calmed down. He apologised as he always did, said someone had wound him up down the pub."

Kev bit his bottom lip and tapped his gun on the desk.

"What happened next?" I asked.

"He gave me a bag of peanuts, dry roasted. Said he was going to tuck Elaine in. I gave it a couple of minutes and followed him upstairs. I crept up to her bedroom and peeped through the crack in the door. The bedsheet was peeled back and he had his hand up her nighty. Christ, she was only nine! I felt sick to the pit of my stomach."

His knuckles were white as he gripped the gun tightly.

"That was the night I killed him."

****

"There you go Pete. Cheers."

As promised, Kevin Davison returned my maths book, much to my surprise.

"Anytime," I said, hoping he would never take me up on it. At least now I was in his good books for a while.

"Right, get your homework books out."

318

Mr Burns must have been nearing retirement. He was a short greying man with a quick temper. I had often been the target of his anger when I didn't do my homework. I had the misfortune to be in both his maths and religious classes and he was also my form teacher. There was no love lost between us. Today he was pleasantly surprised.

"Nice to see you've actually done it for a change Wood. Detention must be doing you some good. Mr Davison, you as well. I think we're going for some sort of record here."

He collected all of the books in and put them on his desk. He then proceeded to embark on a long lecture about Pythagorus or some such thing. Maths would be quite interesting if it wasn't for the teachers. I drifted off as I thought about the swimming lesson that was about to come.

****

"What about the story you gave to the police?"

I edged over to Kev's desk, enthralled by his story.

"It was partly true. He had been drinking whisky. The post mortem would have shown that. He even argued with the man on the moon like I told the police. I think that is what pushed me over the edge. I sat upstairs in my room for hours trying to get my head round what he was doing to his own daughter. It didn't make sense. I headed to the top of the stairs. I was trying to pluck up the courage to ask my Dad why he was messing with my sister and there he was, arguing with the moon's reflection. I ran down the stairs and shoved his head through the glass. That's why I never called the police."

He sat back in the chair and opened his arms wide.

"The thing is Pete, you've come home with this big victim thing hanging over you, thinking you're hard done by. But we're all victims, every one of us. And we're all guilty. It's how you deal with it that matters. I've made my bed and I'll lie in it."

"Do you not feel any remorse for what you've done? I know that your father isn't the only one you have killed."

"Once you've killed one it becomes easier. I had nightmares for a while but once I got older I stopped thinking about it. When it came to sorting out business I didn't think twice before popping someone."

"What about your sister? Does she know what you did to your father?"

"She knows. She wasn't going to say anything because they will have wanted to know why I did it."

"That was Elaine leaving when I got here wasn't it?"

"I had to warn her that you were back, warn her that the secret might come out."

"How is she? What is she doing now?"

"She's on the game. Has been since we were in the foster home together. Used to do hand jobs for the older boys to get a bit of pocket money and progressed from there; blow jobs and eventually full sex. It didn't matter to her. Then the carers became involved. They wanted it for free as usual, thought it was a perk of the job but they paid, eventually."

"Have you never tried to stop her? Surely you have the money so she doesn't have to work?"

"She works for me, one of my best earners."

I sat down, trying to take everything in.

"So how long have you known?" Kev asked as he sat back in his chair with the glass in his left hand and a gun in his right.

I decided to tell him the truth.

"I didn't. Not until you've just told me. I knew something wasn't quite right and God knows I have a lot of stuff on you but this I didn't know."

He just shrugged his shoulders.

"I thought that's why you had come home. You knew that I would kill you so I assumed you were going to try and blackmail me. It make's no difference though. I suppose I had to tell someone."

He drained the crystal tumbler.

"Are you going to kill me then?" I asked.

Kev just shrugged.

****

I wasn't happy to be in the pool after the last incident with Kevin Davison. Up to now the lesson had gone without incident but I was sure it wouldn't last. I was practising my kicking in the shallow end alongside Gilbert when Karen Walker came into pool area.

"Please Miss, Mr Burns wants to see Peter Wood in the entrance hall."

"What does he want to see me for?"

"Do you think he's realised that Kev has copied?" asked Gilbert.

"Don't think so. He's only asked for me not Davison. Maybe it's to praise me for getting one hundred percent."

"Tell Mr Burns that Pete is swimming. He can see him in his own time, not mine."

Whilst I wasn't swimming in the strictest sense of the word I was pleased that Miss Shipp had put Burnsy in his place.

"I'd love to see his face when he's told that, " said Gilbert. We splashed harder as we laughed.

"Right Miss." Karen headed off.

She was back five minutes later.

"Please Miss. Mr Burns says he doesn't care if he's drowning, he wants to see Peter Wood right now."

"Go and get changed, Pete. You have to see Mr Burns in the entrance hall," she shook her head resignedly as I climbed out of the pool.

I was quite pleased to get out of swimming as it meant I avoided the now weekly ritual of getting my towel and underwear thrown in the foot pool. The only other time I had avoided it was when someone noticed Chris Miskell with a semi-erection in the showers. He was immediately branded a poof and the abuse became so bad that his parents eventually removed him from the school.

I dried myself off and changed back into my uniform, placing the wet towel and trunks in the bottom section of my bag to avoid soaking the books. I headed off to the entrance hall.

****

"I don't understand. If it's not for the money, why did he do it?"

Marie was confused. The story hadn't come as a complete surprise. She knew something had been troubling Elvis. He could never lie.

"Revenge I suppose. Davison had really got to us all. This way we got some sort of respect back"

The crowds had now dwindled. Unlike school discos of old, everyone had families to get back to. The last smooch was the domain of the drunk and the foolish. There would be repercussions and recriminations, but for one or two, it would be worth it.

"And you are sure it will work. This isn't going to backfire is it?"

Marie sounded worried.

"It will work. You can guarantee it. It's like he's been planning it from the day he left school. It will all be over now. All we need to do is sit back and wait. Tomorrow we'll be free."

"I hope so."

"Trust me I'm a nerd."

They both laughed as they headed out of the hall past the snogging couples. Elvis hoped he was right. He hung around in the entrance hall awaiting Pete's return. He still needed to ask Pete one final question.

****

A grand plaque listing the high achievers from the school adorned the entrance hall wall. One lad had played football for England schoolboys and another couple had gone to Oxford. The last great achievement appeared to have been in 1973. I'm not sure whether standards had slipped since then or whether the school hadn't bothered updating the board. Mr Burns' face was bright red when I got there. Blood pressure was obviously getting the better of him.

"What do you call this?"

His scream took me by surprise as he threw my exercise book onto the table. My shock was reflected in my answer.

"A book?"

Mr Burns punched the wall just above my head, the plaster cracking and crumbling onto the floor. I'd never seen Burns this angry before, not even that time in Religious.

"A book? I know it's a bloody book! What do you call this?"

He opened the book to the middle pages where there was a drawing. I began to see why he was so upset. Spanning the two pages was a drawing of a giant penis, complete with hairy balls and semen seeping out of the end. I was struck dumb with the extent of Kevin Davison's artistic abilities. Mr Burns dropped the book on the table and pinned me against the wall by my lapels. I glanced down at the picture in front of me. I don't think the reaction would have been quite as strong had Kev not included a very good likeness of Mr Burns licking the cum from the end of the phallus.

My feet dangled from the floor as the blood boiled in his face. I was in trouble and this time it really was serious.

****

"I haven't decided what to do with you yet. It's not exactly your fault that Claire has always loved you. It's not as if you've been bombarding her with love letters over the years; you've hardly been encouraging her. I resent you for what you did but I don't hate you," Kev leaned back in his chair as if pondering his next move. "I was quite impressed with the way that you stitched me up all of those years ago. You wouldn't get away with it again though."

"Nice to hear it but you don't get it do you?" I said.

"Get what?"

"Who do you think stitched you up this time? Who do you think broke up your little relationship with Elizabeth? Do you think anyone cares that much about you to go to the trouble of photographing you with your mistress and then blackmailing you with the photos."

"I've got enemies. You tend to get a few in this business."

"I suspect Ingham will be paying you a visit soon. You want to hope that the Police get here first."

"What have the pigs got to do with it?"

Kev was getting more agitated, swigging from the near empty whisky bottle and fingering the gun.

"I heard they were very interested in your secret computer files. Quite surprised when they ended up on CID's desk this morning"

"I don't get it. What are you on about? What files?"

"The ones with your accounts and the ones of your rubber clad friends."

"How did they get hold of the files? What rubber clad friends?"

"A special present from Elvis."

"That specky cunt what's he got to do with it?"

"Computer whiz-kid our Elvis. Master at tapping into computer systems would you believe? Surprised you didn't know. You seem to take such a keen financial interest in his business."

"You've lost me," Kev leaned forward over his desk.

"You never were very bright were you?"

Any pity I had for him had now faded. I was going to finish this once and for all.

"You know Tim's dead don't you?"

"Who the fuck is Tim? I don't know anybody called Tim."

"He looked out for me and my mates when we were kids, used to drink in the whistle. Bloke with a camera? Now your little soldiers have killed him, burnt his house down."

"They've done what. Why didn't they ask permission? Why do they want to kill somebody like that? He isn't a threat to us."

"Wounded pride I suppose, it's surprising what it does to people."

"I'll fucking kill them."

"Too late, they're already inside. I'm surprised you didn't know."

326

Kev picked up the phone in the office and dialled 1471. It was a number he recognised well, Southwick Police Station.

"Looks like your little empire's falling apart."

I turned and headed for the door.

The noise from the blasts took me by surprise. It was the first time I had heard a gun fired.

****

There was no way I could have explained that the drawing was not done by myself but by Kevin Davison. He would have killed me. I was sat in the headmaster's office alongside my mother. Mr Gutteridge, Mr Burns and Mr Hunter, a representative from the education authority, sat on the opposite side of the desk.

"I'm sorry your husband didn't see fit to come, Mrs Wood."

"He's working but I can assure you that he takes the matter as seriously as I do," she looked disappointedly at me.

"I sincerely hope so, Mrs Wood. This is a very serious matter."

"Can we get on with this?" Mr Burns was getting impatient. "I want him out of here as soon as possible."

"Yes I think we can begin now," Mr Hunter said sternly.

Whilst he was sitting down, he still towered above everybody else in the room. He had a tuft of hair above each ear but was otherwise bald. His thick-rimmed spectacles partially hid his long pointed nose.

"I don't think there's anything to discuss," Mr Burns started proceedings, "he should be expelled. This is a good Catholic School."

"Now hold on," interjected my mother.

"I've got to say I agree," added Mr Gutteridge. "He's a disgrace to the school. We should be making an example of him."

"Can I just say something here?" The gentleman from the authority stood up, using his height to good effect. "Now as a headmaster you should be well aware that you can't expel a child of Pete's age. He is coming up to his O'Levels and you have a responsibility to teach him. Whilst you may want to make an example of him, I am here to ensure that you fulfil your obligations to the Education Authority, your obligation to the parents and, most important of all, your obligation to the pupils."

Mr Gutteridge had been put in his place and was scarlet.

"That's ridiculous," Mr Burns tried to argue but was silenced by an angry stare.

I was beginning to enjoy myself but was brought back down to earth when I learnt the severity of the punishment.

"As you may be aware Mrs Wood, this isn't the first time that your son has shown complete disrespect for this school. You may remember the incident in Religious Studies recently."

He had a point. I was very nearly expelled then however escaped due to the same rules that were keeping me here today.

"What we propose is that instead of expelling Peter, we exclude him from lessons."

"What will that entail?" asked my mother.

"He will not be allowed in any lessons, instead he will be taught separately in a venue yet to be decided. He will have no contact with any pupils or teachers from the school unless specified by myself. Some of the teachers are quite upset at his presence here."

"Too bloody right."

"Mr Burns," Gutteridge raised his voice. "I trust this is ok with you?" He said turning to Mr Hunter.

He nodded his approval.

"Mrs Wood?"

"As long as he still gets his education."

"We'll do the best we can in the circumstances."

The meeting was over

****

Carter's phone smashed against the wall as look of sheer anger spread across his face.

"Bastards!" The whole office stopped and stared. "We've just had a report of gunfire at Davison's house. It's kicking off and we're scratching our arses wondering what's going to happen. Well it's happening now ladies and gentlemen. We've got to move."

Everyone gathered around Carter.

"Who's involved?"

"We don't know. Ingham probably if he's received the same photos as we have today. In fact it could be just about anybody. I wish I knew who sent us this information. I wish I could make some sense of it all."

"What about Couzens? Where does he fit in?"

"I don't know and right now I don't bloody care. We need to get hold of Davison before Ingham does or we'll have one bloody great mess to clean up."

Carter grabbed his phone on the way out of the office.

"I need the armed response unit and I need them now. I don't care, I want every gun in this entire fucking force round at Davison's house in ten minutes flat because we're just about to be caught up in the biggest gun fight since the O.K Corral."

****

I was forced to sit in the chapel and work alone. I wasn't allowed to have lunch or breaks with my friends. I had gained some notoriety amongst my peers but now, as far as everyone was concerned, I didn't exist.

Kevin Davison and his gang pretty much forgot about me and I got a chance to do some work and revise for my exams. Whilst Kev and his mates knew the truth about the drawing he was careful for it not to get out when he realised how strong the punishment was. He wouldn't be able to keep up his reputation if he didn't have an audience.

Although I was grounded forever, Elvis still managed to get in to see me occasionally. After he had his lunch he would slip through the hall and then into the chapel. The teachers were too busy in the staff room to be bothered.

"How's things on the outside?"

"Not good. Kev has given his gang a name, The St Pat's Casuals."

"What, like the football hooligans?" I said.

"Exactly. He's getting right into that scene. I've started believing the stories he tells. They've even got their own calling cards. They leave them with their victims after they've encountered a beating."

"You're joking? Where did they get them done?"

Elvis pointed at himself. "Being the only person apart from you to have the slightest idea what to do with a computer, I was given the job of producing the cards. Couldn't really say no could I?"

I shook my head in disbelief as he handed me one of the cards.

"I was also the first to receive one after I delivered them one day later than promised. My printer wasn't working."

"How's everyone else? Gilbert and Bumper?"

"Gilbert is having a bad time of it," said Elvis. "He's got his own little collection of calling cards now, three in one day."

"Three? How?"

He took a beating for no particular reason, typical Davison stuff. They threw one of the cards down and told him to read it to them. As you know, reading is not one of Gilbert's strong points. They chased him and gave him another beating on the stairs outside the science block. One of the elderly dinner ladies arrived on the scene and found Gilbert on all fours, in tears. When she asked what was up with him, Martin Gelder said that Gilbert had lost his contact lenses. Satisfied with the explanation, she left him to his third beating of the day. Kev's getting out of control, Pete. Somebody's going to have to stop him before it really gets out of hand."

****

Carter was first to the door but it was already open.

"This is the problem with the rich criminal types, all the security in the world and they leave the fucking front door open."

He was now sporting a bulletproof vest and a gun that he'd been trained to use but had never had the need or the desire to fire on active duty. The rest of the armed response unit were lined up at either side of the door. Carter's heart started racing, this was it. Two members of the ARU went in first.

"FREEZE, ARMED POLICE!" the first one shouted as he burst through the door.

Ingham turned and raised his gun to shoulder height.

"Fucking drop it dickhead."

Ingham thought about it for a couple of seconds and then placed the gun on the floor.

"On your knees."

"All right, all right, I'm going."

"Where's Davison?" Carter shouted.

332

"In there," Ingham nodded towards the study.

"It's not pleasant. Looks like someone got to him before I did."

"Save your story for the judge. Someone get him out of my sight."

Carter edged towards the study door.

"What the fuck?" Junior Carling came through from the conservatory when he heard the shouting.

"Freeze! Armed Police!"

Everyone raised their guns again.

"Boss?" Junior looked towards Ingham for inspiration but he was already cuffed.

"BASTARDS!"

A shadow emerged from behind Junior. The bouncer fired his gun towards the front door. Carter let off two rounds and the gunman was dead. The second bouncer came bounding down the stairs but dropped his gun as soon as he saw his friend lying, face down in a pool of blood.

"Check the rest of the house. Make sure there's no more gung-ho heroes waiting to gun us down."

Carter shook his head; he had never aimed his gun at anyone or been fired at in the past, now he had killed a man and two bullets lay in the doorframe behind him.

"Follow me," he said to DC Oliver as he opened the door to the study.

Carter edged in slowly with his gun at shoulder height. The blue flashing lights outside briefly lit the room. Davison sat behind his desk in his swivel chair. The rain on the windows mixed with the police lights to send tear like shadows running down his face. His brains were spread over the wall covering the photo of him and Frank Bruno.

"For fuck's sake."

Carter slid down the wall and held his head in his hands.

"Looks like we've got another murder on our hands. If Ingham is telling the truth and he isn't responsible then what the fuck is going on?"

****

I had to be in the chapel by 8.30 each morning so that I didn't come into contact with any of the pupils on my way to school. Mr Swinbank, the deputy head, was always in early and met me in the entrance hall. After he had left me in the chapel, I was pretty much left to my own devices until about eleven thirty when I went for lunch. I was then put back into the chapel for the rest of the day. Whilst I was given work to do, it took very little time and I filled my mornings by daydreaming.

I started to have a look around the chapel, more out of boredom than a general interest. There wasn't much to see; an altar with a couple of candlesticks and behind red velvet curtains was the tabernacle. This contained the wine and bread that the priest used during mass. It was always locked. On the wall behind the altar was a large vent from the heating duct. I peered in through the grate but there was very little to see as it was so dark. I considered my surroundings. Perhaps, after the outburst in Religious, the school thought it would be appropriate for me to spend time contemplating the error of my ways in a chapel. Maybe they were trying to be ironic.

****

I wandered back into the hall, trying to look as inconspicuous as possible. Elvis grabbed me anxiously as soon as I came through the door.

"Everything okay?" he asked.

"Yeah, it's all over with just as I promised."

It hadn't quite gone as I had expected but I didn't want to worry him. A relieved look spread across his face.

"Now that it's finished with I need to ask you something Pete."

"Go on."

"That money in my account, it's not a mistake by the bank is it?"

"Look, I didn't want to tell you this until it was all over. I wanted you to be doing this for the right reasons. When I sold the company I made a fortune, more money than I could ever hope to spend in one lifetime. I have made arrangements so that you, Bumper and Gilbert all get a share. You'll never need to work again."

"You don't need to do this. I don't need the money; I'll get by. You could have been killed."

"The money was yours whether I decided to go through with it or not. I've turned you all into criminals. You didn't have to get involved; after all you hadn't seen me for fifteen years. The only reason you agreed to it was because I asked you to. That shows great loyalty and it shouldn't go unrewarded."

"Aren't you forgetting something?"

"What?"

"You turned us into criminals a long time ago?"

"When?" I was stumped.

"Southwick library 1986."

"The pass books. I'd forgotten about that."

"There's something I've been bugging me for years about that, " said Elvis.

"What's that?"

"Why didn't you just borrow the books? It was a fucking library."

****

The next day I waited until nine when I knew everybody would be in assembly. They had long since stopped using the hall and now congregated in the gym. I took my pen knife from my inside pocket and unscrewed the vent. Switching on my torch I climbed inside. The heating duct, now partially illuminated by the torch light, extended for about ten yards then gave me the option of going left or right. I shuffled along on my hands and knees careful not to bump my head and decided to go left. There was a flicker of light up ahead and I wanted to see where it came from. I crawled along the tunnel, the metal giving slightly beneath my weight. The light came from the courtyard outside. I decided to continue along the shaft and see where it led. It didn't take long for me to get disorientated. My breathing got faster and I could swear that the sound of my heart beating echoed from the aluminium walls.

I had been crawling for what seemed like hours before I found anything. There were voices and laughter somewhere in the distance so I continued along my path hoping for a clue. As I reached the metal grate and glanced through, I recognised Elvis and the rest of my old class. A quick scan of the classroom identified it as Mr Burns' religious class. He wasn't there but there were a number of bibles, lying unopened on the desks. Tomma was at the black board. I edged along, careful not to make too much noise, so that I got a better view of what he was doing. Much to the amusement of the whole class, he wrote Burns is a puff in big letters across the board. He then rolled the board upward so only a plain black surface was showing. He went back to his desk and I was tempted to wait and see Burns' reaction when he moved the board.

I glanced at my watch. It was already 10.15. I had been crawling through the vent for more than an hour and I wasn't sure how to get back. I pictured where Burns' class was in relation to the chapel and headed a few yards up the tunnel to another cross section so that I could turn around. I got back in just over twenty minutes and carefully replaced the grill. I spent the rest of the afternoon drawing a map. That night I found it hard to sleep. I was at the entrance hall by 8.20 the next morning and was anxious to start exploring again.

The vent took me to a whole new world. I could see into every classroom on the ground floor. The real bonus had been when I discovered the staff room on Wednesday. I got a full view and got to listen to conversations that dispelled the notion that teachers were the adults in the school. They were just as bad as the pupils for skiving and petty squabbles.

Over the next few days I had drawn up a detailed map and timetable of teachers' whereabouts. I spent each day investigating, learning when certain classrooms were full and when they were empty. I had learnt that on Monday mornings, for example, for about two hours after first break, the staff room was completely empty. I'm not sure where the teachers who didn't have lessons went but I was quite happy to take advantage. I listened to boring lessons that now, somehow had a strange fascination. I sometimes just sat and watched Claire for a whole lesson. My map and timetable had now become a diary. Comments made by teachers in the staff room were recorded, timed and dated. Maybe I could use everything I heard to my advantage.

Then I had an idea.

****

I waited until Claire left the school in a taxi then headed into the car park.

"Hello again," Karen was just leaving the hall. "Didn't make the last dance I see. Claire seemed disappointed."

"Was she?"

"Don't tell me that you still hold a torch for her. I thought you were over that."

"I am, promise," I smiled.

"Do you fancy a walk? You can show me that lighthouse you were telling me about."

"Come on then," I opened the passenger door for her. I looked for Elvis but he'd already left. It would have been nice to say goodbye.

I parked the car and we walked along the seafront without speaking. Karen had her arm round me. The waves crashed up over the promenade and the rain had just started coming down again.

"How come your jacket's wet? It wasn't raining earlier was it?" Karen felt my side. "What have you spilt? Can't hold your drink eh?"

"Yes," I answered distantly.

"Yes what. Yes you can't hold your drink? Yes it was raining? Which was it?"

"Mmm....." The answer was non-committal, I was finding it hard to concentrate. I could just about make out the blue lights up ahead.

"Don't go Mr Silent on me. I thought we'd got over that. Come on let's have a look at your jacket," Karen pulled me towards the streetlamp. "Damn orange lights I can't see a thing."

I stumbled as she pulled at my jacket, reaching out desperately for the lamppost. Sweat had now started to gather on my brow as I doubled up against the steel pole.

"What's wrong? You can't be drunk you've hardly drunk anything. Don't tell me it's drugs. I'm walking away now if it is," she looked closer. "It's blood!" Karen screamed.

I was growing tired. If only I could sit down against the lamppost and go to sleep. I knew that she wouldn't let me.

"What happened?" Karen was becoming hysterical. "Is it yours? Where has it come from?"

A couple hurried past on the other side of the road As far as they were concerned it was just another drunken couple arguing and they knew better than to intervene.

"I'll phone for an ambulance," she took her mobile from her bag. "Shit, no signal."

She looked frantically for a phone box but there were none. Karen supported me, thankful that I was still quite small.

"Claire's," Karen shouted. "Her and Kev only live up the road. We can get them to phone an ambulance, come on it's only five minutes away."

We could see the flashing lights in the distance.

****

It was 10.30 on Monday morning as I sat in the heating duct over looking the staff room. As usual, it was full at break time. A lot of coffee was drunk and there were the normal dreary discussions about timetables and exams. Mr Riley, the permanently angry head of Maths approached Mr Burns.

"What do you call this?" he threw a folder on the table, very nearly spilling Miss Lynn's tea all over her.

Mr Burns looked disinterested.

"These are the results for your third year class and they are an absolute, bloody disgrace."

"They are a waste of space," said Burns, "none of them are interested."

"It's your job to make them interested."

The rest of the room had now fallen silent; newspapers had been folded and placed back in briefcases. Mr Burns stood up and stared Riley in the eyes.

"You're not kidding anyone. You are here for exactly the same reasons as me. Long holidays and a decent pay cheque at the end of the month, anything else is irrelevant. It's a long time since anybody has cared for the kids. They are a just a small irritation that we have to put up with. If you want high achievers go and teach at Eton. Until then just accept that you are teaching a bunch of no-hopers in Southwick and get used to it."

Burns was now face to face with Riley. I was trying to record as much of this as I could in my diary.

"Whilst I may not be at Eton," argued Riley, "I am still accountable for the results. If I get a rollicking then by God you are going to get one as well. This is an official warning. If your results don't improve you are out of a job. So get used to that."

He emptied his coffee down the sink and rinsed out his cup.

"Not much to say for yourself now, have you?"

Riley walked past the now seated Burns as he left the staff room missing the two raised fingers behind him.

One by one the teachers left for their lessons. Mr Burns was always the last to leave and today was no exception. He headed for the door but instead of leaving, he locked the door and came back into the staff room.

Shit.

He looked out of the window into the yard to where the fifth form were having a games lesson. The boy's playing football on the field opposite and the girls playing netball in the yard below. He started to rub his crotch against the windowsill then went to sit down in one of the armchairs. Removing his penis from his pants, he started masturbating furiously and ejaculated into his handkerchief within seconds. If anybody found out what he was doing he would be in serious trouble but how could I tell anyone? He did up his fly and headed over to the sink where the teacher's coffee mugs were lying on the draining board. He picked up Mr Riley's mug and rubbed the rim with his sperm covered handkerchief. I forced down the bile as I nearly threw up.

He tucked the handkerchief into his pocket, unlocked the door and left the staff room, locking the door behind him. I sat back against the metal wall trying to take in what I had seen. I nearly forgot why I was there. I gave it a couple of minutes in case Mr Burns came back. When he didn't, I went to work.

****

Blue flashing lights surrounded the house. Red and white plastic tape keeping the crowds back.

"Has there been an accident?"

There were always boy racers flying up and down the seafront. It was one of the few disadvantages of living there. Normally there would be Fire Engines. Where were the cars? And then she saw the guns. Claire jumped out of the taxi.

"What the Fuck are the armed Police doing here?" she cried as she rushed towards her home, towards the gunmen. It wasn't as if she was scared of guns anymore. They had threatened her plenty of times. She made her way through the crowds, through the vultures that always seem to gather at any horrific incident.

"Drug pushing scum," said an overweight woman in her thirties, still in her slippers despite the rain.

"He had it coming," agreed her friend, nursing a half smoked cigarette.

Who do they mean? Has somebody been knocked over? What do they mean drug pushing scum?

Then she caught on.

"Kev!"

She pushed at the crowds.

"Get back," said the obese woman. "We were here first." Her arms folded in an act of defiance.

Claire summoned up all the strength she had inside her and landed a right hook on the chin of the woman who was easily twice her weight.

"Get out of my fucking way," her friend stepped back without resistance.

As Claire ducked under the tape an armed policeman grabbed her.

"Where do you think you're going?" he said with an air of smugness only the Police possess.

"That's my house so let go of my arm before I take that gun and shove it straight up your arse."

Years of ridicule and oppression and finally boiled over and Claire was at breaking point. The Policeman was shocked and temporarily loosened his grip. Claire darted for the gate but he suddenly lunged for her and grabbed her round the waist.

"You don't want to go in there love," the smugness now replaced by a look of panic, "I'll get the Sergeant."

Claire slumped to the floor.

****

I removed the grill from the heating duct and lowered myself into the staff room. Wasting no time I headed for the coat rack. As I suspected nearly all of the teachers had left their wallets in their jackets. I removed them quickly and put them in my bag, checking a couple to make sure that, as expected, teachers earned far more than they would ever let on. A lot of the female teachers had left their handbags lying around the room also. I emptied them quickly and climbed back into the heating duct, replacing the grill.

I scurried along the heating duct until I came to Mr Burns' form room; my old form room before I was excluded. I had checked my timetable carefully and knew it would be empty. I crawled out of the vent and along the floor, being careful not to be spotted by the girls playing netball outside. I got to the desk and placed the bag inside. I had to get back quickly before anybody noticed I was missing.

****

There were armed police everywhere.

"Jesus Pete, what's going on?" Karen stared at the crowds. "I'll get an ambulance."

She made to run for the house, eventually remembering the weight she was carrying. Unbalanced she stumbled and lost her footing on the grass, sending me tumbling to the floor. The grass was wet and cool. I was comfortable, resting my face in the mist damp soil. The blue flashing lights, the orange glow, they all mixed to give a hallucinatory effect. Then the pain came back in my side and I vomited on the grass.

Karen pushed her way through the crowds. The fat ladies moved aside not wanting a repeat of their run in with Claire. She tried to attract the attention of the ambulance driver. He eventually looked up as she got through the cordon.

Somebody grabbed her arm.

"Where are you going love? There's nothing to see here."

"It's Pete, he need's an ambulance."

"Who's Pete?" the Sergeant was confused.

A well built man in his late forties, looking as if he had seen one dead body too many. He looked towards Claire

"Is there someone else in there? Who was with Davison?"

"Not in the house. He's on the grass, bleeding. You have to help him, quickly," Claire looked towards Karen.

"Pete's hurt?"

The Sergeant pushed past the crowd and headed for the grass, Claire and Karen followed. There was nobody there. As they headed back through the crowds Claire started crying. She didn't know if the tears were for Pete or her late husband.

****

The whole operation had taken no more than an hour and I had been settled back into my chair a long while before Mr Swinbank, the deputy head, came into see me.

"Pete, I know you are excluded from lessons but this is an emergency. Can you take this message round to all of the teachers and make sure they all act on it immediately?" He handed me a small piece of folded paper.

I headed across the hall and through the entrance hall. There was a police car outside and two policemen were talking to Mr Burns.

"Can you tell us again, Mr Burns, why you were late for your first lesson after break?"

I tried to keep in my smile but still couldn't help a little smirk.

I took the message around all the teachers and they immediately told everyone to pack up and head for their form rooms. Everybody did so, happy to avoid lessons. My old class weren't so happy as they were in the middle of football and netball games.

"What's going on, Pete?" asked Claire.

I couldn't help noticing how nice she looked in her little netball skirt.

"I've no idea but the police are in the entrance hall interviewing Mr Burns."

"Maybe they've finally caught up with the dirty old pervert," she laughed, "I always knew there was something dodgy about him."

She turned to her friends to let them know the news.

Mr Armstrong rounded up the footballers and also those who had got out of games by producing forged notes. Davison, Tomma and Nick quickly stubbed out their cigarettes as he came round to the bike shed. He had been happy for them to disappear for the lesson, as they were more trouble than they were worth.

****

"Fuck me," exclaimed Bumper as he put down the phone, "we're rich."

"What was that?" Bernie shouted through from the bathroom.

"We're rich." Bumper slumped into his armchair, unable to believe what Elvis had told him. The last weeks had certainly been weird for Bumper. Meeting an old school friend he hadn't seen for fifteen years, getting married, stitching up the local gangster and now this. Not since he had won the chod chucking championships at Tate's had Bumper felt so good.

****

"Quiet," Mr Burns shouted above the rabble and when he got no response he ran his finger nails down the blackboard, the horrible screeching noise ensuring everybody's attention. "You might be wondering why you have been brought back to your form rooms."
"I'm surprised that the police have let you go."
Everyone chuckled. Mr Burns ignored this and continued.
"There has been a very serious crime committed today. A number of items have been taken from the staff room and the police have asked us to complete a desk search to eliminate you all from their enquiries. Everyone open their desks please."
He started walking up the aisle looking into everybody's desk. Burns knew exactly which desk he wanted to look into. The somewhat carelessly misplaced St Pat's casual's calling card found in the staff room could only lead to one person.
Kevin Davison's jaw dropped when he saw the bag inside his desk. The colour drained from his face when he looked inside.

****

Gilbert sat down in his armchair with a cup of tea. He had enjoyed tonight. He had danced with Claire, admittedly he had felt a little guilty as he knew what was happening with Kev and didn't tell her.

348

It was a good idea to have the reunion, he thought, *maybe school wasn't that bad after all.*

He considered what Elvis had told him.

One million pounds.

He wouldn't spend any of it just yet; he was saving it for a rainy day. He knew that the money changed everything though. He had hoped that when Pete had returned home that maybe the old friends would stay together this time. He knew now that Bumper and Elvis were likely to move away and Pete wasn't going to hang about.

Maybe he could get them to rally round one last time; maybe the lads would help him find his father.

****

I left school with four 'o' levels. Quite an achievement considering how little work I had done. With Kev out of the way I decided to come clean about the drawing in the maths book. Burnsy didn't believe me at first but chose to accept my story after I was backed up by my art teacher. She explained that I would be unable to draw a stick man.

The exams came as a bit of an anti climax after what had gone on the previous year. I sailed through the maths and Computers was as easy as expected. Tony Evans may have regretted not taking me up on my offer as he failed miserably. The major surprise was English Literature, despite not attending any of the lessons or reading any of the books I managed to get a 'C'. Luckily the parts of the passbooks I decided to cram into my head the night before the exam were exactly the ones that appeared on the exam paper. The last day of exams should have been a celebration but I found myself strangely deflated. Eggs and flour were thrown and exercise books were ritually burnt on the school field but I didn't feel part of it. Missing the last few months of term had left me even more of an outsider than I had been before. The celebrations went on without me as I watched from a distance.

"Glad to be out of it all?"

It was Mr Burns, realising that he no longer had any power over me, he tried to be human.

"Any idea what you are going to do next? You could go to college and get a few more 'o' levels. You never know what you could achieve if you applied yourself a bit more."

I already knew what I was going to do.

I took one last look at the crowd in the centre of the field, focusing on Claire knowing that this would be the last time I would see her for some time.

"Got to go," I said to Mr Burns.

"Make sure you use the gate and not the fence."

This was his last attempt at authority. I headed for the fence, removed my tie and tied it round one of metal posts. I straddled the railings and looked back one last time. Not only was I leaving St Pat's today, I was also leaving Sunderland. I had no definite plans of where I was going but during all of the celebrations there was one fact I couldn't ignore; Kevin Davison was not going to be in a young offender's institution forever. He was going to come after me and I was tired of fighting, I had to get away.

****

Some say that revenge is a dish best served cold. It isn't, revenge is cold. It's cold, damp and painful and it never turns out the way you thought it would. My legs were becoming weaker now but I was determined to reach the lighthouse. I felt bad leaving Karen like that but it would never have worked out. I've learnt the hard way.

I hoped that Elvis had told the lads about the money now, I hoped it would make things better some how. I felt guilty for not telling Gilbert about his father, I felt guilty for getting Tim killed.

I'd left one of the main lights on in the lighthouse and I could just about make it out as I headed down the pier. The rain was heavier now, lashing in from the sea. Waves swept up the side of the pier and crashed down at my feet.

Not long now.

I didn't mean for anyone to die.

Burns didn't have to hang himself.

The light from the helicopter swept along the coast road as the blue lights of the police cars blinked in the distance. I wondered why I had returned home. Sometimes when you seek something so hard you lose sight of what it is you are actually looking for. A wave crashed up beside me and took my legs from beneath me.

Fuck.

I lay on my stomach and then forced myself onto my knees. I sat back and stared at the sky, the helicopter now hovering behind me with it's searchlight sweeping up the pier towards the weak, pathetic figure I had now become. I thought about Karen, about Claire, about Elvis, Bumper and Gilbert. Did I come back for them? Did I come back for revenge?

All I wanted was to ruin Davison, get him put away for a few years, destroy his business. Why did he have to go and shoot himself? The fucking idiot. Why did he have to shoot me? I had no more answers now than I did when I arrived. I looked down and noticed the pool of blood at my knees.

Not long now.